THE
APARTMENT
UPSTAIRS

Lesley Kara

PENGUIN BOOKS

TRANSWORLD PUBLISHERS
Penguin Random House, One Embassy Gardens,
8 Viaduct Gardens, London SW11 7BW
www.penguin.co.uk

Transworld is part of the Penguin Random House group of companies
whose addresses can be found at global.penguinrandomhouse.com

Penguin
Random House
UK

First published in Great Britain in 2022 by Bantam Press
an imprint of Transworld Publishers
Penguin paperback edition published 2023

A CIP catalogue record for this book
is available from the British Library.

ISBN
9780552177238

Typeset in 11.25/15pt Sabon by Jouve (UK), Milton Keynes.
Printed and bound in Great Britain by Clays Ltd, Elcograf S.p.A.

The authorized representative in the EEA is Penguin Random House
Ireland, Morrison Chambers, 32 Nassau Street, Dublin D02 YH68.

Penguin Random House is committed to a sustainable
future for our business, our readers and our planet. This book
is made from Forest Stewardship Council® certified paper.

Praise for

THE APARTMENT UPSTAIRS

'Startlingly original . . . It's hard to think of a recent novel that can match Kara's for an almost unbearable level of suspense'
Sunday Times

'A palpable sense of dread that builds on every page'
T. M. Logan, author of *The Holiday*

'Twisty and tense, another great read from Lesley Kara'
B. A. Paris, author of *The Therapist*

'Taut, tense, dark and claustrophobic with a creeping sense of menace and a cast of compelling characters'
Gilly Macmillan, author of *The Nanny*

'A twisted plot, believable, well-written characters and loads of nail-biting suspense'
Emma Curtis, author of *Invite Me In*

'Clever and twisty with some brilliant examination of loyalties between friends and within families'
Catherine Cooper, author of *The Chalet*

'A shocking crime, an intriguing cast of suspects and a compelling mystery make this thriller a thoroughly gripping and twisty read'
B.P. Walter, author of *The Dinner Guest*

Also by Lesley Kara

THE RUMOUR
WHO DID YOU TELL?
THE DARE

For Rashid

1

THE BUS IDLED IN traffic. Scarlett rubbed a circle in the steamed-up window. Soon she would be level with the crime scene – the house where the 'bedroom bloodbath' had occurred. At least, that's what it had been called in some of the more lurid headlines. There was nothing the tabloids liked better than a grisly murder.

Scarlett wasn't the only passenger craning her neck to get a better view. The couple on the seat in front of her was looking too, and the old guy in front of them. The police tape had long since gone, but flowers were still heaped on the pavement outside. Scarlett wondered how long it would be before they were cleared away and people stopped gawping as they passed. People like her.

She couldn't recall having seen roadside tributes like these when she was a child, but they were becoming increasingly common. When Fusilier Lee Rigby had been murdered further along this same stretch of road, near Woolwich barracks, the flowers had been there for months on end, flags too, but that had been different. He'd been a young soldier, hacked to death in an act of terrorism. Nobody wanted to forget that. Nobody *would* forget that.

Rebecca Quilter's murder had been equally shocking. A fifty-six-year-old woman beaten to death by her fiancé. Just one of so many women killed by their partners. Scarlett had been reading the statistics, and they were staggering. Two women a week in England and Wales alone. But domestic homicide was soon forgotten in favour of the next big story. In Rebecca's case, the nationals had already moved on.

Scarlett studied the Victorian house with interest, her eyes lingering on the large bay window on the first floor. An involuntary shudder travelled down her spine. They said she'd been attacked as she slept, bludgeoned with the baseball bat she kept under her bed in case of intruders. The reporters had made much of that fact – the irony of it. At least the spineless bastard had finished himself off too. Slit his wrists and bled out. Scarlett closed her eyes and forced the images away.

The bus lurched forward, nosing its way slowly through the traffic. Scarlett hoisted her rucksack over her shoulder and shuffled to the edge of the seat. She pressed the button and waited for the bus to stop before standing up. Some drivers were apt to pull away before she'd made it to the doors. Not all of them noticed her walking cane until it was too late, although since she'd chosen one made from clear acrylic, she couldn't entirely blame them. This afternoon, a woman with a toddler and a buggy to wrestle with meant that Scarlett had plenty of time. She stepped off the bus into the damp October air and called out her usual 'Thank you!'

On the pavement, she did the buttons up on her raincoat and headed back towards the zebra crossing, narrowly avoiding a large puddle from that downpour earlier. She was tired now and her back was starting to ache. She wanted nothing more than to get indoors. Later, when she was feeling more rested, she'd take a long, hot shower in her beautiful bathroom and change into her pyjamas, settle down on the sofa for an evening of mindless TV. Anything would do, as long as it was suitably numbing.

As she neared the house where the murder had taken place, the stench of rotten lilies reached her nostrils. A part of her would have liked to pause and read the messages on the cards, but another part couldn't bear to look. Sympathy for the misfortunes of others was understandable, but when it spilled over into mawkishness it left a sour taste in her mouth.

Her eyes darted in the direction of the house, then back down to the pavement. One of the cellophane-wrapped bouquets had fallen in front of the pathway leading up to the front door – a particularly tasteless arrangement of garish chrysanthemums and frilly carnations. Scarlett nudged it away with her cane.

Her heartbeat quickened. Her brother had been right in one respect. She should never have come here alone. Not this first time. Sometimes Ollie seemed to forget that she was a forty-two-year-old woman and three years older than him. 'You're so stubborn,' he'd said. But he had been wrong about not coming back at all.

She reached into her pocket for her key, walked up to the front door and unlocked it.

This was her home. She had to come back some time.

2

Scarlett stood in the hallway, blood hammering in her ears. She stared at the internal front door on the right leading up to her Aunt Rebecca's apartment, her mind swimming with violent images. She pictured the police forensics team moving steadily and purposefully from room to room, their white suits rustling. What horrors they must have seen up there.

The nausea that was never far from the surface rose up in her once more, but Scarlett willed herself to ignore it. She lifted her walking cane into the air and tentatively prodded the door with it, just to reassure herself it was locked.

Then she turned her head away and walked along the short corridor to her own front door, past the post the police had piled on to the radiator shelf, and let herself in as fast as she could, pressing her back against the closed door and focusing on her breath. *In* to the count of three, *hold* to the count of three, *out* to the count of three. And repeat.

Apart from a slight mustiness – that strange, stuffy sort of smell that came from the place having had no fresh air let in for almost a month – it wasn't as bad as she'd feared. This home had been her sanctuary for so long, she was determined it would remain so, despite what had happened upstairs. Only time would tell if she had the nerve for it.

A strangulated sob erupted from Scarlett's mouth and her cane fell to the floor. She raised her eyes to the ceiling. Little more than six feet from where she now stood, Clive Hamlyn had brutally murdered her aunt. It was horrific. Unimaginable. And yet she *had* been imagining it, in hideous and graphic detail, for how could she not? No matter how hard she tried to resist the compulsion, her mind kept taking her there, forcing her to watch various scenarios unfold, all of them ending the same way, with the baseball bat raining down blows on Rebecca's head. Even now, four weeks later, she still couldn't believe it had happened. Couldn't believe that Rebecca was actually dead.

Scarlett bent down to retrieve her cane. A spasm of pain shot through the back of her left thigh like a red-hot skewer. She hobbled over to her green velvet sofa and sank into its comforting depths, put her legs up on the cushions and laid back. She'd underestimated the stress of returning, the physical and mental toll it would exert on her. Why, after all these years, did her body still take her by surprise?

As she began to relax, her mind returned to Clive. Quiet, ordinary Clive. Not stupid by any means, but hardly a match for Rebecca's intellect. When she'd first learned of their engagement, Scarlett had been surprised. She'd assumed that Rebecca would remain single. Her aunt was, as she herself had freely admitted on more than one occasion, an *acquired taste*. And Clive was nothing like the men she'd previously gone out with. Educated men who'd accompanied her to the theatre, to concerts. Men who'd enjoyed a lively debate with a forthright woman.

Clive had left school at sixteen to work in his father's electrical shop. Took over the business when he died. He was the sort of man who'd rather stay in and watch TV than go into town to see a play. He'd always been polite. Attentive. But there'd been something not quite right about him, that's what Scarlett had told the police when they interviewed her. Something a little *too* attentive. As if he were trying too hard to get his feet under the table, as her dad had been fond of saying. Apparently, one of the neighbours told the police they'd heard him shouting at her in the garden the day it happened, and that they'd heard Rebecca crying.

Scarlett sighed deeply and braced herself for the onslaught of self-recrimination. Why the hell hadn't she said anything? Why hadn't she expressed her reservations? Because Rebecca would have resented her interference, that's why. And when the woman she'd looked up to and loved all her life began to change, became forgetful and volatile, prone to odd delusions, Clive had been there, looking after her, supporting her. His dedication had been . . . convenient. Scarlett closed her eyes. There, she'd admitted it at last.

Scarlett shifted position on the sofa. She'd been eighty miles away in Bedford the night it happened, at a party she hadn't wanted to attend in the first place. Travel exhausted her, and she was never particularly keen on overnight stays in other people's houses. Rebecca had rung her earlier that day, while Scarlett was still on the train. She'd got it into her head that Clive was cheating on her with someone young enough to be his daughter and had made up her mind to call off the engagement. She'd been so lucid on the phone, it had been almost like the old Rebecca again. Scarlett remembered thinking that perhaps it was Clive who'd been making her aunt ill all this time, his presence in her life that had caused her such mental distress. She hadn't even considered how looking after her might affect *his* mental health.

'I know that as soon as I see you I'll start blubbing,' she'd told Scarlett on the phone. 'And I need to be strong. You can help me drown my sorrows when it's all over.'

And now the two of them would never share a bottle of wine again. Never sprawl on Scarlett's sofa and talk long into the night about their lives and their loves and their worries. Clive had seen to that, and

8

then he'd killed himself. It's what men like him always did. Removed themselves from the problem. Weak, gutless men who couldn't cope with rejection.

Scarlett glanced at her wheelchair, tucked neatly into the recess under the peninsular unit that separated the living area from the kitchen. She hadn't needed it for months, but if this pain continued . . .

Slowly, reluctantly, she raised her eyes to the ceiling again, half expecting to see a red stain blooming like a rose. She looked away and shook her head.

It *had* been the right decision to move back in, hadn't it?

Sometime later, her phone woke her. By the time she'd heaved herself off the sofa and across to the kitchen counter where she'd left it, the caller had rung off. It was Ollie.

She rang her brother straight back.

'You okay, Scar?' he said. 'I was worried.'

Scarlett smiled. It always struck her as amusing that 'little Ollie', as she used to call him, the brother she had looked out for all his life, now assumed a protective role towards her.

'I fell asleep. Sorry.'

'Fell asleep?' He sounded incredulous. Scarlett felt a stab of irritation. However protective he was, even after all these years he still didn't get it, how bone-achingly tired she got, how impossible it was to resist her body's need for sleep. Not many people did. But she checked herself before reacting. She might be the one who suffered from chronic pain and fatigue but, mentally, she was the stronger sibling. She took after their father in that respect. Dad had been on her side about coming back. 'I agree with Scarlett,' he'd said when the police had given them the all-clear to return. 'All the work we've done on that place. It's exactly how she wants it. How she *needs* it. To have to start all over again adapting somewhere else would be an unnecessary stress.'

Ollie had stared at his father in disbelief. 'As opposed to the stress of living right beneath where her aunt was murdered, you mean?'

Scarlett's eyes wandered over to her rucksack, still on the floor where she'd left it. Perhaps it *was* too soon. But if she'd stayed with her father and step-mother any longer they'd have ended up falling out. Microtensions had already started to appear. They were all of them too set in their ways. Besides, the longer she put it off, the harder it would be.

'Scar, are you still there?' Ollie's voice sounded urgent in her ear.

She exhaled through her nose. 'Yeah, I'm still here.'

'Do you want me to come round?'

'No, it's fine. If I need you, I'll call.'

'Well, if you change your mind, you know where I am. And let me know how it goes with that funeral firm.'

Scarlett looked at her watch. 'I might phone them now,' she said. 'Get the ball rolling.'

'Promise me you won't do anything stupid.'

'What do you mean?'

'You *know* what I mean. Don't go upstairs. It'll be too upsetting.'

In her mind, Scarlett had already been upstairs. She'd pictured her hands trembling as she turned the key in the lock, seen herself reaching the top of the stairs, her legs aching from the effort. She knew there'd be no blood. The specialist cleaning firm had disposed of the bedding and the mattress, removed the carpet and cleaned the walls. They'd cleaned the ceiling too. A fact she could have done without knowing. But there were bound to be stains, and an act of such brutality – such *savagery* – would surely leave its mark in other, less tangible ways.

'I'll have to go up at some point.'

'Yes, but not on your own. We'll fix a time. Promise me, Scar. I know what you're like.'

Scarlett gave a long, audible sigh. He didn't. He really didn't. Nobody knew what anyone was like, not really. Clive Hamlyn was proof of that.

'I promise,' she said.

3

DEE BOSWELL REPLACED THE office phone in its cradle. This wouldn't be Fond Farewells' first service for a murder victim. Last year, she and Lindsay had conducted a ceremony for a seventeen-year-old boy who'd been stabbed in a gang killing. But it would be their first for a murder victim they'd both met. A long time ago, admittedly, but even so . . .

It was Lindsay, her friend and business partner, who'd made the connection when the news first broke. 'Wasn't she that supply teacher we had when Mrs Bell broke her leg?' she'd said, and instantly Dee had been transported back to 1996, when a frazzled woman in crazy red specs had broken down in tears when they'd refused to get into groups for an A-level English revision class. Miss Patchett, the deputy head, had had to come in and give them all a good telling-off. If it weren't for the unusual surname and the fact that the papers had said she'd been a teacher, Dee doubted they would even have recognized Rebecca Quilter from the photo they'd printed.

She got up and went to the kitchen. This is what came of running a funeral firm in the same patch of south-east London where they'd lived all their lives. Sooner or later, they were bound to have to bury someone they knew. It was, perhaps, more surprising that it hadn't happened before. Not that they'd really *known* the deceased. Was that why she hadn't mentioned it to the niece?

She made herself a cup of coffee and took it out to the backyard – a small square of concrete enclosed by a red brick wall with a gate leading on to the access road. The air still felt damp, but the sun had just come out through a break in the clouds and, with winter fast approaching, Dee wanted to make the most of it.

When she and Lindsay had first moved into these premises they'd pulled up all the weeds from the cracks in the concrete and Lindsay's brother, Jake, who'd been in between acting jobs, had blasted the dirt away with a power-washer. They'd bought plant pots and filled them with ivy, ferns and other shade-loving plants, found a metal bistro table and two chairs from B&Q and one of those Moroccan-looking outdoor mats.

Dee gave the chairs and table a quick wipe with an old towel and sat down with her coffee. She eyed the yard with satisfaction. Just because most people who passed through the gate were either carrying a coffin or inside one, that was no reason not to keep this outdoor space bright and cheerful.

Ever since her beloved grandmother died and Dee had sat through her travesty of a funeral, she had nurtured the idea of doing things differently. She had trained first as a celebrant and then as a funeral director, and when Lindsay had grown tired of her career as a beautician and sought her advice about retraining as a mortuary assistant, the idea for Fond Farewells was born.

Some people might think it was a depressing way for two women to make a living, but they were wrong. Helping people at the saddest, often most stressful time of their lives and giving them power and choice over the arrangements for their loved ones, was just about the most rewarding thing Dee could think of doing.

Lindsay joined her at the table with a can of Diet Coke. 'How's things?'

'I've just been speaking to Scarlett Quilter,' Dee said. Lindsay widened her eyes. 'She wants us to do her aunt's funeral. Now that the police have excluded the possibility of anyone else being involved, the coroner can release the body.' Dee paused. 'I didn't mention we'd met her. Should I have done, do you think?'

Lindsay considered the question, then said, 'I don't suppose it matters, really.' She slugged back her drink, then crumpled the can in her hand. 'You could always mention it at the arrangement meeting. I presume she's coming into the office?'

Dee took a sip of coffee and avoided Lindsay's eyes.

Lindsay stared at her. 'Oh my God, you're not doing a home visit?'

'Yes, she asked me if I would. She has a chronic disability that makes it hard for her to walk sometimes. Apparently, it's flared up again. Anyway, she lives in the flat *below* where it happened. I could hardly say no, could I?'

'S'pose not. Would you like me to come with you?'

Dee shook her head. 'I'll be fine. It's a completely separate flat. She was at pains to point that out.' She took another sip of coffee. 'I do wonder how she can live there, though, knowing what happened upstairs.'

Lindsay grimaced. 'I know what you mean. I'm not sure I could move back in. It's too creepy.'

Lindsay's phone pinged with a notification. She reached into her shirt pocket. 'It's probably Caz. She's been trying to arrange a meet-up.'

Lindsay gave her a worried look. 'It's from Sue. I hope it's not . . .'

Dee swallowed the lump in her throat. 'Only one way to find out.'

She watched Lindsay's face as she opened the message, didn't relax until she saw the tension in her friend's jaw fall away.

'It's okay. She just wants us to go round to update them on progress.'

Dee nodded. A few weeks ago, the Caplins had asked for their help in arranging an anniversary event to mark the date their daughter, Gina, had gone missing. As Gina's oldest and closest friends, Dee and Lindsay had been the Caplins' first choice as event planners. But whenever Sue or Alan Caplin got in touch, they always feared the worst. Deep down, they knew the worst already. Gina had been missing for almost ten years. She was dead. She had to be. But until she was found, hope still lingered.

A plane droned overhead. Dee followed its path with her eyes until it disappeared behind the clouds. The memory was strong and sudden and Dee knew that Lindsay would be remembering the exact same thing: the three of them – Lindsay, Dee and Gina – flying to their favourite holiday destination in Morocco to celebrate three very special occasions: the year they all turned thirty, the opening of Fond Farewells and Gina being accepted on a course to teach dance.

How happy they'd been. How thrilled to be 37,000 feet in the air, drinking vodka and tonic. A whole fortnight of fun and sun in glorious Essaouira to look forward to. What none of them knew was that just three weeks after their return home, all tanned and relaxed and happy, Gina would disappear.

Dee exhaled slowly. It didn't seem possible that in

less than five months' time a whole decade would have passed and there were no more leads. Gina had simply . . . vanished.

'Tell her I'll ring tomorrow with some dates,' she said.

Lindsay tapped out a reply. Then she put her crumpled can into Dee's empty mug, hooked her finger through the handle and stood up. 'Come on, let's get out of here.'

They walked back inside and Dee locked the door behind them. She followed Lindsay to the front of the shop, past the lift that went down to the prep room and the viewing room, past the stairs and the kitchen.

'They'll find her one day,' Lindsay said, opening the main door to the street. 'We have to believe that.'

4

THE FOLLOWING DAY, DEE stood outside the house where Rebecca Quilter had been murdered, wondering why on earth she'd agreed to make a home visit. Surely the niece could have got a cab to the office.

She spent a moment gazing at the makeshift memorial on the pavement. Fresh bouquets alongside decaying ones. Messages on cards – some smudged and blurry from the rain, others protected inside plastic filing pockets. She let her eyes wander. By the looks of things, Rebecca Quilter had been a respected and much-loved member of the community.

R.I.P. Mrs Quilter.
You were the best English teacher I ever had.
Kylie Davidson xxx

To our dear, dear friend and valued soprano, Rebecca
We miss you dearly.
With all our love, the Charlton Cheerfulness Choir

To our kind and lovely neighbour
Every time we see your beautiful roses, we think
  of you
May you be at peace now
From the Joneses at number 49.

Dee took a deep breath and straightened her spine. She'd seen the house and the flowers many times during the last month, but only ever in passing, through the window of her car. Now that she was here on the pavement right outside, the house seemed larger somehow, more ominous. And yet it wasn't markedly different from any of the others on this section of the road. They were all of a type: substantial detached and semi-detached properties set back from the road with large front gardens.

Dee made her way along the path to the front step, noticing the gradually sloping concrete ramp alongside. She pressed the bottom buzzer and waited, aware of curtains twitching in the house next door and a face peering out at her. She turned her head and the face immediately withdrew, the curtains falling back into place. From somewhere inside came the sound of footsteps. A couple of seconds later, the door opened to reveal a tall, slim forty-something woman, dark brown hair hanging damply around her shoulders, her feet bare beneath a loose smock-type garment and leggings.

Dee stepped forwards. 'Ms Quilter?' she said,

extending her right hand, then retracting it with embarrassment. She had failed to spot the see-through walking stick. Her new client would have had to switch it over to her other hand to have been able to shake Dee's. For a second, Dee considered extending her left hand instead, but the whole manoeuvre now seemed clumsy and thoughtless.

'I'm Dee Boswell from Fond Farewells,' she said, aware of a faint blush creeping up her neck.

The woman smiled. 'Please, call me Scarlett. Sorry about the wet hair. I've been a bit slow getting ready this morning.'

Dee studiously avoided looking at the internal front door just off to her right and followed Scarlett Quilter down a little corridor, through another front door and into a spacious, open-plan living area that quite took her breath away. She didn't know what exactly she had been expecting, but this stunning contemporary space with beautiful white oak flooring and gleaming high-end kitchen wasn't it.

Dee never usually commented on clients' homes – it was hardly appropriate under the circumstances in which she visited them – but this place was some-thing else and, almost without her thinking about it, a small 'wow' escaped her lips.

'I know,' Scarlett said, gesturing to a stylish armchair by the window that looked large enough to comfort-ably seat two. Dee sat down, feeling a little like Alice in Wonderland on an oversized piece of furniture.

'My father designed it for me. He's an architect. And my brother's firm did the building work and the decorating.'

Scarlett was in the kitchen now, leaning on the peninsular unit. The morning sun was streaming directly on to her face, and Dee saw the dark circles under her eyes that she'd missed in the hall, the lines on her forehead and around her mouth. Grief did terrible things to a person's face. As did chronic pain. She was still an attractive woman, though.

'Tea or coffee?'

'Coffee, please. If it's not too much trouble.'

Scarlett drew a box of pods out of a cupboard. 'Any particular strength or flavour?'

'Really anything but caramel or vanilla.'

Scarlett pulled a face. 'No such atrocities in this box, you'll be relieved to hear.'

Dee watched as she prepared two coffees and noted her laboured movement around the kitchen, the way she occasionally grabbed the edges of the countertops to help her keep her balance. The transparent walking cane she'd been using earlier had been slotted into a stand by the door as they came in.

Dee wondered if she should offer to carry the coffees through but decided against it. If Scarlett Quilter required assistance, Dee had no doubt that she would ask. Despite her obvious pain and limited mobility, there was something steely about this woman. Sure enough, a few minutes later, a small trolley was rolled out from under a counter and the coffees were wheeled across to where Dee sat, the trolley now doubling as an occasional table placed between the chair and the sofa, on to which Scarlett now lowered herself.

'May I just say how very sorry I am about your aunt's death.' Dee always started these meetings offering her condolences. The age of the deceased varied, and the circumstances of their final moments, but the sentiment remained the same.

The woman sitting opposite her tilted her chin. A small, defiant gesture.

'My aunt's *murder*,' she said.

Dee pressed her lips together and nodded. 'I can't begin to imagine what—'

'Nobody can,' Scarlett said. 'There are no words . . .' Her voice cracked. She stared down at her lap, her hands balled into fists on her thighs, the knuckles white and shiny.

She looked up then and fixed her gaze at a point somewhere above Dee's left shoulder. Her damp hair was starting to curl at the ends as it dried. Dee tried not to stare. There was something about Scarlett Quilter she found strangely compelling.

'My aunt was an exceptional woman,' she said at last. 'I don't want her funeral to dwell on the way she died but on the way she lived. She was so full of life and joy.'

Dee nodded, trying to reconcile the memory of a

fraught, uptight woman barely holding it together in front of a class of seventeen-year-old girls with the very different picture Scarlett Quilter was beginning to paint. But, of course, that had been well over twenty years ago. Perhaps Rebecca had been new to the profession. And they'd been a tough crowd back then. Too full of themselves. Too sarcastic. Any weakness on the part of a new teacher, especially a supply teacher, would have been thoroughly exploited.

Scarlett twisted a strand of hair between her fingers. 'At least, she *was* full of life and joy until fairly recently. Her mental health had started to . . . deteriorate. We think she might have been in the first stages of early-onset dementia, although there'd been no formal diagnosis. It could have been depression. Either way, she wasn't herself. She'd been signed off from work. Extended sick leave. There'd been an . . . *incident* at the school. She could be a little paranoid sometimes, said the oddest things.'

Dee inclined her head, but Scarlett did not elaborate.

'She was a teacher, wasn't she?' Dee asked.

'Yes. Head of English at Riverhill. Do you know it?'

Dee nodded. Riverhill was an independent, fee-paying school. A far cry from the large comprehensive she, Lindsay and Gina had attended.

'I didn't say anything on the phone,' Dee said, 'but I met your aunt once. A long time ago.'

Scarlett Quilter stared at her in astonishment.

23

'Really? You don't mean you were one of her pupils?' Her forehead pleated in a frown. 'Why didn't you say?'

'Oh *no* – well, not exactly. I mean, I didn't go to Riverhill. I went to school in Plumstead. But my business partner and I remember her as a supply teacher we had for a while, when we were in Year Twelve. I'm sorry I didn't say anything earlier. If it weren't for the surname, we wouldn't even have made the connection.'

'She hated supply teaching,' Scarlett said. 'But as soon as she started working at Riverhill, she loved it. And they loved her. We've had some really touching messages from the girls there, and from her colleagues, too. Lots of the pupils she taught kept in touch with her.'

Scarlett sighed and went on, 'The thing is, I want her funeral to reflect the *real* Rebecca. You do understand, don't you? She was such a clever, *interesting* woman. She loved music and sang in the local choir. She wrote a novel, too. I mean, it was never published or anything, but it was a dream of hers once, to be a writer.' She blinked her tears away. 'Rebecca was always there for my brother and me,' she said. 'Our mum died, you see, when I was fourteen and Ollie was eleven. Rebecca was like a surrogate mother to us, but she became so much more than that. She was my closest friend.'

24

Dee gave her a moment to recover. 'Rest assured,' she said, 'we'll do whatever we can to help you celebrate your aunt's life in the most meaningful way for you and your family. Presumably you've had a look at our website? In which case you'll know that the service is something we particularly focus on.'

Scarlett leaned forward for her coffee, then settled back with it on the sofa, tucking her legs up to one side. 'Yes, although I should say now that we won't be going for holding hands in the middle of a forest and chanting or gathering on a beach at sunset and releasing butterflies. As touching and lovely as such ceremonies sound.'

Dee smiled. 'We can, and do, offer more traditional services, if that's what you'd prefer,' she said.

Scarlett shook her head. 'No. We don't want that either. Rebecca wasn't a believer, and neither am I. None of us is. And she hated being ripped off, which is another reason for coming to you and not one of the bigger firms. But, more importantly, you have a good reputation. I've read such glowing testimonials and reviews.'

Dee gave a polite smile. 'Customer service is our top priority.'

'We – the family, that is – just want something plain and simple. Some of her favourite poetry and music.'

Tears ran silently down her face. This time she

didn't even try to blink them away. She flexed her right foot and Dee's eye was drawn to the tiny gold ring on her second toe. She didn't usually like looking at people's bare feet, but Scarlett's were strong and rather beautiful.

'Why don't you tell me some more about Rebecca?' Dee said.

5

SCARLETT QUILTER WAS STILL in full flow. Dee looked at her notes. She'd already got plenty of useful information on Rebecca Quilter, enough to make a start on the eulogy, at any rate. She'd assumed that the family would want to write and deliver their own, or that they'd want to appoint one of Fond Farewells' recommended celebrants to lead the service, but Scarlett had asked if Dee could do it instead. 'I feel a rapport with you already,' she'd said. 'You don't mind, do you?'

Now, they needed to discuss practicalities.

'Ollie and I came to live with her in this house when Dad remarried.' Her brows knitted together in a frown. 'Barely a year after Mum died.'

Dee put her pen down. When people were talking about their loved ones, all sorts of things came out. They couldn't help themselves. Besides, she liked listening to Scarlett's voice.

'He didn't want us to move out, but in the end he

gave in. There were too many rows. And, to be honest, it probably suited him too, to have the two of us out of the way. And I'm sure Claire – our stepmother – was delighted with the decision.'

She unfurled her legs and tucked them up on the other side. 'It was one big house then. Very dated. Nothing like this,' she said, waving her arm around and looking faintly embarrassed by her surroundings. 'It still *is* dated, upstairs.'

'Does your brother still live here?' Dee asked.

'No. I moved out when I went to uni, but he only left a couple of years before the house was converted. He's done very well for himself, has Ollie, after a bit of a shaky start. He's got a place of his own now.' She gave Dee a look that conveyed both indulgence and frustration. 'I'm just hoping he finds a nice woman to settle down with. He's a lovely guy, but he's very much a *player*, if you know what I mean.'

Dee nodded.

'After uni and all through my twenties, I was living in Clapham and commuting into the City. Then I got ill – I had a really bad bout of flu and never recovered. Took me years to get a diagnosis of CFS/ME. Have you heard of it?'

'Chronic Fatigue Syndrome?' Dee said. 'Although I'm not sure what the ME stands for.'

'I'm not surprised. It's Myalgic Encephalomyelitis, hence the acronym. I have a relatively mild version, but it's one of those conditions that comes and goes.

I never know where I am with it half the time. Anyway, Rebecca suggested converting the house into two apartments so I didn't have to use the stairs when I was bad. I think it was also her way of appeasing her brother. My dad,' she added. 'He was a little put out when his parents left the entire house to her. Not that he needed the money. He's a very successful architect, but I think a part of him always thought that was unfair.'

She gave a rueful smile. 'So back I came. It's funny, but I still miss my old place. It wasn't nearly as grand as this, but . . .' Her voice trailed off. 'This is so much more convenient. I work from here too. I'm a self-employed accountant.'

She pointed towards the ceiling. 'Upstairs belongs to Ollie now. Rebecca left it to him in her will.' She drained her cup of coffee and leaned forward to place it on the trolley. 'He's going to try and rent it out. That's if he can find anyone willing to move in.'

'Was your aunt ever married?'

'No. She'd had several boyfriends in the past. *Man* friends, I should say. She was going to marry one of them, until she discovered he was playing around with someone else and had to send him packing.' Scarlett shook her head. 'Andrew Pulteney. Bit of an idiot, in my opinion. The sort of man who posts pictures of his yacht on Facebook and says things like: "Just given the old girl another lick of paint. Isn't she a beauty?"'

Scarlett put her finger in her mouth and pretended to gag. Dee smiled. She had the posh accent spot on.

'Not that Rebecca and I were in the habit of stalking him online, but you know how it is with exes. Every so often, you can't resist having a quick look. Anyway, I was very happy for her when she told us she'd found someone else. Not that she needed a man to complete her or anything like that. She was a feminist through and through. But she *wanted* one.'

Dee jotted down the phrase 'feminist, through and through'. When she looked up, Scarlett was staring into the middle distance.

'If only she hadn't wanted Clive Hamlyn.' She grimaced. 'Poor Rebecca. She'd have been better off if she'd steered well clear of men altogether.'

Dee's mind strayed to her ex. 'The *lovely* Euan', as her mum still insisted on referring to him, in that wistful voice she always used whenever she was discussing Dee's love life, or lack of one. 'He adores you, Dee. I don't know why you can't see that,' she'd said when Dee first told her she'd split up with him. 'Well, I'm not sure I adore him' had been Dee's reply, and her mother had rolled her eyes and shaken her head in exasperation. 'You're too fussy, Dee. Too demanding.' Dee hadn't told her mum the *real* reason they'd split up.

She tuned back to the present. 'Time was,' Scarlett said, 'she'd have found Clive Hamlyn very dull company. But he really seemed to *care* for her.' She twisted her mouth. 'Why do they do it? Men like him. Why do they kill the women they supposedly love? If he didn't want to look after her any more, why didn't he just leave her?'

Dee reached for her bag. She needed to leave soon to start getting ready for another funeral. 'Insecurity, misogyny, jealousy,' she said, closing her notepad and putting it away. 'Lack of positive male role models when they're growing up. It's never about love, is it? They kill because they've lost control.'

As soon as the words were out she couldn't help but think of poor Gina and what might have happened to her at the hands of a man who'd lost control. It didn't take much to nudge Gina out of the shadows. As far as anyone knew, there'd been no love interest on the scene in the weeks and months leading up to her disappearance, but then, she had been infuriatingly secretive at times. Perhaps there *had* been someone. Ten years was a long time, but that was exactly why the Caplins wanted to mark the date with a public event, to remind people that she was still missing in the hope it might jog someone's memory.

Scarlett nodded. 'That's it. That's exactly it.'

It took Dee a moment to realize that Scarlett wasn't talking about Gina but about her aunt. She lifted up her jacket from the arm of the chair and slipped it on, hoping that Scarlett wouldn't notice the tears brimming in her eyes. What on earth was wrong with her? It was so inappropriate to start crying like this, in front of a client. So unprofessional.

But it was too late. Scarlett was peering at her with concern. 'Are you all right?'

The kindness in her voice seemed to flick a switch in Dee's head and the words tumbled out before she could stop them. 'I'm so sorry. I was thinking about my friend, Gina. She . . . she disappeared. Almost ten years ago.'

She pressed her lips together. Why was she talking to this stranger about Gina?

'Oh dear. That must be awful. Not knowing if . . .' Scarlett frowned. 'Gina, did you say? You don't mean Gina Caplin?'

Dee nodded. She'd guessed that Scarlett might recognize the name. Most people did. Gina's disappearance had been a major news story for weeks on end when it happened. There were often articles about her in the press. Fresh inquiries that came to nothing. There'd even been a TV documentary.

'We'd been friends since we were five.'

'I'm so sorry,' Scarlett said. 'There's going to be a big memorial event next year, isn't there? I saw something in the local paper last week.'

'Yes, we're helping her parents organize it.' Dee sighed. 'The chances of finding her alive after all this time are so slim they're virtually non-existent, but until she's found we can't be a hundred per cent certain that she's . . .'

Dee closed her eyes. The thought of Gina still alive but trapped somewhere awful, imprisoned by some kind of monster, was too horrific to contemplate. But, of course, she *did* contemplate it, more often than she cared to – it was impossible not to be tormented by those thoughts and it would be a million times worse for her poor parents.

'I'm afraid I've got to head off,' she said, suddenly anxious to change the subject. In Dee's experience, when people found out that she'd been friends with Gina Caplin, it was all they ever wanted to talk about – some of them just couldn't contain their morbid curiosity. It was a toxic kind of fame that she and Lindsay and everyone close to Gina had had to learn to live with. Although Scarlett Quilter didn't seem like the sort of person to start quizzing her about it. Maybe that's why she'd told her. Besides, the poor woman had enough trauma of her own to deal with. And she'd be on the receiving end of that same toxic fame herself now.

'We've made a good start,' she said. 'I think one more meeting should be enough to discuss the funeral itself and what sort of thing you'd like. Shall we make another appointment?'

Scarlett looked at her watch. 'I didn't realize that was the time. You should have stopped me wittering on.'

'Absolutely not,' Dee said. 'It's important for me to know what kind of person your aunt was so that the eulogy I write is meaningful to you and your family and everyone who knew and loved her.'

'Do you mind if I ring you another time to make the second appointment?' Scarlett said. 'Only I think my father and brother ought to be present for that one.'

'Of course,' Dee said. 'Although I'd strongly recommend that the three of you get together beforehand, to make sure you're all singing from the same hymn sheet, so to speak. I've had meetings with families before where they can't seem to agree on anything, and it can become a little . . . *fraught*.'

As the door clicked shut behind her Dee noticed two things: the gloominess of the hallway after the light-filled interior she'd just left, and the sudden increase in her heart rate. She strode towards the main front door and let herself out as fast as she could. Traffic was building and a 486 had stopped right in front of the house. Curious faces turned their gaze on her as she hurried down the path and on to the street. It felt intrusive and voyeuristic. Poor Scarlett, having to endure this each time she left the house.

When she got back to the office, Lindsay had stuck a yellow Post-it Note on her screen. It said simply: 'Terrible review on Facebook page! Check it out.' Dee frowned. They hadn't had any dissatisfied customers, as far as she could recall. Quite the opposite, in fact. They usually got recommendations and five-star ratings. Scarlett Quilter had mentioned earlier that it was the main reason she'd chosen to use them in the first place.

Dee logged on straight away, her heart sinking when she saw the one-star rating from someone called T. J. Cooper. Who the hell was that? Then she read the message and felt sick. It was malicious, it had to be. Some nasty troll getting kicks at their expense.

Fond Farewells is a terrible, terrible funeral firm. They do not respect the dead. Don't take any notice of the crap on their website. It's all lies, lies, lies.

6

SCARLETT SAT IN SILENCE for a few minutes, then made her way through the kitchen and into the spare bedroom she used as an office. It was about time she eased herself back into her routine and caught up with her accountancy work. First, though, she needed to contact her dad and Ollie. What was it Dee Boswell had said? 'Make sure you're all singing from the same hymn sheet.'

Hmm. Fat chance of that. Since when had anyone in their family agreed on anything?

She settled herself at her desk and reached for the phone. She shouldn't have asked about the missing friend's name. Scarlett had fended off enough enquiries about Rebecca over the past few weeks to know how intrusive it felt when people asked questions. Perhaps that was the reason the poor woman had rushed off. There'd been a stillness about Dee up to that point. A deep sense of compassion. Talking to her had been almost like therapy. Was that why

Scarlett had found herself rabbiting on about her dad and Claire?

Still, she supposed funeral directors were used to relatives going off at a tangent. Even ones who looked far too young to be doing such a job. Scarlett did the maths. Rebecca had done supply teaching when Scarlett was in her first year at uni, living in halls of residence in Edgbaston, so if she'd taught Dee Boswell in Year 12, Dee could only be two years younger than Scarlett herself.

She thought of Dee's fresh, unlined face and large, clear eyes, her mouse-coloured hair cropped short in a flattering elfin style, not to mention those giraffe-patterned socks peeking out from the bottom of her trousers – the sort of socks one might buy for a child. How astonishing that she was forty years old. Scarlett smiled. She wondered what her dad would make of Dee Boswell, funeral director. He'd be expecting a man, knowing him.

Three hours later, Scarlett yawned and rubbed her eyes. She'd decluttered her inbox, prioritized her tasks in order of importance *and* arranged a meeting with her dad and Ollie for this evening. She'd also managed to get some possible dates from them both for a meeting with Dee Boswell. It was time for lunch now. After that, she needed to get on to the council to see if they'd remove the flowers outside the house. It seemed callous to get rid of them – they were, after all, a tribute to Rebecca – but people would be less inclined to gawp once they were gone.

After picking at a bowl of pasta and cheese and throwing most of it away, it wasn't long before she was on the phone to Ollie again. 'Apparently, it's *our* responsibility to clear the flowers. Even though we didn't put them there. Just like it was our responsibility to get that cleaning firm in. It's outrageous.'

'Don't worry. I'll get one of the lads to come round in a van.' Ollie always called the men who worked for him 'lads', unless they were much older, in which case he called them 'blokes'. 'I'm thinking you don't want to keep any of the cards and messages?'

Scarlett considered this for a moment. 'Maybe I *should* look at them. Perhaps one or two could be read out at the funeral.'

'Okay. No worries,' he said. 'It'll probably be Mickey who does it. Is that okay?'

Scarlett felt her neck flush. 'Just so long as he doesn't expect tea and biscuits.'

Ollie made a harumphing noise. 'I'll get him to post any cards through the letterbox.'

When the phone call was over, Scarlett wondered what, if anything, her brother knew. The way he'd said, 'Is that okay?' had worried her slightly. No, Mickey wouldn't have said anything. Surely he wouldn't. It had been years ago. Ollie would have mentioned it before now.

*

That evening, Ollie arrived first. But there was nothing unusual in that. Her father was always late. Scarlett felt sorry for his put-upon PA, who was always ringing ahead to apologize on his behalf.

'He'll be with you in five,' Jane said on the phone now, in her breathy, slightly anxious-sounding voice.

Scarlett sighed. Why was the poor woman still at the office at this time in the evening anyway? Scarlett thanked her and said goodbye.

'What was the point in that?' she asked Ollie. 'He could have called me himself.'

Ollie shrugged. 'I'm surprised he still wipes his own arse, to be honest. It's a status thing, isn't it? Why keep a dog and bark yourself?'

'But we're family. His own flesh and blood. And this isn't work. We're arranging his sister's funeral.'

'Everything's work to him. You should know that by now.' Ollie stretched his legs out in front of him and stared at his phone. 'How long do you reckon this will take?'

Scarlett shot him a furious look. 'Not you, too. Got something more important on, have you?'

'Of course not. How can you say that? It's just that I said I'd meet this girl for a drink. I need to let her know I'll be late.'

Scarlett sighed. Was he already seeing someone else? 'What's happened to Nikki, then?' she said. Of all her brother's girlfriends, Nikki had been the one she'd liked the most. She'd been hoping he felt the same way.

Ollie didn't look up. 'Nothing. She's still around.'

Scarlett sighed. 'Aren't you getting a bit old for all this, Ollie?'

'Old? What are you talking about? And what do you mean, "all this"?' He stared at her, the hurt in his eyes making her wish she'd kept her mouth shut. 'If you mean having my first night out, my first *down* time, after the kind of month no sane person would wish on their very worst enemy, then no, I don't think I'm *a bit old* for that.'

The pain in his voice tore at Scarlett's heart, because it was her pain too. 'I'm sorry. I didn't mean to make you feel bad.'

They heard the front door open and close, then their father's voice. 'Fucking traffic!'

When Scarlett peered into the hall, she caught him standing in front of Rebecca's door, staring at it warily the same way she had done when she'd first returned.

'Shit!' he said. 'This is all so . . .'

For a second or two, she thought he was going to break down. She'd heard him weeping once or twice, behind the closed door of his and Claire's bedroom, but so far he'd managed to hold himself together in front of her.

'Come on, Dad. Let's get you a drink.'

7

Scarlett poured herself another glass of red and tried not to look at her father's appalled expression. Two minutes ago, he'd been delighted at her suggestion of adding 'Dido's Lament' to the music list. Then she'd told him what version she wanted.

'Alison *Moyet*?' he said, the surname exploding out of his mouth. 'Are you serious?'

Ollie muttered something under his breath that Scarlett felt sure was 'Fuck's sake'. She gave him a pointed look. If he was so keen to get to the pub and see this new *girl* of his, why the hell wouldn't he back her up?

'Have you ever heard her sing it, Dad?' she said, reaching for her iPad. 'Here, I'll play it for you. It's a fabulous bluesy rendition. Rebecca loved it. She always said how much more emotional impact it had than a classical performance.'

'Balderdash! You need to listen to Janet Baker sing it. Or Sarah Connolly.'

Ollie sat up at last. 'For God's sake, Dad! We know opera is your *thing*, but it's not *your* funeral we're arranging, is it? It's Rebecca's.' He slumped back down again. 'Why does any of this matter, anyway? It won't bring her back, will it?'

The two of them stared at each other in anger. Scarlett wanted to scream at them both to fuck right off if they were going to turn this into one of their stupid stand-offs. What was *wrong* with them? Now really wasn't the time. Instead, she found what she was looking for and pressed play. The sudden orchestral swell did the trick and broke the unbearable tension.

Her dad scowled. 'She's got a good voice, I'll grant you that,' he said. 'But it isn't right for an aria. Purcell would turn in his grave.'

'Purcell wouldn't give a shit,' Ollie said.

Peter Quilter glared at his son. 'Do you have to be so consistently flippant about *everything*?'

'No. Do you have to be so consistently——'

Scarlett's patience snapped. 'Will you two please shut up?' she said, slapping her iPad shut and tossing it on to the end of the sofa in a temper. Dee Boswell had been right. Thank God they weren't having this discussion, if that's what it was, in front of her.

'You asked me to take the lead in organizing this funeral, and that's what I'm doing. If we don't get this sorted tonight, when *are* we going to sort it?'

'Scar's right, Dad. And what would Rebecca think if she could see us all shouting at each other like this? Haven't we been through enough? The shock of losing her – of losing her *like that* – it's horrific.' Ollie's eyes shone with unshed tears. 'And then there's all the rest of it. Being interviewed by the police. How people look at us – you can see it in their eyes, some of them, the questions they want to ask.' He dragged his fingers through his hair. 'Let's just get this done, yeah?'

Scarlett gave her brother a grateful look. He was right. This last month had taken its toll on all of them.

Peter Quilter threw his hands up in the air in defeat. 'Okay, okay. I'm sorry.'

Scarlett looked down at her list. Only two items crossed off and they'd been here half an hour already. It was going to be a long evening.

Scarlett watched from the window as her dad climbed into the waiting taxi. They'd opened a second bottle of wine in the end, which meant that neither he nor Ollie could drive themselves home. Ollie had turned down the offer of a ride and insisted on walking. And he had the cheek to call *her* the stubborn one.

Scarlett locked up, then wheeled the dirty glasses into the kitchen on the trolley and washed them up by hand. She poured herself a tumbler of water, took it through to her bedroom. An hour later and she was still wide awake. She'd wanted a direct cremation for Rebecca, followed by a small private gathering in her dad and Claire's house – it was plenty big enough to accommodate the family and Rebecca's friends – but apparently Claire had put the kibosh on that. The silly cow probably didn't want them all traipsing through her show-house rooms with their outdoor shoes on. And they couldn't have it here, for obvious reasons.

'Okay, so why don't we hire a private function room in a hotel or something?' she'd suggested instead, but her dad had insisted on 'doing it properly' at the crematorium, so that anyone who knew Rebecca and wanted to pay their respects could come along – which was exactly the scenario Scarlett had been hoping to avoid. She didn't want a load of random schoolgirls *emoting* all over the place. Ollie, much to her annoyance, had sat on the fence.

She got out of bed and put on her dressing gown, wandered back into the living room and put the TV on, ended up watching *Naked Attraction*, of all things, and muttering at the sheer lunacy of it. Every so often, when a particularly unpleasant set of genitals filled the screen, she stared up at the ceiling. It had become a compulsion, this perpetual looking up.

'I don't suppose any of it really matters, does it?' she said aloud, and imagined her aunt smiling sadly and shaking her head.

'Turn that rubbish off and go back to bed,' Rebecca said, as if she were right there in the room with her.

Scarlett did as she was told.

In the bathroom, she sat on the loo and wondered when Mickey North would be round to clear the flowers. Ever since Ollie had mentioned his name, she thought of him every time she came in here, the way his T-shirt had ridden up as he lay on the floor disconnecting the pipes under the old bathtub. It had been a moment of madness, coming on to him like that. *Mickey North*, of all people. The same Mickey North who'd got into so much trouble as a youngster. Nothing too serious – the odd fight with some other lads, a bit of shoplifting – but enough to get him cautioned a couple of times.

Their dad had been furious when Ollie got mixed up in some of that too. But as Rebecca had tried to tell him, Ollie was a good boy with a heart of gold who'd lost his mum and gone off the rails for a while. He needed to be patient with him. As for Mickey, she'd said, why, you only had to look at his home life to see what a poor start the boy had had.

Rebecca, ever the peacekeeper. Ever the kind heart. And she'd been right, hadn't she? Mickey had come good in the end. They both had. Mickey had worked for Ollie ever since Ollie had started the firm. He was one of his most loyal employees.

But after what had happened between them, here in this bathroom, and then afterwards in the bedroom, Scarlett had done her best to avoid him. It hadn't been all that difficult. Close as they were, Scarlett rarely socialized with her brother outside of family occasions. And besides, it had been such a long time ago.

She flushed the loo and went back to bed. Was that why Rebecca had allowed Clive Hamlyn into her life? Because he'd been an attractive man? Because he was more straightforward and down to earth than some of her more *cultured* male friends – the Andrew Pulteneys of this world? Men like her dad, who could wax lyrical about opera and be great dinner-party guests but who must be pretty tiresome to actually *live* with.

She turned off her lamp and settled down under the duvet, but now that Clive Hamlyn had invaded her thoughts, all she could think of was what he'd done to her poor aunt, not six feet from where she now lay.

And now something else was running amok in her head. It would be totally inappropriate to play 'Dido's Lament' at Rebecca's funeral, no matter how much her aunt had loved it. Dido had killed herself out of grief when her lover, Aeneas, set sail for Italy and abandoned her. Rebecca hadn't loved Clive Hamlyn. Not in the end. She'd wanted to break off their engagement, said he'd done something unforgiveable. She'd wanted rid of him, and he'd killed her in cold blood.

Scarlett punched her pillow in frustration and wept. If only she'd voiced her concerns about him sooner, maybe Rebecca would still be alive.

8

As soon as she'd read that awful review, Dee trawled through the Fond Farewells database to check for the name T. J. Cooper, but it wasn't there. She'd known it wouldn't be. If a previous client had been *that* dissatisfied with them, she and Lindsay would almost certainly have known about it.

Lindsay was on her hands and knees in the prep room, her head stuck in one of the lower cupboards, when Dee went down to talk to her.

'I've just read it,' Dee said.

Lindsay shuffled out backwards and stood up, her cheeks pink from the exertion of scrubbing. 'It's *awful*, isn't it?' She peeled off her rubber gloves and flung them into the sink. 'I didn't know whether to report it to Facebook. Do you think we should?' she said. 'Get it removed?'

'Maybe, but that might take ages and, in the meantime, potential customers will see it and be put off.'

47

Lindsay frowned. 'Okay, let's think logically about this. What would you do if it was an ordinary sort of complaint, like, good firm but their urns are a bit pricey?'

Dee thought about this. 'I'd respond as politely as possible. Thank them for their review and explain how we commission a local ceramic artist to make our urns, that they're hand-crafted originals, hence the price, but that we do supply more affordable receptacles for ashes, and clients are, of course, at liberty to provide their own.'

Lindsay grinned. 'I love the way that just tripped off your tongue,' she said. 'That's why you're in the office and I'm down here with my head stuck in a cupboard and my arse in the air.'

Dee smiled. It was true, they both had their own areas of expertise, and though they could each assume the other's role when necessary, there was no denying that Dee's skills lay firmly in communication and administration. Dee spent her days filing death certificates and getting permits – all the paper-pushing exercises that enabled them to work within the law and fulfil their obligations. She took responsibility for the arrangement meetings and liaised with celebrants and ministers and crematorium staff. She oversaw the funerals, sometimes even delivered them herself.

Whereas Lindsay (and one or other of their small but loyal band of part-timers, including her godsend of a brother, Jake) dealt primarily with the bodies. She picked them up from nursing homes or hospital mortuaries and prepared them for burial or cremation. Plus, she looked after the shopfront and the graphics on their website and social media accounts.

Back in the office, Dee typed out a reply, cross with herself that she'd let her emotions temporarily cloud her judgement. Her fingers flew over the keyboard. '*We are very sorry and, frankly, shocked, to read this review of our services. We try our utmost to respect the wishes of all our clients and their families and pride ourselves on providing exactly the sort of service they request. We are afraid that we do not recognize your name from our records, so I would ask you please to contact us directly so that we can look into the details of your complaint and rectify any misunderstanding.*'

'Take *that*, T. J. Cooper,' she said.

The rest of the day flew by. Dee barely had time to grab a bite to eat before heading out to Kent for a woodland burial she'd been helping a family from Lewisham arrange. It was a beautiful location with sweeping views over the Swale estuary. She and Lindsay had used similar sites for quite a few clients in the past, only one of which had involved holding hands and chanting, or whatever Scarlett Quilter had said would not be appropriate for her aunt.

The important thing was that more and more

people were now opting for green funerals, liking the fact that their loved ones could be laid to rest in biodegradable coffins among native trees and wild-flowers with only the simplest of natural grave markings rather than a headstone. Not all of them realized that they couldn't bury their nearest and dearest actually *under* a tree, but once it had been explained to them about the roots growing up through the body they were usually quite happy to settle for a more appropriate position within sight of the trees.

This afternoon's service had gone well and the family had all thanked Dee personally for the sim-plicity of the occasion. But as she sat in heavy traffic on the A2 heading back into London, her thoughts returned to the mysterious T. J. Cooper and that dreadful review. The more she thought about it, the more spiteful it seemed. The more personal. As if someone out there had some kind of grudge against them.

By the time she pulled into her space in the Labur-num Court car park, she was tired and hungry. She pressed her fob key against the heavy steel door and went inside. When she'd left home first thing this morning, the stairwell had reeked of urine. Now it smelled of disinfectant. She took the stairs up to the fourth floor – she hadn't taken the lift since that time she'd been stuck in it for almost forty minutes – and turned into the external communal walkway. Mrs

Kowalski's bucket and mop were still outside her front door, and so were her orange Crocs. She waved at Dee from her kitchen window and Dee waved back. Mrs Kowalski had been waving to her more often lately.

As usual, the front door was on the latch.

'All right, love?' her dad called from the kitchen. 'How'd it go today?'

'Bloody hell,' he said, when she told him about taking on Rebecca Quilter's funeral. 'You sure you're okay with that?'

'Can't afford to turn work down, Dad.'

He handed her a mug of tea. 'It's going to be a tough one,' he said. 'I mean, funerals are never easy, but . . .' He shook his head. 'Something like that – the horrible way she was killed . . .'

'Her niece wants it to be a celebration of her life. She says she was a good woman. Full of life and joy.'

John Boswell nodded and Dee waited for him to come out with his favourite cliché – 'It's always the good who die before their time' – but instead he said: 'Eva thinks it's a wonderful job you're doing, helping people remember their loved ones.'

Dee frowned. 'Who's Eva?'

He tipped his head at the wall. 'Mrs Kowalski. I was talking to her the other day.'

Dee glanced at him. There was a studied careless-ness in his voice. Was something going on between her dad and their neighbour? It had been two years since her parents had got divorced, and now that her mum had moved to Scotland with her new man, it was about time her dad got his life back.

'I see she's cleaned the stairwell again,' Dee said.

'You should have heard her slag off that cleaning company.' Her dad grinned. 'She was magnificent.'

Dee caught his eye but he immediately leaned down and plucked a handful of old newspapers from the floor, started leafing through them. At last, he found what he was looking for and opened one of them up on the table. The faces of Rebecca Quilter and Clive Hamlyn stared out from the front page under the headline: MURDER-SUICIDE: CLEANER MAKES GRUESOME DISCOVERY.

Dee read the first few paragraphs. Certain phrases leapt out at her. 'Bloody footprints matched fiancé's slippers', 'Fiancé's DNA found on handle of baseball bat', 'Neighbours report an altercation in the garden earlier in the day.'

Dee studied the man smiling up at her from the paper.

'He looks so ordinary, doesn't he? So normal,' she said.

Her dad gave a wry laugh. 'They all do, love. They all do.'

Dee scanned the rest of the article. 'Says here the family are claiming the antidepressants he was on made him suicidal, that the stress of caring for someone with dementia was too much for him.'

Her dad snorted. 'Why didn't he just kill himself then? Why did he have to kill her too?'

Later that evening, Dee remembered Sue Caplin's WhatsApp message and called her straight away.

'Sue, how are you? Sorry it's taken me so long to get back to you.'

'No worries, hon. I know how busy you and Lindsay are.'

The familiar voice in her ear was like a direct line to the past, when she and Lindsay would go back to Gina's house after school. The three of them had been inseparable since primary school.

'I was just wondering if you'd like to come round next Saturday afternoon,' Sue said. 'We want to update you on what the police said about the gathering in March.'

Dee noted Sue's use of the word 'gathering' and decided that that's what they'd call it from now on.

'I'm sure that'll be fine. I'll have a chat with Lindsay and get back to you.'

Dee WhatsApped Lindsay as soon as the call was over.

'On tinder date let's talk tomoz' came the instant response.

Dee sent a thumbs-up in reply. Then she plugged her phone into the charger by her bed and changed into her Gizmo Gremlins pyjamas. Sitting in a crowded bar with a stranger wasn't her idea of fun, but Lindsay seemed to love it. The thrill of the chase, she called it, not wanting to actually catch someone for good, or be caught herself. It scared Dee, knowing that Lindsay sometimes had sex with men she hardly knew, but then, maybe she was right not to let fear dictate her lifestyle. Maybe Dee's own reluctance to leave home and get her own place, to *start living*, as Lindsay would say, was just as much a reaction to Gina's disappearance as Lindsay's determination to live life to the full and to hell with the risks.

She climbed into bed and switched her TV on. Perhaps this *gathering* for Gina was exactly what they both needed in order to move on with their lives. What Sue and Alan needed, too. A tacit assumption that wherever Gina was and whatever it was that had happened to her, she wasn't coming back. Not after all this time.

9

Lindsay was already there when Dee arrived at work the next morning. Dee took in her friend's smudged eye make-up and tired eyes. Her normally straightened blonde hair was looking somewhat frizzy and wild, but the truth was, even hungover, she looked good.

'I take it last night was a success then?'

Lindsay gave her a sheepish grin which soon turned into a yawn. 'We went on to a club. He's a really good dancer.' Her voice was hoarse.

Dee gave her an enquiring look. 'And?'

'And nothing. We drank. We danced. We snogged. Then he put me in a cab and I went home.'

'Do you think you'll see him again?'

'Yes. Tomorrow. Look, he's texted already.'

She took out her phone and showed Dee his photo.

Dee gave an appreciative 'mm', but the strong-necked guy staring moodily at the camera wasn't really her type. Lindsay was a sucker for a chiselled face and a six-pack.

'I spoke to Sue last night,' she said.

Lindsay closed her eyes. 'Shit. Sorry. I forgot all about that.'

Dee relayed the gist of the conversation. 'She wants us to drop round next weekend.'

'Phew. I thought for a minute you were going to say tomorrow. I wanted to spend the afternoon getting ready for my date.'

'What's his name, then?'

'Callum. Callum Jeffreys. Want me to ask if he's got a mate going spare?'

Dee gave her a pointed look. 'Don't you dare. I'm perfectly capable of finding my own dates, thank you very much.'

'So you keep saying, but where's the evidence?'

Dee stuck her middle finger in the air and Lindsay laughed. 'Seriously, Dee. You need to get out more. It's been, what, eight years since you were in a proper relationship? You know what they say: all work and no play makes Dee a—'

Dee held her hand up in front of her, palm outwards. 'Perfectly happy girl,' she said, hoping the words would somehow make it so. Had it really been eight years since she and Euan had split up? It didn't seem possible.

*

Dee was halfway through a rough draft of Rebecca Quilter's eulogy when the phone rang. It was Scarlett, wanting to arrange the second meeting.

'Let me have a look in the diary,' Dee said, when Scarlett had reeled off the options. It wouldn't do to give the impression that Fond Farewells didn't have that much work on right now. In any case, it wouldn't last. Clients were like buses. A long wait, then three turned up at once. Just so long as that bad review didn't put people off.

After a suitable pause, she plumped for the following Tuesday. Lindsay popped her head round the door just as she was putting the phone down.

'Fancy a walk round the park? I could murder an egg-and-bacon sarnie from the café. We can talk more about the anniversary.'

Dee stood up and stretched. 'Good idea. If Sue and Alan want updating on progress, we'd better make sure we've got something positive to share with them.'

The air was crisp and cold, but the sun was bright and golden. A perfect autumn day. As usual, Lindsay set a punishing pace and Dee kept having to remind her to slow down. Eventually, they found their rhythm. Walking together had been what got the two of them through those first dreadful weeks after Gina had gone missing. The weeks when they'd feared the worst, but hoped, and prayed, for the best. They had walked, the two of them, to all the places they'd hung out as teenagers, as if by revisiting their youth they might somehow, miraculously, return to a safer, more innocent time. But the weeks had turned into months, and the months into years, and Gina was still gone.

They'd carried on walking, though, all this time. It was their thing. Their ritual.

'Sue's started referring to Gina's event as a gathering,' Dee said.

Lindsay made an approving noise at the back of her throat. 'I suppose that's better than calling it an anniversary event, which has always struck me as sounding more like a celebration. And "memorial" implies she's dead.'

Dee nodded. '"Remembrance" is just as bad. I mean, it shouldn't be. Just because we're remembering her, it doesn't mean we think she's gone for good.'

Lindsay kicked a conker along the path in front of her. 'But we kind of do, don't we?'

Dee swallowed hard. It was the first time either of them had said this out loud.

'Sorry,' Lindsay said, her voice cracking.

'No, it's me who should apologize. For not being brave enough to say it first.'

'I can go for days and days without thinking of her at all,' Lindsay said. 'Then something happens, some little thing that reminds me, and it's the worst feeling in the world. Because it's all mixed up with guilt for forgetting.'

'Not thinking about her all the time doesn't mean you've forgotten.'

'I know that, but knowing something in theory doesn't help, does it?'

'Maybe having this service will be like drawing a line under the past.'

'Not a line, exactly,' Lindsay said. 'More like the asterisk you sometimes get in books, to signify the end of a scene.'

'Yes,' Dee said. 'That's exactly what it's like.'

In the café, they filled each other in on the progress they had made. Dee had brought the Caplins' wish list with her and was ticking items off as they covered each one.

'I've spoken to our old school about using the hall,' she said. 'They said they'll lease it to us for free and they'll provide someone to oversee the audio-visuals so we can play the original TV reconstruction, that's if the BBC let us have it.'

'Good work,' Lindsay said. 'And I've talked to Jake about fundraising ideas for the missing-persons charity Sue supports. He's going to talk to the lads in the football team about putting on a special match. He's already sounded Euan out and he thinks it's a great idea.' She looked at Dee across the top of her coffee cup. 'Euan and his girlfriend have split up, did you hear? She's going home to Germany.'

Dee shrugged. 'Yeah, Jake mentioned it when he

dropped by last week. Although why either of you thinks I'm the least bit interested in what Euan's up to, I really don't know. Just because we used to go out together doesn't mean I need to know every single detail about his life.'

Lindsay gave an exaggerated sigh. 'You make it sound like you just went out on a couple of dates. You were engaged to be *married*, Dee! Jake reckons he's never really got over breaking up with you.'

Dee gave Lindsay a warning look.

'Okay, okay. I'll shut up. I just worry about you sometimes.'

'Well, there's no need. I'm perfectly happy on my own.' Dee plopped a sugar cube into her coffee. She didn't actually take sugar any more, but every so often it was nice. A little treat. 'And if anyone needs to be worried, it's me,' she said as she stirred it in. 'About *you*.'

'Why on earth would you worry about me?'

Dee rolled her eyes. Lindsay could be exasperating. She knew damn well what Dee was talking about.

'Meeting strangers on Tinder. Having sex with them too fast.'

Lindsay smirked. 'Nothing wrong with fast sex.'

'Too soon, I meant, and you know it. It's dangerous. And I'm not the only one who worries about you. Jake does too.'

Lindsay sighed, and Dee knew she'd hit a nerve.

'You want to be careful,' she'd heard Lindsay's brother say to her on more than one occasion. 'I've heard the way blokes talk about girls they hook up with on Tinder, and it isn't nice. *They* aren't nice.'

Dee softened her voice. 'You don't even know them, Lins. They could be anyone, they could be—'

Lindsay reached across the table and rested her hand gently on Dee's wrist. 'I'm not stupid, Dee. I never go back to their place, and I always make out the lodger's in her room.' She withdrew her hand.

'You don't have a lodger.'

'Duh!'

'Oh, I see.'

Lindsay finished her sandwich and Dee opened the packet on her saucer to eat the cinnamon biscuit. Lindsay gave her the one from her saucer, too.

'*You* could be my lodger – I keep telling you. Or if you think that's too much, us working *and* living together, you could just move in while you're look-ing for somewhere more permanent. Think about it, Dee. It'd be fun. I know you and your dad are close but, for crying out loud, isn't it about time you left home?'

Dee snapped the biscuit in half. It would be so easy to say yes. She wanted to, more than anything, but listening to Lindsay having sex in the next room would be torture.

'All right,' she said. 'I'll think about it.'

'One more thing,' Lindsay said. 'I'm going to

arrange for us to meet up with Jake and Euan one evening next week. Just the four of us.' Dee opened her mouth to protest. 'And before you say anything, it's for Gina, okay? To fill them in on the arrangements for next March and see what plans are in place for the football match. I thought maybe the Dial Arch?'

Dee sighed. She could hardly say no. Jake and Euan were Gina's friends, too. They'd all been at school together and, as they'd got older, had become a supportive group of friends. 'The Famous Five', as Dee's dad used to call them. Jake and Gina had even dated for a while, when they were in their early twenties, before Gina went off to dance school and Jake fell in love with Hayley and got married. Then Euan and Dee had hooked up some years later. Just because they were no longer an item didn't change their shared history. Lindsay was right. They were doing this for Gina.

10

THE FOLLOWING TUESDAY, DEE parked in the nearest side street and walked to Scarlett Quilter's house. Most, if not all, of the flowers on the pavement were now dead, the leaves and petals dried and curling beneath the cellophane. Someone had left an empty bottle of beer slap bang in the middle of the display, a deliberate act of disrespect that made the muscles in Dee's jaw tighten. She marched towards the front door, anxious to get inside. She stumbled on the concrete ramp, just as the door swung open to reveal a broad-shouldered man in jeans and a tight-fitting T-shirt that showed off his muscles. He reached out to break her fall.

'Whoa, you okay?'

Dee nodded, embarrassed.

'You must be the funeral director. I'm Ollie. The nephew,' he said. 'Scarlett's brother.'

An annoying blush stained Dee's cheeks. Trust her to make a fool of herself like that. She gave him a brisk smile and shook his hand, keen to reassert her professionalism as quickly as possible. Ollie Quilter shared the same hair colouring and facial features as his sister. The high forehead and long nose, the deep-set brown eyes. Like her, there were dark circles under his eyes, but his seemed more pronounced. If she hadn't known he was Scarlett's younger brother, Dee would have thought him older than her.

'Must be a great ice-breaker at parties,' he said.

Scarlett appeared in her doorway and gave Dee a quick nod by way of greeting. 'What must?'

Ollie stepped aside to let Dee in. 'Saying she's an undertaker.'

'It does tend to raise a few eyebrows,' Dee said and, once more, she stepped into the bright, spacious kitchen wishing she'd arranged for the meeting to be at the office instead. Scarlett had taken it for granted that Dee would come to the house, and Dee hadn't thought to suggest otherwise.

'Dee, this is my father, Peter Quilter.' Scarlett gestured to an older, silver-haired man standing in front of the coffee machine and frowning at a selection of coloured pods.

For a moment, he looked bemused at the sight of her. Then he sprang forward, hand outstretched, his face transformed by a generous smile.

'So good of you to come,' he said warmly, as if this were a social occasion and not a meeting to arrange the funeral of his dead sister. His murdered sister. But then, if there was one thing Dee had learned above all else from her time in the funeral industry, it was that everyone reacted differently to the trauma of death and grief.

She remembered the family of the young man who'd been hit and killed by a van while riding his motorbike. His parents and girlfriend had been more worried about whether to put his favourite crash helmet in the coffin with him than what type of funeral service to have. In the end, they'd chosen to commemorate his life by inviting friends and relatives to go bowling in his honour at the local alley, where he'd been a keen team member. They had swigged cans of Coke and eaten French fries with tomato ketchup. Tears had been shed, but they'd been mingled with fun and laughter.

Dee shook Peter Quilter's hand. There was no *right* way to behave, only the way that felt most natural to the individuals concerned.

'I must say, I was a little taken aback when Scarlett suggested using an *alternative* funeral company,' he said. 'I'm more of a traditionalist myself.'

There was, Dee thought, something faintly derisory about his emphasis on the word 'alternative', but somehow he'd managed to smooth it over with a disarming smile. He was one of those men who gave the impression of being at ease with themselves and the world, confident of their place in it. Someone who liked the sound of their own voice and was sure in their opinions.

He glanced back at the coffee pods and then directly at Scarlett. 'For instance, what's wrong with good old-fashioned filter coffee?'

Scarlett gave Dee a look that seemed to say *See what I have to put up with?* and Dee felt that same sense of connection she'd experienced at their first meeting, like a pulse of energy travelling between them.

'Try one of the purple or black ones, Dad. You'll be surprised.'

'Let's attend to our visitor first, shall we?' He picked up one of the pods and held it up for Dee's approval.

'Perfect,' she said, and went to sit in the armchair Scarlett was directing her to, the same oversized one she'd sat in before, except everything felt different today. The atmosphere was heavier, somehow. Laden with tension.

The brother, Ollie, was now sprawled on the floor, his back against one end of the green velvet sofa, his legs sticking out in front of him. He looked up at her briefly then continued scrolling on his phone.

'This is one of the drawbacks of these wretched machines,' Peter said from the kitchen. 'You can't just pour everyone a cup in one go. You have to stand here, faffing about with handles and pods, and by the time they're all ready, the one you made first is already cold.'

Scarlett sighed in exasperation. 'For God's sake, Dad! Go and sit down and let me do it.'

'They're an odd family,' Dee told Lindsay that evening. The two of them were refreshing their window display. Or rather, Lindsay was refreshing it while Dee perched on one corner of the display shelf watching her. Outside, it was starting to get dark. The fifth of November was still two weeks away, but someone, somewhere, was letting off fireworks.

'How so?'

Dee wrinkled her nose. 'It's hard to explain. It's the way they communicate with each other.'

Lindsay crouched in the window, her back to the street, and made a few last tweaks to an impressive arrangement of autumn flowers and foliage. When they'd first started the business, they'd studied the window displays of their competitors and found them sadly clichéd and wanting. Granite and marble headstones on crumpled purple velvet. Sad displays of faded artificial flowers and those dreadful fans of glossy pamphlets selling funeral plans.

'People don't want to look at headstones,' Lindsay had said. 'We need to create something fresh and original, something that keeps changing that people will look forward to seeing as they walk past.'

So they'd plumped for flowers and hanging voile panels and brightly painted ceramic urns created by a local artist, rearranging them and rotating them to create different colour schemes. Fond Farewells' ever-changing window display had become a talking point in the neighbourhood. It had even featured in the local paper.

Lindsay stood up and teetered slightly. For one awful moment, Dee imagined her falling backwards into the glass and crashing through it on to the street. One of the passers-by stopped – a man hunched into a waxed waterproof jacket. It was Ollie Quilter.

He moved towards the door and tried to come in.

'We're closed,' Lindsay said, shaking her head at him apologetically.

'It's okay,' Dee said, sliding off the display shelf. 'It's Rebecca Quilter's nephew. I'd better see what he wants.'

She unlocked the door and stuck her head outside.

'Sorry, didn't mean to disturb you,' he said. 'I just wanted to apologize about my dad this morning. All that stuff he came out with about not wanting to use your company. Just take all that with a pinch of salt. He can be a bit . . . ' – he shrugged – 'you know.'

'There's no need to apologize,' Dee said. 'I wasn't in the least bit offended.'

Ollie Quilter stood there, hands thrust deep into the pockets of his jacket. Lindsay had now climbed out of the window and was standing next to Dee at the door. Dee noticed his eyes flick over her.

'Good,' he said. 'By the way, my sister tells me you were taught by my aunt.'

'That's right,' Dee said. 'Only for a term, but we remember her.'

Ollie looked at Lindsay again. He paused, as if he wasn't quite sure what to say next. 'Right, well, I'll be off then.' He started to walk away, then called back over his shoulder. 'Nice window, by the way.'

Lindsay looked at Dee and grinned. 'You didn't tell me he was gorgeous.'

Dee locked the door. 'I didn't think he was.'

Lindsay arched her eyebrows. 'Are you serious? And what was all that about the dad?'

They moved back into the window for Lindsay to finish what she'd been doing.

'I've no idea. I mean, he did say something about being taken aback that Scarlett had hired us, but he was perfectly civil about it. It certainly wasn't worthy of an apology.'

Lindsay smiled. 'Maybe it was just an excuse to come in and speak to you.'

'Don't be daft. Anyway, he's a *client*.'

Lindsay did one of her exaggerated eyerolls. 'There's absolutely nothing in the funeral director's code to say you can't date a client. Unless they're dead, of course. That's never a good idea. Seriously, though, Dee, he's *hot*. I can't believe you haven't noticed.'

'I didn't *say* I hadn't noticed. But he's not my type.

Anyway, according to his sister, he's a commitment-phobe.'

'She told you that?'

'No. But she said he was a player. Same thing, isn't it?'

'Maybe he just hasn't found the right woman yet,' Lindsay said, a teasing tone creeping into her voice. 'Maybe what he's been searching for all these years is a funeral director who'll take him in hand and make an honest man out of him.'

Dee laughed. 'From the way he looked at you just now, I'd say there's only one funeral director he's interested in, and it isn't me.'

'It was *you* he came in to talk to.'

'And *you* who got the sly once-over. Don't pretend you didn't notice. He probably saw you bending over in the window and all that apology nonsense was just an excuse to come in and be introduced to you.'

'Except you didn't, did you?'

'What?'

'Introduce me.'

'Oh God, you're serious, aren't you? You fancy him.'

'Yeah, I do a bit. Are you sure you don't? Because I'd hate to—'

'I don't fancy him, Lindsay. And even if I did, there's no way I'd . . . Anyway, what's happened to Callum?'

'Nothing. But he's into bondage. I had enough of all that with that personal trainer last year. Why don't men just want ordinary sex any more? Why have they always got to have *extras*?'

Dee stared at her in disbelief. 'You let that personal trainer tie you up? Fucking hell, Lindsay, you hardly knew him. Why have you never told me this?'

'Because I knew you'd freak out, that's why.'

'I thought you said you were always careful.'

Lindsay made the last few adjustments to her display. 'I *am* always careful. He used my tights, hon, not cable ties. And it was kind of fun, to start with. We had a safe word and everything.'

Dee shook her head. 'I can't believe you put yourself at risk like that, not after what happened to Gina.'

Lindsay sighed. 'We don't *know* what happened to Gina.'

'No, but we *do* know it must have been something really bad.'

Lindsay turned to face her, and Dee knew exactly what she was going to say because they'd had this same conversation, or versions of it, more times than she cared to remember. 'And you think that by putting your own life on hold you can somehow stop bad things happening? Is that it?'

'No. Yes. Maybe. Anyway, it's no more stupid than deliberately *inviting* danger into your life.'

Lindsay started tidying up all the bits of discarded

twine she'd been using to secure the flower arrangements. 'I'm just trying to have a good time, Dee. To live life to the full instead of hiding myself away from it. I spend my days working with dead bodies and people who've been bereaved. I need an outlet, and so do you.'

Dee held the wastepaper bin out for Lindsay to drop the bits of twine into. 'So what was your safe word?' she asked, keen to stop the lecture before Lindsay really got going. 'Just out of interest.'

The corners of Lindsay's mouth twitched. 'Well, if you must know, it was "moussaka".'

And within seconds they were helpless with laughter like a couple of kids.

11

SCARLETT SCOOPED UP AN armful of dirty washing from the wicker basket outside her bedroom and carried it through to the washing machine. It was Friday morning, and a perfect day for hanging laundry outside – bright and sunny, with a light breeze. No sooner had she thought this than Rebecca's voice came into her head, all breezy and sing-song: 'A fine day is a line day.' It brought a lump to Scarlett's throat.

Forty minutes later, she was walking up the garden with a basket of wet clothes in her hands. She felt stronger today. Less reliant on her cane. That was the weird thing about ME. Some days she felt fine; others she was virtually bedridden. It's what made it so difficult to explain to people.

The air had that peaty, autumnal smell. It was the first time she'd been out here since returning home and everything she saw reminded her of Rebecca. The terracotta pots her aunt had emptied of old compost and stacked up by the fence. The wind chimes she'd hung on the apple tree, and the apples themselves, rotting away on the grass, apples that would by now – if Rebecca were still alive – have been peeled and sliced and made into apple crumbles and pies or puréed and frozen for the months to come.

Or maybe not. Rebecca hadn't been herself for months before she died. Scarlett rested the laundry basket on the ground as a wave of grief rocked through her. Once, not so long ago, Scarlett had seen her aunt standing in the garden early one morning, still in her nightclothes, her back to the house, hugging herself and swaying. When she'd gone out to see what was wrong, Rebecca had stared at her as if she didn't know who she was. All she kept saying was: 'It's a secret. I'm not allowed to tell.' Some childhood memory, no doubt. Isn't that what happened with dementia? You remembered things from long ago with more clarity than what had happened yesterday.

Scarlett turned to look back at the house, allowing her eyes to move slowly and reluctantly to the first floor, half expecting, half dreading, to see her aunt's face looking down at her from the sitting-room window.

She shook her head and looked away, lifted the basket once more and made her way down the garden, the soles of her old wellies squelching in the sodden grass. It was a heavy clay soil – sticky and wet in the winter, dry as a bone in the summer. Rebecca had paid for the lawn to be professionally aerated after all the work had been done on the house. Workmen had trampled all over it and it had ended up looking more like a muddy field than a garden. But that had been almost ten years ago. It needed doing again.

Scarlett reached the rotary drier, the pegs still on it, and took a lungful of air. It smelled surprisingly fresh, considering the proximity of the South Circular. And then it hit her: the realization that all hundred by forty feet of this garden was now her responsibility. Rebecca had signed the ground-floor apartment and garden over to Scarlett as soon as the conversion was completed, but on the mutual understanding that Rebecca would continue to take the lead on garden-related decisions.

It had been the perfect arrangement. Scarlett loved being in the garden but wasn't particularly interested in the work associated with it. She couldn't have managed it anyway, not with her fluctuating health. Now, she would either have to employ someone to do it for her or neglect it and watch nature take its course until the weeds and brambles reigned supreme in Rebecca's carefully tended borders. No, she could never do that.

She pegged out the clothes, then carried on walking to the bottom of the garden. The grass was even boggier down here, on account of the dip in the lawn. She eyed the raised beds at the end. Rebecca had planted beetroot every June, along with runner beans and tomatoes she'd grown on her window-sills from seed. Scarlett tugged one of the beets up, remembering the fuss her aunt had made about get-ting these raised beds put in. 'She's going a bit loopy,' Scarlett had said to her brother. 'Keeps saying the soil in the borders is *contaminated*.'

Had she really called her aunt 'loopy'? It shamed her to remember this. She hadn't been loopy at all; she'd been ill, poor woman. Dementia was a disease every bit as real as cancer or heart disease. As some-one who suffered from ME, a condition that many people, even doctors, still don't fully understand, Scarlett should have been more respectful. It had only been a throwaway comment, she hadn't truly meant it, but still . . .

Scarlett had no desire to harvest this lot, let alone eat them, but she owed it to Rebecca, didn't she? She looked at the summer house. There was bound to be an old trug or something in there. She carried the empty basket to the house and picked up the key from its hook on the back door. She probably shouldn't be doing this – she didn't want to overtire herself – but when she felt this good, this strong, it seemed a shame not to capitalize on it.

Back at the summer house, she pushed an old cast-iron chair out of the way and opened the door, the glazed top half of which had a large crack running through it. She surveyed the deckchairs and various pieces of old garden furniture stacked up inside. It had originally been intended as a haven to sit in and enjoy afternoon tea or, better still, early-evening 'snifters', as her aunt had called them. But Scarlett could count on the fingers of one hand the number of times Rebecca had actually sat in here.

'Perhaps if it was nearer the house, I'd go in there more often,' her aunt had said whenever Scarlett had mentioned how seldom they used it. But even when it had been the height of summer and the grass was parched, Rebecca had still turned her nose up when Scarlett suggested they have a glass of Prosecco in there one evening. 'What's the point?' she'd said. 'We might as well sit here by the house,' and Scarlett had bitten her lip to keep the retort inside. The one she'd never quite plucked up the courage to say aloud: *What was the point in having it built in the first place?*

Scarlett scraped the wet mud from the bottom of her boots on the iron grid in front of the door and stepped inside. She looked around, but the gardening trug was nowhere to be seen. Why was she even worrying about the beetroots, anyway?

She was about to leave when she had an idea. An old chest of drawers stood against one wall – a relic from the original sitting room that was now her open-plan kitchen-diner. One of the deep bottom drawers would make a perfect container. She would struggle to carry it back to the house, but she could leave it in here and get Ollie to bring it in next time he came round.

The drawers were stiff, and when she finally wrenched one free she was surprised to see that it was full of bulging manila folders. She opened one of them up and had a closer look at what was inside. An old manuscript, by the looks of things. She skim-read a few paragraphs and recognized her aunt's distinctive voice. This must be the novel she'd tried, and failed, to get published. Scarlett had assumed it would be up in her aunt's study somewhere, but here it was, mouldering away in an abandoned chest of drawers.

She lifted the folders out, one by one, and plonked them on top of the chest. It made her sad just looking at them. All those words and sentences that Rebecca had painstakingly typed out and printed over the years. These bulging folders full of yellowing paper represented her aunt's dreams. Her lifetime's ambition.

'But you *are* a writer,' Scarlett had told her whenever her aunt had despaired over yet another rejection from a literary agent. The last one had been ages ago. She hadn't mentioned anything to do with her writing for years.

Scarlett removed the empty drawer. A small envelope that had been slit open at the top lay on the floor in the space where the drawer had been. It must have fallen down the back. She reached down for it and drew out a greetings card. On the front was a picture of a group of ballet dancers in blue tutus. A print of an Impressionist painting. Inside was written: *'Thank you so much for sharing your first draft with me, Rebecca. I absolutely loved it and can't wait to discuss it with you. I bet mine won't be anywhere near as good! Best wishes, Gina.'*

12

SCARLETT READ THE CARD again and frowned. The only Gina that came into her head right now was Gina Caplin. Dee Boswell's missing friend. Scarlett thought about that for a moment. If Dee and her business partner remembered being taught by Rebecca, then wasn't there a possibility that Rebecca had taught Gina, too? Her aunt had kept in touch with quite a few of her former students over the years. Lame ducks she'd taken under her wing, or those she thought had a gift for creative writing.

But Rebecca would have told her if she'd known Gina Caplin, and Dee would almost certainly have known about it too. She would have said something, surely. No, this Gina must be someone from one of her aunt's old writing groups. She picked the card up and slid it into the back pocket of her jeans.

When she'd finished digging up the beetroots, she stashed them in the drawer and put it into a dark corner in the summer house. That was enough activity for one day. She'd overstretched herself. She could feel it already, the familiar weariness weighing her down. Usually the tiredness came on the next day, but every so often it was like this and happened almost immediately. When would she ever learn?

Back at her desk, she phoned Ollie to ask him when Mickey North was coming round to clear the flowers from the pavement, hoping he'd asked someone else instead.

'As soon as I can spare him,' he said. 'We're incredibly busy at the moment. Everyone wants stuff completed by Christmas.'

'Okay. No worries. By the way, did you ever hear Rebecca mention someone called Gina?'

Ollie would have more of a take on what was going on in their aunt's life back then than Scarlett would. Scarlett had been so busy in her twenties, working long hours at an accountancy firm while studying for her ACCA qualifications, and although Clapham wasn't a million miles away from here, it was a tedious journey by public transport and she'd never learned to drive. Her visits had been fairly sporadic. Ollie, meanwhile, had carried on living with Rebecca until his business took off and he bought a place of his own.

'No. Why?'

'I found a card, that's all. In the summer house.'

She told him about finding their aunt's old manuscript, annoyed that she hadn't thought to bring it back to the house. 'It's looking pretty ancient now, I must say. I'm wondering whether we should destroy it or read it. What do you think? I must admit, I'm kind of curious.'

There was a pause as Ollie thought about this. 'If she'd wanted us to read it, she'd have given it to us before, wouldn't she?'

'I suppose so.'

'You could ask Dad, I suppose, but I don't expect he'll have an opinion one way or the other.'

'Maybe we could put it in the coffin with her.'

'What? Bit extreme, isn't it?'

'It seems kinder than throwing it away.'

'I'm sure Fond Farewells will be happy to arrange it. They seem like a nice couple of girls.'

'They're not *girls*, Ollie, they're women. And what do you mean? You've only met one of them.'

'I've met both of them, actually. I was passing their shop, if that's what you call it, the other evening, and they were doing their window display. Stopped and had a quick word. The other one's really pretty.'

'Don't even think about it, Ollie.'

He laughed. 'Christ, sis, what do you take me for?'

'I was thinking earlier how strange it was that Rebecca made such a big thing about getting a summer house built and then hardly ever used it. I might start clearing it out.'

'That boggy grass didn't help. I should have laid a path. I promised her I would,' Ollie said, regret in his voice. 'Listen, don't you go overtiring yourself.' *Too late for that,* she thought. 'I'll try and clear it out for you sometime soon if you want to start using it. Get it ready for next year.'

She yawned. 'I thought you were busy.'

'I am. But I can always find time for my darling sister.'

As soon as she put the phone down, Scarlett knew she'd have to go and lie down. A migraine was brewing. She felt her brain push against her skull, the familiar ache behind her left eyeball growing in intensity. If she didn't take some painkillers, it would get worse.

She rummaged in her medicine drawer for her tablets, then knocked one back with a glass of water, frustrated at the prospect of yet another wasted day. She slipped out of her trousers and climbed into bed. Some people thought that ME was a form of depression, and it was true that despair and dejection had been her regular companions over the years, but that was because of the disconnect between her mind and her body. If she really was depressed, she would *want* to crawl under her duvet and hide from the world. But she still had a long list of work-related tasks she wanted to complete. Going to bed in the middle of the day was the last thing she wanted, but she had no choice. Sleep beckoned like a friend she both loved and detested.

*

In her dreams, Scarlett sat in the summer house, surrounded by her family. Ollie was there, and so was Rebecca. Her father and Claire were there too, as was her late mother, which nobody except Scarlett seemed to find in the least bit odd. The summer house had been cleared of all the junk and the inside had been painted a soft, buttery yellow. All of them were sitting round a table, laughing and drinking wine, like old friends. Her mother looked so healthy and beautiful, exactly how she'd looked before cancer had slowly ravaged her from the inside out.

But underneath the jolliness, underneath the shared jokes and familiar anecdotes and gentle teasing, something dark and dangerous fizzed and sparked like an electric current, and only Scarlett could feel it. She was the outsider here. The ghost at the feast.

When the dream began to dissolve and she found herself in that surreal limbo between sleep and wakefulness, strange fragments of conversation revolved in her head, random words whispered in her ears. 'It's a secret. I'm not allowed to tell.' When she woke, her skin was drenched in sweat and her hair stuck to her forehead and the back of her neck. The dream had spun away from her entirely now, leaving only the sensation of dread.

Scarlett got out of bed on legs that felt like lead. Nauseated and weak, she pulled on her dressing gown, found a pair of warm slipper socks and went into the kitchen. She tried to look on the bright side. The migraine was now just an annoying headache and some of the nausea was almost certainly due to hunger. She hadn't eaten anything since breakfast.

She set about opening a carton of soup and heating it in a pan. She'd lived with this bastard of a condition long enough to recognize when she'd crashed, and there was nothing she could do but ride it out. Drink her soup, rest on the sofa and watch TV.

It was late afternoon when she woke for a second time, the empty soup bowl still on her lap, the cold spoon stuck to the cushion beside her. She felt better, though. Still dog-tired, but the headache had gone and so had the nausea. She fancied something else to eat. Some carbohydrates. So she popped a couple of crumpets in the toaster and made some tea while she was waiting for them to pop up. Another one of Rebecca's little sayings came back to her, something ludicrous, but strangely comforting, about there being very little in life that a hot, buttered crumpet and a pot of tea couldn't solve. Then she remembered what she'd said about the secret.

Scarlett took her crumpets and tea back to the sofa and wished her aunt were here right now. Talking to her in that reassuringly steady voice. Allaying her fears. 'Of *course* I didn't know Gina Caplin, you silly thing.'

She could almost feel her aunt's hand stroking her

hair, smoothing it back from her face. 'Oh, Scarlett. Dear Scarlett. Don't you think I'd have told you if I had?'

When the tea and crumpets had done their work, Scarlett turned the lights off and went back to her bedroom. Her jeans were still in a little heap on the floor where she'd left them. As she was hanging them up, something fell out of the back pocket. It was the envelope with the card inside. She reached down to pick it up and saw something she'd missed before, one of those pre-printed mini address labels stuck on the back. But it wasn't the address that froze her to the spot. It was the name above it: Gina Caplin.

She staggered back on to her bed and sat there holding it for a long time, maybe twenty minutes, while the light faded and the sky beyond her bedroom window turned a deep navy blue.

13

THE DIAL ARCH WAS, Dee thought, grudgingly, a
good choice for a meeting place. Lots of space and
more than enough seating. Exposed brickwork and
high ceilings. Chandeliers and pendant lights hanging from the wooden rafters. Once upon a time, it
had been a munitions factory. Now, it was a popular
pub and restaurant, slap bang in the middle of the
Royal Arsenal Riverside Development, one of Europe's
largest regeneration projects. This part of Woolwich
was fast becoming unrecognizable. 'We've missed the
boat,' her dad often said. 'The likes of you and me
would be lucky to afford a garage round here now.'

Dee and Lindsay looked around to see if Jake and
Euan had arrived yet but couldn't see them anywhere, so Dee bagged a table and a couple of sofas
and Lindsay went to get them something to drink.

'Just a small one,' Dee called over her shoulder.
She'd already made up her mind that she wasn't going
to drink more than one glass of wine. She wanted to

do what they'd come here to do and then get back home as soon as she could.

When Lindsay returned with the drinks, she was accompanied by Jake and Euan, both carrying pints of beer.

'Look who I bumped into,' she said.

Jake grinned. 'Wotcha, mate.' He was wearing a smart pair of jeans and a long-sleeved black shirt, open at the neck to reveal the last traces of his summer tan. His thick blond hair looked longer and untidier than usual and Dee couldn't help noticing that he hadn't shaved.

He gave her a sheepish look. 'I've got an audition in a couple of weeks. It's for a homeless guy.'

Dee laughed. 'I wasn't going to say anything.'

'You didn't need to,' he said, a smile in his voice. 'I could see it in your eyes.'

'How's Hayley? It's only a couple of months now, isn't it?'

Jake mimed a massive bump over his stomach. 'She's the size of a small elephant, but don't tell her I said that.'

'All right?' Euan said.

Dee had been aware of him hovering awkwardly while she greeted Jake. In terms of appearance, he was the polar opposite to Lindsay's brother. Closely cropped dark hair and clean-shaven. Skin as pale as Dee's. Where Jake was broad-shouldered and powerfully built, Euan was much skinnier. Dee had a sudden and unwanted memory of them in bed together, limbs entwined. She blinked to dispel the image before more arrived in her head and made her blush.

He stepped forward and pecked her lightly on the cheek. Dee wasn't quite sure what to do with her face, or her hands. It was always slightly embarrassing, seeing him again. Some people managed to stay relaxed and friendly after a break-up, like Jake and Gina always had. But Dee found it hard to forget that she and Euan had seen each other naked, that they'd been intimate with each other.

'Yeah,' she said. 'You?'

He shrugged, not quite looking her in the eye. At least he found meeting up again as excruciating as she did. Dee wasn't sure she could have coped if he'd been in any way *laddish* about it. 'Oh, you know, not so bad,' he said.

'I was sorry to hear about you and Sabine,' Dee said, and immediately wished she'd kept her mouth shut. It was probably the last thing he wanted to talk about.

He scratched the side of his neck and wrinkled his nose. 'Yeah, well, these things happen. She was missing her family too much and I didn't want to move to Germany, so . . .'

Dee saw Jake and Lindsay exchange a glance and

tried to ignore it. She hated the fact that she and Euan were probably being scrutinized for any signs of lingering attraction, their body language interpreted. She could, of course, end all such speculation once and for all by doing what she should have done years ago. By being honest with them. Why was that so difficult?

They moved over to the sofas and sat down, Dee and Lindsay on one, Jake and Euan on the other.

'Still living in Plumstead?' Euan said.

'Yup.' Dee knew what he really meant was 'Are you still living with your dad?' It had been a bone of contention between the two of them that she wouldn't leave home and move in with him. She'd kept telling him she wanted to wait until they were married, but he'd never understood her reasoning, and she couldn't blame him for that. He knew she wasn't religious.

'I heard about your grandmother,' she said. 'I'm really sorry.'

Euan looked down at his feet. 'Thanks. I couldn't believe it when she left me her house.' He looked up then and Dee wondered if that was code for 'See what you could have had if you'd stayed with me.'

'Yeah, he's a filthy-rich landlord now,' Jake quipped.

Dee pulled out her notepad and pen before this whole situation became even more uncomfortable. 'Right then, how are you getting on with arranging this football match? Have you decided on a date yet?'

Jake raised an eyebrow. 'Bloody hell, Dee. You don't hang about. We've only just sat down.'

'Sorry, but I can only stay an hour.'

Euan caught her eye. 'Going on somewhere nice?'

Dee felt her cheeks redden. 'No, not really. I just—'

Lindsay came to her rescue. 'Okay, we might as well get the business side of things out of the way first – shouldn't take too long, should it? And then we can get another round in before you have to go.'

Dee crossed her legs. Lindsay could get another round in if she wanted, but she was sticking to her one small glass of wine. Although when she brought it to her lips for another sip she saw that she'd drunk half of it already. She would have to slow down.

Jake and Lindsay did most of the talking, with Euan chipping in every now and again. Dee made notes. She started to relax and focus on the discussion. Before long, she'd filled two pages of her pad with bulletpoints and, almost without her realizing it, an hour had passed, and it wasn't as bad as she'd thought it would be, although, somehow or other, she'd ended up with another glass of wine. A large one this time.

'The lads in the team are all more than happy to do it,' Jake said, leaning back into the sofa, legs spread wide. 'They want to help as much as they can.'

Euan nodded. 'Even the younger players who never knew her. They're all going to spread the word.'

Dee glanced at Euan. Sometimes, on occasions

like this, when she'd had a little too much to drink, she wondered what her life would be like if she'd made the decision to stay with him, to carry on pretending. Euan was a good man. A kind man. And he'd loved her. Maybe Lindsay and Jake were right and he still did. She could have been married with kids now. Living a completely different life. But she wouldn't have been happy. She'd have been living a lie. And it wouldn't have been fair on Euan either. He deserved someone who was laid-back and fun, someone who wouldn't have to fake it in bed.

She took another slug of wine. The trouble was, she was *still* living a lie. And she still wasn't happy.

'Rob's going to take photos,' Jake said. 'And his little lad, Billy, he's going to be our mascot.'

'That's great,' Dee said. 'Really good work, guys. The Caplins are going to be so grateful.' She took another gulp of her wine, suddenly awash with emotion. 'And if Gina were here, *she'd* be grateful, too.'

They all nodded and looked down at the table for a few seconds. When Dee raised her head, she saw a tear slide from the corner of Jake's eye. Lindsay must have noticed it too, because her hand snaked across the table and landed on her brother's, gave it a brief squeeze.

When Gina first went missing, the police had questioned them all at length: Dee, Lindsay, Jake, Euan. Gina's parents. Dee's and Lindsay's parents. Everyone Gina had come into contact with on a regular basis. But, of course, it was the men who'd felt the weight of those questions more. Jake, in particular. 'They think I'm a fucking suspect!' he'd complained.

Dee looked at her watch. 'I'd better go,' she said, reaching for her bag and getting to her feet. She wasn't drunk, exactly, but her head was fuzzier than she liked it, and the lights seemed far too bright.

'Do you want me to walk you to the bus stop?' Euan said.

For a moment, she thought she might say yes, but changed her mind at the last second. 'No, I'm fine, thanks. You stay here with Jake and Lins.'

But Jake was already springing to his feet. 'Tell you what, we'll all walk to the bus stop together. How about that?'

Dee breathed a sigh of relief. She hadn't much fancied weaving her way across those cobblestones and crossing over to General Gordon Square all on her own, not when she didn't feel in full control of her faculties. Euan would have been a gentleman and waited with her until her bus came. He wouldn't have tried it on or said anything to put her on the spot, she knew he wouldn't, but she'd have felt self-conscious all the same. Besides, everything always seemed so much easier and more relaxed when Jake was around. No wonder Hayley adored him. No wonder Lindsay did, too.

Lindsay tried to get up off the sofa, groaning at the effort. Euan laughed and pulled her up. Then the four of them left the pub together – Dee and Jake linking arms in front, and Lindsay and Euan goofing around and bringing up the rear. It was almost like old times, before Jake had married Hayley. Before Dee and Euan had the slightest inkling they'd be a couple one day. Before Gina went missing and changed their lives for ever.

They weren't the Famous Five any more, and hadn't been for a very long time.

14

DEE UNCLIPPED HER SEATBELT. Sue Caplin had the front door open before Lindsay had even finished parking. Dee gave her a wave.

'She's lost even more weight,' Lindsay said. 'Poor Sue. I don't know how she keeps going, I really don't.'

They got out of the car and walked up the front path. The Caplins still lived in the same house they'd lived in when Gina was at school. A neat two-up two-down Victorian terrace that Alan had lovingly restored over the years. Dee remembered the night that she, Lindsay and Gina had got back late from a house party a little the worse for wear – they must have been about sixteen – and Gina had thrown up on the quarry-tiled front step just as Alan opened the door in his dressing gown. Some of her vomit had splashed on to his slippers and he'd been cross with her. But Dee could tell he wasn't *that* cross, not really. He was just relieved that she was back in one piece, that they all were. Dee and Lindsay had stayed over that night, camped out on the floor in Gina's bedroom, just like the sleepovers they used to have as children.

'Alan!' Sue called over her shoulder. 'The girls are here.'

The girls. She still called them that. Only now, of course, there were only two of them, and neither of them was *her* girl.

They hugged in the hallway, then went and sat in the small front room on the striped sofa. Alan had baked scones for them.

'He does more baking than me now,' Sue said, with amusement.

For the first fifteen or twenty minutes, they chatted about this and that: Alan's retirement and Sue's latest attempts at needle felting. By now, Dee and Lindsay were on to their second scone and Alan had been despatched into the kitchen to make another pot of tea.

When he returned and their cups had been refilled, Sue cleared her throat.

'So, we've had a long chat with the police, and they're keen to use the gathering as an opportunity to appeal for new witnesses,' she said. 'It will coincide with their yearly review of the case.'

Alan put his arm around her shoulders. 'But we mustn't get our hopes up, must we, love?'

Sue pressed her lips together and shook her head. Sometimes Dee wondered how the two of them had managed to stay sane all these years, not knowing what had happened to their daughter. It was worse than bereavement; it had to be. At least with death came certainty.

Alan reached over to a side table and picked up a white envelope. He passed it to Dee. 'I know you said you didn't want any money for helping us organize things, but we want you to have this.'

Dee looked at Lindsay and the two of them immediately shook their heads.

'Absolutely not,' Lindsay said. 'You won't pay us a single penny.'

'Yes, we will,' Alan said gently. 'You're running a business and we want your services. We don't expect you to do it for nothing.'

Lindsay's eyes glistened with tears. 'But we *want* to do it for nothing, don't we, Dee?'

Dee nodded, even though she knew Alan was right. They'd already spent a lot of time planning things and there was loads more to do. Lindsay was still looking at her. 'We can't accept this,' she said, handing it back.

But Alan refused to take it. He turned to face his wife. 'Told you we'd have trouble with these two, didn't I?'

Sue laughed through her tears. 'It's what we used to say when we saw the two of you walk up the front path, when you were little. Here comes trouble.'

Dee proceeded to fill them in on the good news

about the school letting them have the hall for free, and about Jake's idea for a fundraising football match. Then Lindsay outlined her plans for a social media campaign to raise awareness.

'That's wonderful,' Alan said, squeezing his wife's hand.

'And I'm waiting to hear back from the BBC about getting hold of a copy of the reconstruction video. If that's a possibility, we'll play that first, and follow it up with tributes and messages from family and friends, that kind of thing, followed by a simple buffet—'

'We can arrange the caterers for that,' Lindsay said.

'I've let the council know as well, just to be on the safe side, especially with the candlelight vigil in the evening. We were thinking a procession from the school to the park, and then some more tributes and words there, too?'

'That sounds perfect,' Sue said. She wrung her hands in her lap. 'Wouldn't it be amazing if it worked, if new evidence came to light after all this time?'

'It'd be wonderful,' Dee said, her throat clogged with emotion.

Alan whispered something in Sue's ear and she nodded. 'I almost forgot,' she said. 'There's something else we wanted to talk to you about.'

She got up and went over to the sideboard, opened one of the cupboards and drew out a large brown envelope. 'I don't know if either of you were aware of this, but Gina wrote a novel.'

Lindsay and Dee stared at each other in surprise, then at the brown envelope Sue was holding out towards them. Dee took it from her in awe. 'She never mentioned it.'

Sue and Alan exchanged a glance. 'We didn't say anything before because, well, it was obviously something she was keeping to herself. We didn't think she'd want people to know. I'd hate her to be embarrassed about us sharing it like this, but . . . seeing as it's been so long now . . . we thought . . .'

'Have you read it?' Lindsay asked.

'Yes. We didn't want to, at first. It seemed wrong. But, in the end, we decided we would. Just in case there were any . . . I don't know, *clues* as to where she might have gone. The police had a look at it too, but it's just a novel. Romantic fiction. It's . . .' Sue smiled. 'It's rather good, actually. We were wondering whether we should try to get it published. Apparently, you can put stuff on Amazon yourself now. Upload it on to something called Kindle Direct? We thought we could try to raise some money for the missing-persons charity I work with, only we're not sure either of us have the technical knowhow to do something like that. So we were wondering whether one of you could . . . or maybe you might know someone who would . . .'

'We'll look into it for you,' Lindsay said.

Sue exhaled in relief. 'Thank you. We'd really appreciate that. There's no rush, obviously. No rush at all. The gathering is the most important thing . . .'

'But I guess it would be good to get this on Kindle round about the same time if at all possible,' Dee said. 'More publicity that way.'

Sue smiled at Alan, tears brimming in her eyes. 'I told you the girls would know what to do.'

Later, as she and Lindsay walked back to the car, Dee felt ashamed by the relief that washed through her. Relief at leaving the Caplins and their grief behind. She clutched the two envelopes to her chest. The large brown one containing Gina's novel, and the small white one containing a cheque.

'Think I need a drink,' she said.

Lindsay pointed her keys at the car to unlock it. 'Me too. Although I'm meeting Callum at eight.'

'Oh, right. He's back on the scene, is he?'

Lindsay grinned. 'Just until someone better comes along. The thing is, I won't be able to drive you home if we have a drink. You don't mind, do you?'

'I can always get the bus.'

'That's settled then. I've got some wine in the fridge. You can help me choose what to wear.'

Lindsay drove them back to her place in Wool-wich. A flat-fronted terrace in a narrow street near the huge Tesco. She'd managed to scrape together a deposit with the help of her parents and had applied for a mortgage just before she'd resigned from her job as a beautician and gone into business with Dee. That was before prices in this part of London shot up. The regeneration programme and the Crossrail project had seen to that.

Dee took the large glass of white wine Lindsay had poured her and carried it through to the tiny living room, which was, as usual, cluttered with glossy magazines and dirty mugs and sweet wrappers. Sometimes Dee wondered whether the real reason Lindsay kept on at her to move in and be her lodger was that she'd have someone to help her keep the place clean and tidy.

She sat on the old but incredibly comfortable sofa and tucked her legs under her bottom. Lindsay switched the gas fire on and sat on a large floor cushion in front of it. She split open a bag of Kettle crisps, as if they were in the pub, and the two of them dug in. Despite the mess, Dee had to admit she liked being in Lindsay's house. Who was she kidding? It wasn't the house. She liked being with Lindsay. The two of them had been friends for so long they knew each other's thought patterns, could finish each other's sentences and, right now, they needed to deconstruct this afternoon's meeting with the Caplins.

'It's too much,' Lindsay said, looking at the cheque.

Dee scooped up a handful of crisps. 'Somehow, I don't think Alan will take no for an answer. It'll offend him if we give it back. And cash isn't exactly flowing at the moment. I think we should accept it.'

'You're probably right.' Lindsay took a slug of her wine. 'Fancy Gina never telling us she'd written a novel. Romantic fiction, eh?'

'I know,' Dee said. 'Maybe we didn't know her as well as we thought we did.'

15

DEE BOOKED AN UBER. Lindsay's wine glasses were the ultra-large variety, and she'd drunk more than she'd intended. When the car arrived she gave Lindsay a hug and made her promise she'd be careful tonight.

'And I don't just mean condoms,' she said, regretting her words straight away, because they came out far too loud and the Uber driver heard her and smirked. Damn. Would he see that she was tipsy and take advantage? Lock the doors and drive off somewhere remote with her?

She gave herself a little pep talk. *Just calm down and get in. Most men aren't rapists and murderers. You can't go through life worrying about danger at every turn.*

Lindsay had given her a plastic bag to put Gina's novel in, and she sat with it on her lap for the whole journey. If she put it down on the seat beside her, there was every chance that she'd leave it in the car.

She'd lost enough items in taxis over the years. Jackets, umbrellas, even her purse once. Sue and Alan would never forgive her if she lost their missing daughter's precious novel, although presumably there was still a copy on her laptop. When on earth had Gina found the time to write a novel?

Dee took her phone out and called her dad, told him she was in an Uber and that she'd be home in about ten minutes. It always made her feel safer doing that, letting the driver know that someone was expecting her and that they'd worry if she didn't come straight home. Honestly, what was she like! It was drinking that wine that had made her feel so uneasy. It wasn't even eight o'clock, and here she was, carrying on as if it were two in the morning. Then again, Gina had gone missing in broad daylight.

When the car pulled into the Laburnum Court car park and Dee climbed out she saw her dad standing on the balcony with Mrs Kowalski, smoking a roll-up. But it was only after she'd climbed the four flights of stairs and was walking towards them that she realized they were actually *sharing* a roll-up. Dee had never been much of a smoker herself, but in her limited experience you only ever shared a smoke with someone you knew pretty well, or wanted to.

'How was it today?' her dad said. 'With the Caplins.'

'It was . . . okay,' Dee said. 'They both send their love.'

He nodded gravely. 'I've been telling Eva about it,' he said.

Eva gave her a sad smile. 'Such a terrible, terrible thing to happen,' she said.

Dee agreed with her that yes, it was. Then she made her excuses and went into the flat. It didn't feel right discussing Gina in front of a neighbour, even if that neighbour was closer to her dad than maybe Dee had realized.

She dropped the bag with the novel in it on top of her bed and cast her eyes around her bedroom, the one she'd slept in since she was a child. She even had the same curtains. Lindsay was right. She should have moved out years ago. It didn't matter that she wasn't the only one, that there were, apparently, loads of people like her, still living in the parental home, or having returned there after their lives and finances went tits up. But she had no excuse. She ran her own business. She had savings. Staying at Laburnum Court with her dad was just an excuse for not moving on with her life. For not growing up.

It had been a wrench leaving Lindsay's this evening. But could she really move in with her? No. If she was going to leave home, she needed to find her own place. She was too old to be someone's lodger.

She imagined herself living in a flat like Scarlett Quilter's. An *apartment*. Wasn't that how the Quilters always referred to it? Drifting into that gorgeous kitchen in her pyjamas every morning. Not her

Gizmo Gremlins pyjamas, but sophisticated, silky ones. Helping herself to a freshly brewed coffee en route to the sun-filled living room. But that was just a fantasy. An impossible dream. She'd never be able to afford somewhere like that. People like the Quilters moved in a different world to the likes of her. She'd just about qualify for a mortgage on a cramped studio flat – that's if she could even scrape together a big enough deposit.

In that moment, she saw her future stretching out before her. Wet laundry drying on a clothes horse. A bed, a sofa, a folding table for one and, horror of horrors, a kitchenette. Long, lonely evenings in front of a box set, half-written eulogies scattered across the floor. But at least it would be her own space. Hers and hers alone. She could paint it brilliant white to make it look bigger. Buy the most comfortable sofa she could afford and one of those small double beds, to give her more space. She could, at a push, manage with a single, or was that too sad?

She would buy house plants and have them trailing from high shelves, maybe some succulents on a tray. And, one day, if the business continued to grow – and why wouldn't it? People were never going to stop dying – maybe she'd be able to afford a place with its own separate bedroom.

'Don't get carried away,' she said aloud. Oh dear, she'd started talking to herself. And with sarcasm too. Now all she needed was a couple of cats and her life would be complete.

Dee flopped down on to her bed.

'Dee? Is that you?'

Her dad put his head around the door.

She laughed. 'Who else could it be?'

'Sounded like you had a friend in there with you.'

Dee sat up on the bed. 'I was on the phone,' she lied.

He nodded. 'How *is* Lindsay these days?'

Dee's heart sank. Was that the immediate conclusion he'd come to, that if she was talking to someone on the phone, then it was almost certain to be Lindsay? As if Lindsay were the only real friend she had. Mind you, he wouldn't be far off the mark if he *did* think that. Caz and some of their other friends were fun to meet up with every now and again, but they'd been Lindsay's friends first – women she'd met from her days as a beautician. They had assimilated Dee into their group with enthusiasm and kindness, and she was fond of them all, but Dee still felt like the outsider sometimes. The slightly odd one who'd rather stay in than go out, given the choice. They never let her, of course. They always dragged her out in the end.

'She's fine,' Dee said. She pointed to the manuscript on the bed. 'Sue and Alan gave us something of Gina's. It's a novel she wrote. Sue wants us to try and publish it, to raise money for the missing-persons charity she supports.'

'That's a great idea, isn't it?'

'But how do we know whether Gina would have wanted it made public?'

Her dad came and sat next to her on the edge of the bed. 'Hmm. I guess we'll never know the answer to that. But if Sue and Alan are okay with it, and if it's for a good cause, then . . .'

'Yeah, you're probably right. I've just got to psych myself up for it. I feel weird about reading stuff she's written. Private stuff.'

'But it's fiction, isn't it?'

'It came from her mind, though, didn't it? Her subconscious. She didn't even tell us she was writing a novel, and we were supposed to be her best friends. I'm worried I'll hear her voice and . . .' Dee's throat started to close up.

'And what?'

'And it'll be sad.' Her voice broke on the last word and her dad put his arm around her shoulders and drew her to his side, holding her close.

'Well, of course it will be sad. But that doesn't mean you shouldn't read it. Sadness is part of life, Dee. You know that more than anyone. And maybe it will help you.'

'Help me how?'

'Help you work through your grief, love.'

Dee began to sob into her dad's shoulder. How

could she tell him she wasn't just crying for Gina and the life her friend had lost, she was crying for herself, too, and the life she wasn't living and probably never would. Lindsay loved her as a friend, but she would never love her the way Dee wanted her to. She'd never look at her the way she'd just seen her dad look at Mrs Kowalski.

16

IT WAS SUNDAY EVENING and Scarlett was having another early night. Not that it would do her any good. Even when she was lucky enough to get an unbroken eight hours' sleep, it never totally refreshed her.

Ever since seeing the name Gina Caplin on that printed address label on Friday, she'd driven herself half mad trying to work out what it meant and what on earth she should do with her new-found knowledge. And whenever Scarlett stressed out over something, her physical health invariably suffered. She'd been fit for nothing all weekend.

She lay on her back, listening, or rather trying to listen, to a sleep app she'd downloaded on to her phone. She focussed on the calm, steady voice now instructing her to visualize an empty beach, to hear the sound of waves lapping gently at the shore, feel the soft, warm breeze on her skin. But it was no good. She couldn't switch off. Why had Rebecca never told her that she'd once been friendly with a woman whose mysterious disappearance had been so much in the public eye that Scarlett reckoned she could stop any random stranger in the street and they'd recognize the name Gina Caplin instantly? It seemed so unlike her aunt to keep such a thing to herself.

Several times over the last two days she'd almost called her dad and Ollie and asked them to come round so that they could have a family conference about it. But she was so damn tired, and every time she'd picked up the phone a little voice had talked her out of it. If her aunt hadn't even wanted *her* to know about the friendship, when the two of them had been so close, it was unlikely she'd have wanted any other member of the family to know about it either. Besides, Scarlett had already asked Ollie if he knew of a friend called Gina, and he'd said no. She hadn't realized then, of course, that the card was from Gina Caplin.

She rolled over on to her side. Dee Boswell had said that Rebecca had been her supply teacher in Year 12. Scarlett had already worked out that that made Dee forty. So if Gina Caplin had gone to the same secondary school as Dee, and there was every chance that she had, considering Dee had said they'd known each other since they were five, then that meant the card could have been sent, and Rebecca's manuscript read, at any point in the thirteen-year

111

period before Gina went missing. The period that coincided with Scarlett's years away from the house, first when she was at university in Birmingham and then when she was living in Clapham.

But it was very unlikely that Rebecca would have sought feedback on her precious novel from a pupil she'd only recently taught, a girl in her late teens. It was far more probable that she'd kept in touch with her for some reason and that their friendship had grown as Gina matured, or that the two of them had renewed their acquaintance when Gina was older. Either way, Rebecca would have been shocked and upset to hear of her disappearance. And yet she'd said absolutely nothing about knowing her. Nothing at all.

Scarlett turned the app off and threw her duvet back in frustration. Questions darted back and forth in her mind like rats in a maze. Dee obviously didn't know anything about their friendship, or she'd have said something, wouldn't she? It was another connection, after all, beyond that of her remembering Rebecca as a supply teacher. She would ask her anyway, the next time they spoke.

Scarlett went into the kitchen and poured herself a glass of milk. She unlocked the back door and took a lungful of cold night air. She did this sometimes when she couldn't sleep. It was so still and quiet. So otherworldly. It helped her think. Once upon a time, she might have smoked a Marlboro Light, but it had been over two years since she'd last had a cigarette. She used to keep a packet of ten at the back of her medicine drawer, just for emergencies. Then they'd stopped selling them and she'd drawn the line at buying twenty. As long as there were cigarettes in the drawer, Scarlett would find an excuse to smoke them.

An upstairs light was on in the house at the end of the garden. The light illuminated the roof of the summer house. If only she'd had the sense to bring that manuscript in, her aunt's novel. Scarlett briefly considered going out there now, to fetch it. She could read it in bed. But the thought of trudging up the garden in the cold and the dark put her off, and she'd only just started to feel better after her exertions on Friday. She didn't want to set herself back. It would have to wait until morning. If she felt strong enough, she also wanted to look upstairs in Rebecca's apartment, to see if she could find her aunt's old diaries. Rebecca had rarely thrown things like that away, so there was every chance she might be able to find a reference to Gina Caplin and work out when exactly the two of them had been in touch, and how often they had met.

Not that that would solve the mystery of why Rebecca had never mentioned knowing her. But it might put her mind at ease if it turned out to be a long while before Gina went missing, and if Scarlett couldn't find anything else to suggest that their friendship had continued it might be slightly easier to explain her aunt's reticence. Rebecca had had an awful lot to contend with ten years ago. The emotional stress and humiliation of finding out that Andrew Pulteney had been cheating on her and having to call off the wedding; the conversion of this house into two separate apartments and all the upheaval that had caused, not to mention her anxiety about Scarlett's health. Rebecca wouldn't have wanted to burden her with anything else.

Scarlett cast her mind back to that time. Her memories were, understandably, sketchy. It had been hard, admitting defeat and returning to live with her aunt. Even a brand-new, self-contained, state-of-the-art home couldn't quite make up for losing her old life. Her flat in Clapham. Her job in the City. She'd been depressed. She wouldn't have called it that at the time – she'd have said she felt low – but, in hindsight, it was obvious. ME had succeeded in cleaving her life into two distinct parts, before and after, and in those early days she still hadn't relinquished the 'before' part.

Scarlett stepped into the kitchen and locked the door. It wouldn't do to start getting all weepy about things. She got her quilt from the bedroom and carried it to the sofa. Then she put the TV on and tried not to think any more. If she was going to go back into the summer house tomorrow, she needed to get some rest.

17

SCARLETT WOKE AT FIRST light on Monday morning, feeling so much better. It was raining heavily, which meant her trip to the summer house for Rebecca's novel would have to wait. There was, however, nothing to stop her going upstairs and having a look around.

Nothing except her own fear, of course.

Forensics had been all over the place, but they'd only been looking for evidence relating to the deaths of Rebecca and Clive. They wouldn't have had cause to investigate a link between her aunt and a young woman who'd disappeared almost a decade ago. Why would they?

As she stepped into the hallway, her heartbeat quickened. She'd promised Ollie she wouldn't go up there on her own, but that was before she'd found out Rebecca had known Gina Caplin. She slid the key into the lock and turned it to the right, feeling at once scared and guilty. Scarlett wasn't in the least bit superstitious. She didn't believe in malevolent spirits, and if she didn't believe in something, then how could she possibly be scared of it? And yet she was. Entering the apartment where her aunt had been murdered in bed was enough to put the frighteners on anyone.

The guilt issue was a little more complicated. Yes, she had a spare key, but the apartment belonged to Ollie now – at least, it would do as soon as probate was granted. And she'd promised him she wouldn't do it.

She closed the door behind her and began the slow climb to the top. She was mad to even consider doing this after the weekend she'd just had, but she knew she'd never be able to settle down to her work until she had. As long as she paced herself, she'd be okay.

Once at the top of the stairs, she waited until her heart rate returned to something approaching normal. Then she walked with determination into her aunt's sitting room, aware of the closed door of the bedroom at the front of the house. The bedroom she had to face some time. She would work her way up to it, room by room.

The curtains in the sitting room were hooked behind brass tie-backs. The police must have opened them, because Rebecca would never have bunched them up so roughly. Scarlett adjusted the heavy brocade fabric so that it hung better, then turned her back on the window and contemplated the familiar room. The grey light of dawn made it look dull and shadowy, and that fusty smell she'd noticed in her own apartment when she'd first returned was up here too, but even stronger and more pronounced.

Scarlett would have liked to fling open the window and turn on the lamps, but she didn't want to draw any attention to the fact that she was here. There was something about the clandestine nature of her search, about what it was she was searching *for*, that made her more anxious than normal. She felt like an intruder, which, in some respects, she was.

This room, like the rest of the apartment, had been decorated by Rebecca herself. The walls were a deep, dark blue, the floorboards sanded and stained. She hadn't decorated properly, as Ollie was forever pointing out. If you peered behind the radiators you could still see the original wallpaper where she hadn't been able to reach it with the roller. And, in places, some of the stain from the floorboards had splashed on to the once white, now yellowing, skirting boards, and hadn't been removed or painted over. But then, as her aunt had been fond of saying, if you couldn't live with imperfection, you were setting yourself up for a lifetime of disappointment.

With its dated but good-quality furniture, its groaning bookshelves and dusty, cluttered mantelpiece, its occasional tables adorned with dome-shaped Tiffany lamps and its assorted magazine and book towers rearing up like stalagmites from one of the overlapping Persian rugs, the sitting room looked like it might have belonged to an elderly academic. Or a writer. Or a late-middle-aged schoolteacher who should, perhaps, have been one or both of those things.

Scarlett eyed the walnut writing bureau in the corner. It was a logical place to start. She turned the brass key, opened up the pull-down desk and peered into all of the little compartments and drawers to confirm what she already knew she would see: notelets and writing paper, treasury tags and paperclips, fountain pens, biros and pencils. She had a brief surge of excitement when she found a handful of slimline diaries, but they were for the last three years only.

She checked the larger drawers at the bottom of the bureau and they, too, were exactly as she remembered, full of old envelopes and Jiffy bags. The bottom drawer was entirely filled with Christmas-tree decorations, as had always been the case. Her aunt had not been the sort of person to reorganize her drawers unnecessarily. She had viewed the current obsession with decluttering as not only a complete and utter waste of time but a particularly ruthless and potentially heart-breaking task. And all for what, she had said, if you threw away something you might later want or need? Which is what gave Scarlett hope that somewhere in these rooms, if she looked hard enough, she might find some older diaries.

She worked her way systematically through the rest of the sitting room. Then she moved into the study and tackled the box files stacked up on the floor. These were all labelled in black felt-tip pen in her aunt's neat capital letters. Scarlett riffled through each one, but found only old paperwork relating to the house and various teaching resources.

She went back into the corridor. They weren't likely to be in the kitchen so there was only one room left to search. The bedroom. She felt sick at the thought of going in. Of seeing the bed where Rebecca had been murdered. She couldn't give up now, though. She just couldn't. She'd never forgive herself for being so weak.

But as she stood outside the closed door she had the most appalling sense of terror. She took a step back. She thought she knew all there was to know about herself, that nothing she could do or think would ever surprise her, but she was wrong. There was evil in that room. She felt it in her bones.

She straightened her spine and took a steadying breath to calm herself down. She was not, and never would be, the sort of person to flinch from a difficult task. Nor would she allow herself to be cowed by her own primal fears. Because that's all these were. Having resolved to search Rebecca's bedroom, she was determined to go through with it.

Her hand was on the doorknob when the sound

of her phone ringing made her jump in alarm. She reached into the back pocket of her jeans, heart pounding, and pulled it out. It was Dee Boswell. Scarlett backed away from the bedroom door. Her hand shook as she answered the call.

Dee's voice sounded unnaturally loud in the stillness of the air. 'Hello, Scarlett,' she said. 'I hope it's not too early for you?'

Scarlett checked the time, astonished to see that it was already five past nine. She'd been up here for almost two hours.

'Not at all,' she said, still staring at the closed door of Rebecca's bedroom as she moved back to the sitting room. 'How can I help?'

'I just wanted to ask you something I should have asked before.'

'Fire away,' she said, her jaunty, confident tone a deliberate ploy to chase away her fears. Not that it was working. She sat down on one of her aunt's wingback armchairs, aware that her whole body was trembling.

'Will you be wanting your aunt's ashes returned to you?'

Scarlett took a moment to answer, unable to quite get her head around her aunt being reduced to a pile of ashes. 'We haven't actually discussed that, but yes, I'd say yes, we do. What happens to them otherwise?'

'They'd be scattered in the garden of remembrance

at the cemetery,' Dee said. There was a small pause. 'We sell a variety of urns – you can have a look on our website – but if you prefer, you can provide your own receptacle. It can be anything, really – a freezer bag, if you're not sentimental.'

Scarlett almost laughed. She felt light-headed with relief at the interruption. 'I think even *I* draw the line at a freezer bag.' She moistened her lips with her tongue. 'I was just wondering about something,' she said, not entirely sure *what* she was about to say but hoping her brain would come up with the right words. She wanted to find out if Dee knew anything about Gina keeping in touch with Rebecca without actually asking her outright.

'What's that?' Dee said.

'I was wondering if you . . . if you have any memories of my aunt, from when she taught at your school.' Scarlett chewed the inside of her lip. Somehow, she had to bring the conversation round to Gina Caplin, without sounding as if she were prying. 'I only really have contact with the pupils and staff from River-hill, you see. Tell me, Dee, did you like her lessons? You and your friends? Can you remember much about her?'

There was a slight pause. 'I don't remember much, to be honest,' Dee said. 'I think she probably found us lot a bit challenging. It was a large school in a fairly deprived area. We must have been a nightmare to teach.'

Scarlett expelled her breath. 'Oh, well, it was just a thought. By the way, I've been meaning to apologize for asking you about your friend when you first visited. It's been playing on my mind. I didn't mean to be intrusive. I hope I didn't upset you.' She was aware of the short pause before Dee responded.

'No, no, it's fine, honestly. No need to apologize. I brought the subject up, after all.'

Scarlett battled on. She'd come this far, so she might as well chance her arm. 'I guess my aunt must have known her, too, then. Strange old world, isn't it?'

'Yes, yes, it is. Hang on,' Dee said, and she started to laugh. 'I *do* remember something. She insisted on reading out one of Gina's short stories to the whole class. Gina was *so* embarrassed. We kept teasing her about it. She was pleased, too, though. I do remember that.'

Scarlett waited for her to continue. Dee clearly had no idea that Gina had kept in touch with Rebecca. Should she tell her?

'She was a nice woman, your aunt,' Dee said. 'And a very good teacher.'

Scarlett tried to speak, but her mouth had gone dry. If she told Dee about the card she'd found, Dee might start wondering why it was that Rebecca had never told her family about knowing Gina. Her mind might start whirring with implications, just as Scarlett's was doing right now.

'So you'll let me know about the urn then?'

122

'Yes,' Scarlett said. 'I'll let you know. Thanks, Dee.'

Scarlett took one last look at the closed door of Rebecca's bedroom and went downstairs. If she didn't get on with her work, she'd have disgruntled clients to cope with, on top of everything else.

'Making excuses again?' said a familiar voice. Scarlett started. It sounded so real, almost as if Rebecca were right behind her.

18

No sooner had Dee said goodbye to Scarlett Quilter than Lindsay messaged her from downstairs.

'Another bad review. Even worse than the last one.'

Dee logged on to their Facebook page. This time, it was from someone calling themselves Polly Beardsley. Her fists clenched as she read it. 'This firm is a complete rip-off. They take your money and then screw you over. They have no morals whatsoever. Take it from me – a dissatisfied customer: DON'T USE THEIR SERVICES. They won't be around much longer anyway. Not when the truth comes out.'

Dee didn't even need to check the database, but she did anyway. She scrolled down the list of all their previous clients, but it was just as she'd thought. There were no Beardsleys and no Pollys, just as there were no T. J. Coopers. No Coopers at all, in fact.

She stood up and marched out of the office and down to the prep room. Lindsay was perched on her high lab chair, biting the skin around her fingernails. The Facebook page was open on her laptop.

Dee read it again over Lindsay's shoulder. 'This is getting serious now,' she said. 'Maybe we should remove the review section altogether.'

Lindsay frowned. 'But won't that look bad as well? Not giving people – *genuine clients* – the chance to leave feedback?'

'Not as bad as someone looking us up and reading *this*. Someone must be targeting us on purpose.'

'We need to report it,' Lindsay said. She clicked on the three horizontal dots to the right of the review and stared at the options. 'What do you think? Unfair recommendation or harassment?'

'Harassment. That's what it is, isn't it? It's more than unfair, it's *untrue*. It's libellous.'

Lindsay clicked harassment. 'You haven't made any enemies lately, have you?'

'No, of course not. Have *you*?'

'Not that I know of. Let's report the other one, too, while we're at it.'

Lindsay repeated the reporting procedure for T. J. Cooper. Then Dee dictated a response to the Polly Beardsley review while Lindsay typed it out with two fingers.

'Of course, what I really want to say is *Fuck right off, you pathetic troll. You're not even a real person.*'

Lindsay laughed. 'I love it when you swear. You should do it more often.' She swung her legs round so she was facing Dee. 'I wonder if we should speak to that local reporter who did the piece on Gina's event. See if he'll write something up about our anger and dismay at being unfairly targeted. You know what they say, even bad publicity can be good publicity if it's handled the right way.'

'Hmm,' Dee said. 'I'm not so sure about that. It could draw people's attention to it when they might not otherwise have noticed. And I don't want the Caplins or any of our current clients getting wind of it. No, I think it's better to keep a dignified silence. At least for the time being.'

The rest of the day passed uneventfully. But no matter how hard she tried, Dee couldn't stop thinking about those awful reviews. It was maddening to think that some nasty piece of work they'd never even met could ruin their hard-earned reputation on a whim.

She wandered out to reception and looked out of the glazed front door on to the street beyond. Could it be a competitor trying to sabotage their business? It wouldn't be one of the big boys – Fond Farewells was no threat to the likes of the Co-op and Dignity. Another small independent, maybe? It was possible, but unlikely. Before setting up Fond Farewells, Dee had worked for most of them at one time or another in her capacity as a self-employed funeral celebrant. None of the firms she'd had dealings with would stoop this low.

But it couldn't be anyone completely random either, could it? Those phrases they'd used were highly charged. Vindictive. This was someone with an axe to grind.

She went back into the office and called up the client database again. She already knew the names Cooper and Beardsley wouldn't be there, but maybe if she scrolled through it slowly, a memory would spark. Had they arranged any funerals where there'd been disagreements within the family about what kind of service to have?

Dee remembered the odd heated discussion over venue and religious content, conflicting opinions as to what the deceased would, or would not, have wanted. But she was pretty good at facilitating such meetings; sometimes she felt more like a mediator than a funeral director, and surely if anyone had felt aggrieved that their opinions weren't taken into account, they'd take it out on the family member who was the point of contact for organizing the funeral in the first place, not the funeral firm itself.

When Lindsay appeared at lunchtime, Dee told her what she'd been doing. Lindsay gave her a doubtful look.

'So what happens if you *do* manage to remember something?' she said. 'What are you going to do about it? Phone up the point of contact and ask them if someone in their family is posting bad reviews about us?'

Dee opened her mouth to reply, then closed it again. Lindsay was right. Even if she *did* track down a possible culprit, there was nothing she'd be able to do about it.

'Of course not,' she said. 'But at least we'd know who it was. We'd have an explanation. This is so ...' She struggled to find the right word. 'So *unfair*.'

Lindsay came into the office. 'Oh, hon, there are so many things we'll never know. Sometimes we just have to accept that life *is* unfair.'

Dee logged out of the database and stood up. 'I know, I know. I've wasted enough time on this pointless task anyway. I don't know what came over me.' She put on her coat. 'Come on, let's get out of here and get some fresh air.'

They entered the park and set off on their usual route. 'So when are we picking up Rebecca Quilter?' Lindsay said.

'Not sure yet. We're still waiting for the cremation order to be finalized by the coroner.'

'I'm presuming the family won't want a viewing.'

'No, they want to remember her as she was.'

'Wise choice. I was dreading having to embalm her.'

'I bet,' Dee said.

Embalming wasn't something they did very often. Not unless a family specifically requested it. Embalming fluid was a cocktail of harmful chemicals, potential carcinogens. When Dee explained to new clients – those of them who asked her about it – what an invasive process it actually was and how the chemicals leached into the air and the soil and the water table, most of them were dissuaded. Although the typical Fond Farewells client tended to want a greener funeral anyway.

'And as for a facial reconstruction,' Lindsay said, 'her injuries must have been horrendous. I'm good at what I do, but something like that would be a real challenge.'

Dee tried not to imagine what Rebecca Quilter's face must look like.

'Oh, I meant to tell you,' she said. 'The niece asked me if there was anything we could remember about Rebecca from when she taught us.'

'I take it you didn't tell her we reduced the poor woman to tears.'

'No, I kept that shameful little nugget to myself. I did tell her that she read one of Gina's short stories out to the class, though.'

'So she did. I'd forgotten that. Maybe it's not so surprising that Gina wrote a novel, after all. Talking of which, have you read it yet?'

'Yes, I finished it at the weekend.'

'And?'

'And it's exactly as Sue described it. Romantic fiction. About a singer who falls in love with a married man. A piano teacher.'

'Two questions,' Lindsay said. 'Will it need much editing, and is there any sex in it?'

'Yes, and yes. Although the sex scenes are a bit . . .'
Dee pulled a face.

'What?'

'You know, cringey stuff. "Her nipples grazed his shoulder blades", some "ecstatic shuddering", that kind of thing.'

Lindsay giggled.

It was, Dee supposed, hardly surprising that Gina had chosen to write a romance. Whenever the three of them had been on holiday together and sunbathing by a pool, Gina had always had her nose in a book like that. As had Dee herself, for a while. But ever since Gina had gone missing Dee had been in a reading slump. She'd lost her taste for feel-good, humorous novels. For a while, she'd dabbled in crime fiction, but that had just filled her mind with all the terrible things that might have happened to her friend, terrible things that might *still* be happening to her and that could happen to other people she knew and loved, and to herself.

So she'd taken solace in fantasy instead. Thrown herself into stories about witches and wizards, with a few vampires and werewolves thrown in for good measure. Anything that took place in a different type of world, or another dimension. You knew where you were with a fantasy novel. Or rather, you knew where you weren't.

'Let's just say,' Dee said, 'we'd be teasing her about them if she were still a—'

She pinched the bridge of her nose and sighed. 'If she were still around,' she said at last. 'Listen, I don't mind sorting out some of the grammar and punctuation issues, if you don't mind working out how to get it on Kindle.'

'No problem,' Lindsay said. 'Maybe we could set up a Facebook page to promote it. People are more likely to buy a copy if they know the story behind it and that the proceeds are going to charity.'

They walked in silence for a few minutes, each absorbed in their own thoughts.

Dee sighed. 'I was a bit disappointed, if I'm honest.'

'With the novel, you mean?'

'No, not really. It was . . . good. Kind of . . . sweet. It's just that I thought I might learn something new about her, what was occupying her mind, that kind of thing. Not that we even know when she wrote it. I kept hoping I'd find something Sue and Alan and the police might have missed. Some little clue.'

Lindsay hung back and looked up at the sky. 'Maybe we just have to accept that when it comes to Gina, there are no clues. Not any more.'

19

SCARLETT DRUMMED HER FINGERS on her desk and stared at the quarterly VAT return on her screen, her early-morning visit to Rebecca's apartment still weighing heavily on her mind. She was already behind with her work. Her clients had been more than understanding, but HMRC would be less so.

The figures began to blur in front of her eyes. It didn't help that practically all her work these days was screen-based, with everything she needed from her clients collected digitally. When she was on form, this worked well and was so much easier than it had been in the past, when she'd had to plough through mountains of paper receipts and bank statements. Right now, though, with her mind elsewhere and having to switch between two screens and the various webpages open on each one, she found herself temporarily yearning for the old analogue days. Back then, she'd also had colleagues to interact with and meetings to attend. There would have been more to distract her from her current worries. Sometimes, she really missed that office vibe.

When the doorbell rang, she considered ignoring it. Then she remembered she'd ordered some clothes online a few days ago. But it wasn't a package of clothes that awaited her at the front door, it was Ollie. With a box of chocolates in his hands.

'Hi, Scar. Just thought I'd drop these round. They're from Shaz at the office. For you. There's a sympathy card as well. She was in two minds about the chocolates, thought they might be *inappropriate*.'

He held out the box and Scarlett took it. A card was taped to the front. 'I told her chocolates were *never* inappropriate. Not where my sister is concerned.'

Scarlett smiled.

'I haven't disturbed you, have I?'

'Not really,' she said. 'I can't seem to get much done today.'

'Join the club,' he said.

He followed her inside and gestured to the coffee machine. 'Mind if I . . . ?'

'Help yourself,' she said, opening the box of chocolates and setting them down on the counter. 'You might as well have a few of these while you're here. I'll only eat them all otherwise.'

Ollie made himself a double espresso and studied the selection card as if he were cramming for an exam.

Scarlett studied *him*. He looked tired and washed

out. Not for the first time, she thought he wasn't really cut out for running his own business, the stress of keeping it all going, the responsibility for the people he employed. It was their dad who'd put pressure on him to go down this route. Ollie would probably have been happier being a jobbing builder and plumber like Mickey, but that would never have been good enough for their father.

'You been sleeping okay?' she said.

'Me? Yeah, fine. I'm worried about you, actually. All this funeral stuff. I can make some of the phone calls, if you want? Fire off a few emails. I don't see why you should shoulder the whole burden. She was my aunt, too, you know.'

His face was hard as he said this, his tone fierce, but Scarlett knew her brother too well. Ever since their mother had died he'd bottled up all his emotions. Sealed them in tight.

She put her arms around his chest and gave him a hug. Rebecca had been the one constant in their lives. More of a parent to them than their own father. But while Rebecca and Scarlett's relationship had evolved from that of aunt and niece to a friendship between equals, Scarlett now realized that, for Ollie, losing Rebecca was like losing his mum all over again. He might be the owner of a successful building and decorating firm but, deep down, he was still that same little boy who'd crept into her bed at night when he couldn't sleep.

She looked at his sad face. It was almost as if he'd been sleepwalking through the last six weeks and had only just woken up and discovered it wasn't a nightmare, after all. It really had happened.

'I don't mind doing it,' she said. 'And, besides, there's not much left to do.'

Ollie massaged his temples with his thumb and middle finger. 'You haven't got any headache tablets, have you?'

She opened her medicine drawer. 'Take your pick.'

'Fucking hell, Scar! You could open a pharmacy with this lot.'

She watched as he washed a couple of ibuprofen down with a glass of water.

'Listen, I've got to get on with some work. Why don't you have a quick kip on the sofa? You look as if you could do with one. Shaz can hold the fort for a bit, can't she?'

He rubbed his face with both hands and exhaled wearily.

Maybe she would do it now – tell him about the connection she'd discovered between Rebecca and Gina Caplin, see what he made of it. But he was already flinging himself down on her sofa. Knowing Ollie, he'd probably had a bit too much to drink last night. She'd finish dealing with her emails, then make them both some lunch. They could talk about it then.

But when Scarlett came back into the kitchen a

little while later, Ollie had already gone. She put the blister pack of tablets he'd left out on the counter back in the drawer. Maybe he'd just needed that hug. That was the thing with Ollie. All those girlfriends, but no one he could turn to when he needed a bit of comfort. A bit of unconditional love. It was Rebecca who'd provided him with that.

She picked up the local paper from where it had been lying by the coffee machine for the past two weeks. It was still folded over on the page about Gina Caplin's ten-year-anniversary event. Scarlett looked at the familiar photo – the pretty, smiling face, tanned and make-up free, her shoulder-length wavy blonde hair. She reminded Scarlett of someone, but she couldn't for the life of her think who. Or maybe it was because she'd seen this same photo so many times before. Yes, that must be the reason. It was the one that always appeared in papers and on the TV.

It unnerved Scarlett to think that Gina Caplin might have visited this very house. Maybe more than once. She raised her eyes to the ceiling. 'Why didn't you talk to me, Rebecca?' she said aloud. 'Why didn't you tell me about her?'

For a few seconds she waited, half expecting a reply. But if her aunt hadn't spoken to her about it when she was alive, she was hardly going to answer her now that she was dead.

Scarlett opened the drawer that housed her recycling bins and dropped the paper into its designated compartment. Something had certainly been troubling Rebecca during the course of the last year, something that Scarlett, Clive and the rest of the family had put down to her deteriorating mental health. Might it have been something to do with Gina?

There'd been an incident not so long ago, at the school where she used to work. Rebecca had never told Scarlett exactly what happened. All she'd said was that she had got very confused one day, thought one of the pupils was somebody else. Whatever it was she'd said or done, it had unnerved the girl in question and been enough for the head to insist she take sick leave. Scarlett had a hunch it was the opportunity the school had been looking for. Rebecca hadn't been herself for some considerable time.

Whenever Scarlett tried to get to the bottom of what had actually happened, Rebecca became agitated and she'd had to give up. 'I don't *know*,' her aunt had said. 'This girl, that girl. There's always *some* girl. Don't keep asking me these questions, Scarlett!'

Scarlett looked out of the window in the back door. Something didn't feel right.

Maybe she'd find an answer in Rebecca's fiction. Isn't that what novelists did? Stole snippets from their own lives and hid them in their stories? And even if she didn't find an answer, it would be a comfort to read her aunt's words, to hear her voice again.

But it was still raining far too heavily for her to go out and fetch the manuscript. She'd have to wait until tomorrow.

20

It had been a week since her meeting with the Quilter family, but it didn't surprise Dee that Scarlett hadn't come back to her yet to confirm dates. The bureaucracy of death could be a nightmare at the best of times, but when that death had been a murder . . . Dee made a note to give her a call later that day. Then she threw herself into her admin. When the door buzzer went, it made her jump.

She walked through to the reception area and there, outside the door, stood a youngish man with a crash helmet under his arm. She hesitated before opening up. Only two kinds of visitors usually came to this door without a prior appointment: people delivering packages that wouldn't fit through the letterbox or which needed a signature or, rarely, the recently bereaved who hadn't thought to ring first. They also got the odd enquiry about self-arranged funerals, but, generally, people tended to phone ahead or use the contact form on the website.

This man had no obvious letter or parcel in his hands so Dee assumed it must be an enquiry. She unlocked the door, hoping the expression on her face – compassionate, interested – betrayed nothing of the slight apprehension she felt inside. The same apprehension she always felt when opening the door to a lone man when she was on her own.

Not that she *was* on her own. Lindsay was down-stairs in the prep room, doing a stocktake. But she would have her music on loud, knowing her.

'Morning,' she said. 'Can I help you?'

The man cleared his throat. 'I hope so. I wanted to talk to you about a funeral.'

Dee felt herself relax. 'Of course.' *Yes, Dee, you idiot*, she thought. Why else would he be here? She stepped aside and gestured for him to come in and sit down. 'I can take some preliminary details now if you'd like, and then if you decide to go ahead with us, we can make an appointment.'

He perched on the edge of the sofa and put his crash helmet down next to him. The layout of the reception area mirrored that of a sitting room: a sofa and two easy chairs with a coffee table in the middle. Dee sat on one of the easy chairs and gave him a small, encouraging smile.

He stared at his knees. 'I'm not quite sure where to start,' he said, a slight wobble in his voice.

Dee moistened her lips. 'Please, take your time.'

He nodded, still not meeting her eyes.

'It's about my friend,' he said. 'He died in a road accident.'

'I'm very sorry to hear that,' Dee said. 'Very sorry indeed.'

He looked up then, met her eyes. 'We grew up together,' he said. 'Best mates since nursery school.'

Dee inclined her head to let him know she was listening. This part of the job was a little like being a counsellor. Giving people space and time. Not rushing in to ask questions straight away but letting the details unspool gently. The apprehension she'd felt earlier was gone. Here was a man steeped in grief for his friend, a man who clearly wasn't used to showing his emotions. She waited for him to go on.

'I still can't fully believe he's gone.'

Dee leaned forwards slightly, her hands loosely clasped in her lap. 'It's always very difficult when someone dies young,' she said.

He was back to looking at his knees again. Dee watched his shoulders rise and fall with his breath.

'Has the family asked you to help them arrange the funeral?' she said.

He shook his head. 'He's already been buried.'

Dee tucked a strand of hair behind her ear. Whatever she'd anticipated him saying, it hadn't been that.

'I see,' she said, her apprehension seeping back. 'Then may I ask how Fond Farewells can help you today?'

He reached into his jacket pocket and brought out a photo of a twenty-something black man with his arm loosely hanging around the shoulders of a similarly aged white man. They were both grinning widely and wore identical red T-shirts with some kind of logo on the front. Dee soon worked out that the white man in the photo was a younger version of the man now sitting in front of her. The T-shirt looked familiar, and so did his friend.

Then she remembered. It was one of the first jobs she and Lindsay had taken on when they started the company, just a few weeks after Gina went missing. She'd thought about it only recently. The young man whose funeral took place in a bowling alley. But that had been almost ten years ago.

Dee shifted in her seat. 'Would you like me to give you the name of a bereavement counsellor? It's never too late to start processing your grief.'

He shook his head. 'We supported each other, me and the rest of the lads in the team. We still talk about him, have a drink on his birthday. We even changed the name of our team in his honour. We're Gabe's Gang now. Always will be.'

Gabe. That's right. His name had been Gabriel Abiodun. Knocked down by a van on Eltham High Street while riding his motorbike. Dee remembered his mother and girlfriend sitting on this very sofa.

His friend was looking directly at her now, holding her gaze. His face had darkened. What the hell was going on here? What did he want after all this time?

'I wasn't happy with how things were done,' he said.

Dee's palms began to sweat. What was he talking about? Admittedly, it had been an unusual service. Not really a service at all; the members of his team had gone bowling at their local alley, cheered on by his family and friends. That's probably why it had stuck in her mind. But everything had gone off exactly as the family wanted. Dee probably still had the thank-you card from the mother pinned on the massive noticeboard in her office. She never threw thank-you cards away.

'May I ask what your name is?' she said.

'Trevor. Trevor James Cooper.' Dee's heart missed a beat. His earlier awkwardness had been replaced by a look of defiance. Even his voice sounded stronger. 'You asked me to contact you directly.'

21

DEE STRAIGHTENED HER SPINE and took a deep breath. She needed to get Lindsay up here fast. She didn't want to have to deal with this on her own. Whatever *this* turned out to be.

'Would you mind waiting here a moment, Mr Cooper?' she said. 'I just need to find the relevant file from the office.'

She'd barely stood up when he started speaking again. This time, his words tumbled out in an indignant rush.

'Gabe's mum and girlfriend wanted him buried with his crash helmet and leather jacket. They bought one of those big American-style caskets, remember? Cost a fortune, but that's what they wanted.'

Dee did remember that. They'd had to order it from a supplier they hadn't intended using. Their preference, and that of most of their clients, was for simple coffins made out of plain wood or other environmentally friendly materials like willow, wool or cardboard, but Gabriel Abiodun had been a very large young man and, what with the crash helmet and all the biker gear the family wanted him buried in – his bulky leather jacket and boots – not to mention the ten-pin-bowling trophies his girlfriend had insisted on putting in there with him, they'd needed something bigger.

'We all clubbed together to help them pay for it. They'd never have been able to afford it otherwise.'

'Mr Cooper, can you give me a moment? Would you like a cup of coffee or something?'

'I haven't come here to sit around drinking coffee,' he said. 'I've come here to find out why you didn't respect their wishes. Why you stole Gabe's helmet, and probably his jacket too.'

Dee stared at him in disbelief. In horror.

He sneered at her. 'Except I know the reason already. Because you worked out the value. It was a top-quality lid. Composite carbon shell. Worth about seven hundred quid.'

'What on earth are you talking about? We would never, ever—'

'What happened after the family came to view the body? You thought you'd help yourself, did you?'

'I can assure you, Mr Cooper, we carried out the wishes of Gabriel's family to the letter. What makes you think we didn't?'

'Because I found it on eBay a couple of weeks ago. The exact same helmet.'

Dee stared at him crossly. This was some kind of elaborate wind-up, it had to be. 'How do you *know* it was the exact same one?'

Trevor Cooper took his phone out of his back pocket and after a few seconds searching for something held it out for her to see. 'Gabe had it customized. Got his initials engraved on it. And a picture of an angel's wings. Same as the tattoo he had on his arm.'

Dee stared at the initials G.A. and the set of white wings next to them. She remembered that tattoo. Remembered seeing him laid out in the prep room.

'I thought that's what I could see when I first looked at the photo, but I wasn't a hundred per cent sure so I asked the seller to zoom in and take another picture. It's Gabe's lid. No doubt about it. I drew out some of my savings and bought it myself. It's in my hallway at home. You can come round and check for yourself, if you want.'

Dee sat back down again, still holding Trevor Cooper's phone and staring at the photo. This wasn't possible. There had to be some mistake. She should go downstairs and speak to Lindsay about it right now. But if the helmet in this picture *was* Gabriel Abiodun's – the same one his girlfriend had brought into reception – then Trevor Cooper must be right. How else to explain Gabriel's initials and wing design turning up on a motorcycle helmet on eBay almost ten years later?

She looked up to see him studying her from the

sofa. 'Does the name Polly Beardsley mean anything to you?' she said.

He looked away. 'It's a fake account. It wouldn't let me leave a second review.'

Dee chewed the inside of her bottom lip while she considered what to do. 'May I take your contact details, please? I need to speak to my business partner and see if I can get to the bottom of this. Trust me, Mr Cooper, if it turns out that the crash helmet in your possession really is the one your friend should have been buried with, this will have repercussions. Not just for us as a business, but for Gabriel's family, too.'

Trevor Cooper turned to face her. 'Believe me,' he said, 'the last thing I want to do is cause any more grief to Gabe's family. Especially his mum.'

Dee locked eyes with him for a moment. 'I'm very glad to hear that. Something like this would be so upsetting for her. For all of them.'

'It's very upsetting for me too,' he said.

Dee nodded. 'Yes, yes, I can see that.'

He leaned over for the clipboard and paper on the table, the one Dee had picked up intending to make notes on, and wrote his details on it. He stood up and handed it to her.

'I look forward to hearing from you,' he said.

He took hold of his own crash helmet and walked towards the door.

'What do you want me to do if it turns out your allegation is correct?' Dee asked.

He was almost at the door now and turned around so that he was looking directly at her. Dee didn't like the look in his eyes. 'It's not an allegation. That lid is Gabe's. I'd stake my life on it. I don't know what I want you to do, but maybe you should have a long, hard think about those *repercussions* you mentioned and what you can do to prevent this going any further.'

And with that, he left, leaving Dee standing in reception clutching the clipboard and staring after him.

22

IT HAD STOPPED RAINING at last. Scarlett pulled on her wellies, but when she straightened up and reached for the key to the summer house she saw that it wasn't on its hook. That was odd, although, now she came to think of it, she couldn't actually remember locking the door the last time she'd been out there. She'd been so worn out after hanging out the washing and then pulling up all those beetroots she'd just wanted to get back inside as soon as possible.

She plodded up the garden. There wasn't anything valuable in there, so it didn't really matter. But as she approached, she could see that the key wasn't in the lock. She tried the handle, thinking she might have left it inside, but the door was locked. Damn. She must have dropped the key somewhere on the grass then.

She followed her normal route back to the house, her eyes sweeping from side to side as she walked, but there was nothing glinting up at her from the boggy grass. Back in the kitchen, she stared at the empty hook and sighed in frustration. She wasn't normally so careless with keys, and what made it even more annoying was that there wasn't another one. Rebecca had mislaid hers some while back. Scarlett's key had been the spare. The 'one and only', Rebecca used to call it.

She stood in the kitchen, unsure what to do next. No doubt she could get another lock fitted, but that would take time. Or she could phone Ollie – he'd be able to sort it – but she didn't like to bother him when he was so busy. And she didn't want to be the type of woman who always called on a man to help her out, even if that man was her brother.

She thought of the crack running through the window. Presumably, it would be fairly easy to push the glass through and, if she stood on a chair, she'd be able to climb in easily enough. It was a bit risky, but if she went straight inside afterwards and had a rest, she'd be fine.

You won't. You know you won't. It's too much for you. The sensible side of herself tried in vain to dissuade her, but as usual, she ignored it. She really *did* want to read Rebecca's novel.

Fifteen minutes later, having watched a YouTube video on how to break a window safely, she grabbed a roll of black bin bags from the cupboard under the sink, two pairs of rubber gloves, the dustpan and brush, a roll of duct tape and some kitchen scissors. She put the whole lot into a carrier bag and fetched her walking cane from its holder by the door. Her legs felt strong today, but it was going to come in very useful in a moment.

Once she was outside the summer house again, she looked over her shoulder at the upstairs windows of the neighbouring houses. Trees obscured her view on both sides, so she figured if she couldn't see them, they probably couldn't see her and, even if they could, so what? This was her property. If she wanted to smash a window, she bloody well would. The glass had to be taken out anyway or sooner or later it might shatter and do her an injury.

She spread the bin bags over the decked platform in front of the double doors and went to get a brick from behind the raised beds. Then she pulled on both pairs of rubber gloves, cut strips of duct tape off and criss-crossed them all over the glass. The window was much larger than the one in the You-Tube video, but if this was what it took to ensure the glass didn't fly off in all directions, then so be it.

She took a step back and shoved the brick into the glass until it caved in. Then she lifted her walking cane into the air and jabbed it hard into the remaining shards until they had all peeled away and fallen inside. She ran her cane along each of the four edges of the frame, sweeping away the last jagged pieces.

Now for the tricky bit. She dragged the old

cast-iron chair under the window. This could go one of two ways. She'd either climb through successfully without injuring herself or she'd end up crashing down on to the broken glass, cutting herself badly and breaking her leg in the process. Then she'd be trapped in the locked summer house. She patted her back pocket to reassure herself that her phone was still there. Why was she even doing this? It was madness.

A familiar voice started up in her head. 'You've started now, so stop catastrophizing and get on with it!' Only this time, Scarlett wasn't sure whether it was Rebecca's voice she could hear or her own. She peered through the open space where the pane of glass had been and estimated the distance between the bottom of the window frame and the floor of the summer house. It was probably just under two feet, the height of a washing machine. She could do this. She knew she could. Besides, it was stupid to give up after going to all the effort of smashing the window.

She hooked her walking cane over the edge of the window frame, stood on the chair and, grabbing on to the sides of the frame with her gloved hands, put first one foot then another on the bottom of the frame until she was in a precarious crouching position. For one awful moment, she thought she was going to fall backwards on to the chair and the decking and break her neck. Then, having steadied herself, she groped for her cane and held it out in front of her, unfurled her right leg and lowered it tentatively down on to the carpet of broken glass and duct tape.

This had to be the most stupid thing she'd ever done, and she was bound to suffer for it later. She always did. But she'd done it now. She'd broken into the summer house, all by herself. A woman with ME and a walking cane.

23

DEE STARED AT THE retreating figure of Trevor Cooper. For a few moments she felt frozen in time, almost as if he'd put some kind of spell on her. It couldn't be true. Surely Lindsay wouldn't do something like that? And yet how else to explain Gabriel Abiodun's expensive customized crash helmet turning up on eBay after all these years? And if the helmet had been stolen, did that mean his leather jacket had too?

She went back into her office and closed the door. It had to be someone else. Someone who'd had access to the body. One of the part-timers, perhaps? But they vetted everyone so carefully and, besides, they never worked unsupervised.

Her mind strayed to Jake, but no, that was almost as unthinkable as it being Lindsay. Jake was as honest as they come. Dee put her elbows on her desk and rested her head in her hands. If anyone had told her earlier that day that something like this would happen, she'd have said there was only one thing to do and that was to go downstairs right now and talk to Lindsay, tell her what had happened. After all, the reputation of Fond Farewells was at stake. Who knew what Trevor Cooper might do next?

But if she did that, Dee would know straight away if this outrageous accusation was true. She'd see it on Lindsay's face, she knew she would. Lindsay was pretty transparent. Dee didn't think she could bear it if it turned out to be true. Stealing anything was bad enough, but stealing from the dead? Going against the wishes of his family? Jeopardizing the business?

Just then, she heard the door to the basement opening and footsteps running up the stairs. Dee got up and put her coat on. She would keep this to herself for now.

Lindsay stuck her head around the door. 'Ready for a walk?' she said. 'I certainly am.'

'Sorry, I've got a dentist's appointment. I forgot to tell you.'

Lindsay grimaced. 'Nothing horrible, I hope?'

Dee couldn't quite look her in the face. 'Just a filling.'

'Oh no, you poor thing.'

Dee hung her bag over her shoulder, grabbed her car keys from the little dish on her desk and headed for the door.

'I'm not sure how long it'll take,' she said. 'I'll let you know.'

Outside, she practically ran to the side street

where she'd parked her car. It felt wrong, lying to Lindsay, but if Trevor Cooper was right, then Lindsay had lied to her, and to Gabriel Abiodun's family. Lied about something a whole lot worse than going to the dentist's.

It was, she supposed, inevitable that she'd find herself driving home. She had to talk to someone and, since she couldn't speak to Lindsay, the next best person was her dad. Her mum would either over react or she'd start telling her what to do. She never listened, not properly. In any case, her mum would be at work now, doing whatever it was she did in the planning and building department of Perth and Kinross Council.

She was on the third flight of stairs up to the flat when she remembered the *thing* between her dad and Mrs Kowalski. She stopped before the final flight and fished her phone out of her bag. The last thing she wanted was to walk in on them *doing* it. The very thought made her shudder.

Her dad answered after a couple of rings. 'Dee? Everything all right?'

'Not exactly,' she said. 'Are you free for lunch?'

'Of course. Do you want me to come and meet you somewhere?'

'I'm here now, in the stairwell.'

'Oh, right. I'll put the kettle on then.'

*

156

They sat at the kitchen table, each with a plate of cheese-and-tomato sandwiches and a mug of tea in front of them. Her dad hadn't said a word the whole time she'd been speaking. Now, he leaned forward and folded his arms on the table.

'That's a serious accusation,' he said.

'What shall I do, Dad? I can't just ignore it.'

'No, love, you can't.' He took a sip of tea and frowned. 'Is there any chance this Trevor Cooper might be bluffing?'

Dee shook her head. 'I don't think so. I saw the photo. You could quite clearly see Gabriel's initials and the angel wings design. It was exactly the same as his tattoo.' Dee pushed her plate to one side. 'I've seen lots of dead bodies with tattoos, and I never usually remember the designs. But Gabriel's stuck in my mind because it was white. I'd never seen a white tattoo before, and Gabriel was black, so it really stood out.'

'And this Trevor says he's bought the crash helmet and has it at home, yeah?'

'Yeah. He said I could go round and see for myself if I didn't believe him.'

Her dad frowned. 'I wouldn't do that, love.'

'Don't worry, I'm not going to. But I am going to have to speak to him again.' She got up to throw the remainder of her sandwich away. 'After I've spoken to Lindsay.'

24

SCARLETT WOKE AT 4.23 a.m., certain she'd heard something in the back garden, right outside her bedroom window. She sat up in bed. It had sounded like a scraping noise on the patio, almost like a shoe scuffing on the stone slabs. It was probably just a dream. Once, a while back, she'd been convinced that someone had rung the doorbell at six o'clock in the morning, but when she'd got up there was nobody there and no sign of anyone in the street. She'd told Rebecca about it later that day – they often used to chat about their dreams. 'I think that means an opportunity is beckoning, but you're not sure whether to take it,' her aunt had said, and at the time that interpretation had seemed to make sense. Scarlett wondered what Rebecca would have made of her dream about the summer house.

She strained her ears. There it was again. Quieter this time, but worryingly like a footstep. She turned back the duvet and pages of her aunt's manuscript fluttered to the floor. She must have fallen asleep reading it. She sat on the edge of the bed until her eyes had adjusted to the dark. Then she walked over to the curtains and gently hooked a finger around the outer edge of the one on the right. She only had a partial view of the garden from here, on account of the old tool shed, but there was nothing untoward in that bit of it she could see.

It must have been a dream then, or maybe a fox skulking about, nudging something with its snout. All sorts of nocturnal creatures were out there right now, scuffling and scurrying and darting about under cover of darkness. Foraging for food. Mating.

She was about to collect the fallen pages and get back into bed when a thin beam of white light caught her eye. But no sooner had she noticed it dancing on the periphery of her vision than it disappeared. Her body tensed. Was someone really out there?

She moved towards the bedroom door, her heart knocking painfully against her ribcage. She'd get a better view from the back door. She picked up her phone from the bedside table, almost dropping it, her hands were shaking so much. She wouldn't phone the police yet, not until she knew for sure. It could be one of the neighbours, doing something in their garden. Although what anyone could be doing out there this early in the morning, she really didn't know.

She groped her way to the kitchen. If she didn't put the lights on, hopefully she would remain unseen.

Then again, if she *did* put the lights on, it might scare them off and she could go back to bed. She hesitated at the switch. Maybe she didn't *want* to scare them off. Not yet, anyway. Maybe she was curious to see what they were doing.

Admit it, Scarlett, she thought. *You* are *curious*.

She took a few more steps into the kitchen, inching her way to the back door. With her body still tucked behind the wall, she moved her head to one side and peeped out of the glazed panel at the top. She gasped. A figure dressed in black – a man – was moving steadily away from the house, walking up the left-hand side of the garden, as close to the tall hedge as he could get without actually brushing against it.

Scarlett edged out from her hiding place and moved her face closer to the window until her nose almost touched the glass. She followed the figure's progress. Was this one of those opportunist burglars, working his way through the back gardens, preying on forgetful or careless homeowners who'd left a window open or a door unlocked? What was he planning to do next? Climb over the fence at the bottom?

She scrolled up for the home screen, was about to tap the green phone icon and dial 999, when the beam of light came back on. It was directly in front of the summer house now. He must have nipped across the lawn while she was fiddling with her phone. She stood, transfixed, as he stuck his head through the space where the window had been.

You won't find anything of value in there, mate, she thought. *Not unless you're into freshly dug beetroot.* He put a hand into his pocket and drew something out. Her mouth went dry. No, it couldn't be. It wasn't . . .

A few seconds later the door of the summer house opened and the man stepped inside. The beam of light swept from left to right. Scarlett narrowed her eyes. There was something familiar about the height and shape of this person.

The floor lurched beneath her feet. With trembling fingers, she dropped her phone on to the counter and stared in disbelief. Ollie had just let himself into the summer house at half past four in the morning with the missing key. The 'one and only'.

She backed away from the door, heart racing. There was only one explanation. He must have taken it when he came round yesterday. But why would he have done that? If he'd wanted to look in the summer house, he could have just asked her. What on earth could be in there that he was prepared to creep around searching for, like a thief in the night?

Unless . . . unless he was looking for the same thing *she'd* been looking for. Was it Rebecca's manuscript he wanted? He hadn't sounded that interested in it when they'd spoken on the phone, and if he'd changed his mind about wanting to read it, he only had to ask her and she'd have given it to him.

She recalled something else about their conversation, something she hadn't given any thought to before now. Hadn't he offered to come round and clear the summer house out for her sometime soon, to get it ready for next year, even though he'd made a point of telling her how busy he and his men were with all the jobs people wanted done by Christmas.

Then another thought struck her. Her legs almost buckled beneath her and she had to grab on to the counter to steady herself. Perhaps it was her mention of the card from Gina that had compelled him to visit. He'd denied any knowledge of hearing Rebecca mention a Gina, but ... maybe he was lying. Maybe he *did* know about their friendship. Maybe *he'd* known Gina, too.

Sweat broke out on the back of Scarlett's neck and her stomach turned to water. She made it to the bathroom just in time to throw up in the toilet.

25

DEE'S DAD KNOCKED ON her bedroom door. She was already awake and sitting up in bed with her laptop open.

'Come in,' she said.

He gave her a mug of tea, then stood with his back to the radiator. 'I was just thinking. Didn't Lindsay have a few problems raising the deposit for her house?'

'Your mind's on the same track as mine,' Dee said. 'She was a few thousand short, yes. According to Trevor Cooper, that crash helmet was worth about seven hundred pounds. And if she stole the jacket too . . .'

Her dad came and sat on the end of her bed. 'Perhaps it was too much of a temptation,' he said. 'I don't want to believe it of her, but . . .'

'I don't want to believe it either, Dad, but I'm afraid we might have to.'

'When was Gabriel's funeral?'

Dee pointed to the spreadsheet open on her laptop. 'Sixteenth of April 2009. A month after Gina went missing. It was one of our first jobs.'

'And when did she put the offer on her house? Can you remember?'

Dee thought about that for a moment. 'I think it was round about the same time.' Tears welled up behind her eyes.

Her dad nodded. 'I wonder where she got the rest of the money.'

'I always assumed her parents lent it to her.'

'Neither of you were in a particularly good place back then. You had a lot on your plate, worrying about Gina and trying to get your business off the ground.'

'I know, I was thinking that too. We were both struggling to keep it together.' Dee raked her fingers through her hair. 'I'm going to have to talk to her, aren't I? I can't put it off any longer.'

Her dad gave her a sad little smile. 'No, love, you can't.'

Dee sat at her desk and tried to psych herself up. It felt strange being in the office this early, but she'd wanted to be sure she was here first so that she could broach the subject as soon as Lindsay arrived.

She'd never been good with conflict, had spent most of her life avoiding it at all costs. But letting unprofessional, unethical behaviour go unchallenged was not an option. In any case, if she didn't tell Lindsay about Trevor Cooper's accusation soon, he would come back another time and end up telling her himself. One way or another, Lindsay needed to know what had happened.

When the door finally swung open and Lindsay came in, Dee took a deep breath to steady her nerves. She felt sick at the thought of what was coming.

Lindsay looked surprised. 'Makes a change for you to be in before me,' she said, shrugging off her coat and hanging it on one of the hooks outside the office. 'Bad night?'

'You could say that, yes.'

Lindsay came into the office and peered at Dee closely from under her eyebrows, as if she were a nurse checking for symptoms. 'Is your tooth playing up?' Then her expression changed into one of anxiety. 'Oh no, we haven't had another one of those reviews, have we? I'm going to take that whole section down. This is too much.'

'No, we haven't had another one. At least, I hope not. I haven't actually looked yet.'

'So what is it? You look really worried about something.'

'I am, and you're right in a way. It is related to those reviews.' She clenched her toes. 'I had a visitor yesterday. T. J. Cooper.'

Lindsay's eyes widened. 'What? Why are you only telling me this now? Who is it? What did they want?'

'His name is Trevor James Cooper. He's a friend of someone we buried.'

Lindsay frowned. 'Who?'

'Gabriel Abiodun. Remember him?'

Lindsay's face went very still. She sat on the chair opposite Dee and dropped her bag on to the floor beside her. 'Big black guy. The service was at Hollywood Bowl in Surrey Quays. It was *years* ago. Jake had to stand in as a pallbearer when one of Gabriel's mates broke his wrist.'

Dee nodded. 'That's right. Remember anything else?'

Lindsay narrowed her eyes. 'Yes,' she said. 'We had to order an American-style casket because of his size and all the extras the family wanted in there with him.' She frowned again. 'What's this about, Dee?'

This was it. She needed to say it.

'Trevor Cooper has found one of those "extras" for sale on eBay. Gabriel's crash helmet.'

Lindsay's mouth dropped open.

'He showed me a photo of it. He's bought it. Says it's in his hallway at home and we can go and look at it and see for ourselves. He knows it's Gabriel's because it was customized with his initials and a set of white angel wings. Just like his tattoo.'

Dee watched Lindsay's face as her words landed. She didn't look guilty so much as gobsmacked. No, she looked . . . devastated.

Tears stung the back of Dee's eyes. This was Lindsay. Her best friend. The friend she'd known since primary school. The friend who'd always looked out for her and had her back. The friend she'd laughed and cried with. The friend she'd worked alongside for the past ten years. And, with Gina gone, the only person in the world, apart from her dad, that Dee truly trusted and loved. Hurting Lindsay, challenging her like this, was the worst thing she'd ever had to do.

'Did you take it off him after the viewing?' she asked. 'Did you sell Gabriel Abiodun's crash helmet?'

Lindsay stared at her lap. Dee watched the tears roll down her cheeks.

'Yes,' she said at last, so quietly Dee almost missed it. 'I'm so sorry. It was an awful thing to do. The very worst. But I was going to lose the house if I couldn't find the rest of the deposit. I only needed another fifteen hundred pounds. I got five hundred for it, and a couple of hundred for the jacket. My parents lent me the rest.'

Dee closed her eyes. So she'd stolen the jacket, too. At least she'd confessed to that without being asked.

Lindsay lifted her head. Her eyes were wet, her expression wretched. 'I'm so sorry, Dee. I've regretted it ever since.'

26

THE DOORBELL RANG AT a little after 9 a.m. Scarlett had a horrible feeling it would be Ollie. It was the first time in her life she'd ever felt nervous about seeing her own brother.

'What's this, an early-morning check-up?' she said, the words coming out before she could stop them.

He looked momentarily thrown by the question, as if he'd been rumbled. She tried to ignore the uneasy feeling in her stomach. He'd had no right to steal that key, to enter her garden at night without her knowledge. But why had he come back so soon? What was the purpose of this second visit?

'Thought I'd take a look at the summer house on my way to work, get an idea of how long it'll take to clear the junk out. You don't mind, do you? I won't be long.'

He strode to the back door before she could answer and swiped at the hook. Scarlett could hardly believe what she was seeing. He was actually pretending to pluck the key when he must already have it in his hand. He was opening the door and on his way out in a matter of seconds. She stared at his retreating back, frozen to the spot. If she weren't already so freaked out by his behaviour, Scarlett would have been impressed at his ingenuity.

'Shall I make us some coffee?' she called after him, realizing that now, when he asked her about the broken window, which he was sure to do, she wouldn't be able to use the excuse of not having been able to find the key. Not unless she confronted him about stealing it and turning up last night.

'Yeah, great,' he said.

She watched him walk up the garden. Straight down the middle this time, not creeping along, tucked into the hedge, like before. She saw him stop abruptly, about fifteen feet from the summer house, as if in surprise, and then walk even faster towards it. Scarlett knew this charade was purely for her benefit, in case she was watching him. He'd obviously thought this through.

Once again, she saw him stick his head through the space where the window had been, as if it were the first time he'd done this. Scarlett rocked slowly on the heels and balls of her feet. Had he come back because he wanted to ask her about the missing window and the only way he could do that without admitting to having come earlier was if he went out there again? Or maybe he hadn't found what he was looking for during his torchlight search and wanted another go in the daylight.

Was it the card from Gina he wanted or the manuscript? Maybe both. She hadn't told him she'd brought them into the house, so perhaps he was assuming she'd left them out there. But why hadn't he just asked her if he'd wanted to see them? It didn't make sense.

Unless he was looking for something else entirely? Something she might have missed? Because he sure as hell hadn't come here to estimate the length of time it would take to clear the junk out.

Scarlett kept her vigil at the back door. If he found something and pocketed it, she probably wouldn't see from this distance. Even so, she couldn't tear herself away. She only moved when he came out and started walking back to the house. By the time he came into the kitchen she was busying herself at the coffee machine, anxiety fluttering around her breastbone like a trapped bird.

'What happened?' he said. 'Why's the window missing?'

'Thought you'd ask that,' she said, her voice as careless as she could make it. 'I decided to read Rebecca's novel after all. Went all the way up there, then realized I'd left the key on the hook.'

Ollie looked at her as if she were mad, even though

he must have known that the key wouldn't have been there. 'So instead of coming back to get it, you decided you'd smash the window in?'

She laughed. 'Sort of.'

It was a ridiculously improbable story, but there was no way back from it now and, anyway, so what if he thought she was mad? His nocturnal behaviour was hardly that of a sane individual.

'It was already badly cracked. I meant to tell you. I thought I'd save you a job, seeing as you're so busy, so I pushed it in with my cane. I was going to try and board it up, but by the time I'd climbed in, got the manuscript and swept the glass up, I was exhausted.' She was jabbering now, in a voice that wasn't her own. She needed to calm down, to relax.

'How the hell did you climb in?'

'How do you think? I stood on a garden chair and levered myself through.'

'But . . . but you could have cut yourself. Or broken a leg or something. Don't you think that was a pretty stupid thing to do?'

She shrugged. 'Probably. But you know me. Once I set my mind on something . . .'

Ollie sighed. 'I'll ask Mickey to come round and fix it. Don't think I can spare any glaziers right now, but Mickey can handle it. He can do it the same day he gets rid of the flowers.'

Damn. Now Mickey would be here for even

longer. Scarlett gave her brother a grateful smile. It killed her to do it because what she really wanted to do was prod him in the chest and remind him that it was her fucking summer house and she'd do what she wanted and would he please stop treating her like a child and why was he pretending this was the first he knew about the broken window when he'd already seen it at four thirty this morning?

But this wasn't the time to put him on the spot. If Ollie knew something about Rebecca and Gina Caplin, if he knew why Rebecca had kept their friendship a secret, then that was seriously worrying. She needed more time to think things through.

'That would be great,' she said. 'When do you think he'll drop by?'

Now it was Ollie's turn to shrug. 'I'll have a look at the work diary and let you know.'

He took the coffee she offered him. 'Was it any good, Rebecca's novel?'

'I don't know. I only started reading it last night.'

He shook his head and rolled his eyes. 'All that trouble to get it, and you haven't even read it yet.'

'I would have done if I didn't have such a backlog of work.'

'Tell me about it,' he said. 'We're inundated with jobs right now.'

She looked at him over the top of her coffee cup. 'Can't be that busy if you've got time to worry about an old summer house.' She couldn't resist it.

He looked uncomfortable. 'Yeah, well, family comes first.'

Family comes first. It wasn't until Ollie had left and Scarlett was rinsing out the coffee cups that she remembered Rebecca saying that to her once. It had been shortly after she'd moved into this apartment and she'd been completely overwhelmed at how beautiful it was. How perfectly suited to her needs. She'd actually burst into tears, like one of those people on house-makeover shows on TV. Her dad had been there, and Ollie too, plus some of Ollie's men who'd carried out most of the work.

Rebecca had hugged her and said, 'Hush now, you silly thing. Family comes first.'

27

When Scarlett saw Mickey North standing on the doorstep the next morning, it was like being teleported back in time. He handed her the cards he'd salvaged from the pavement. Apart from a few lines on his face, he looked exactly the same. Same Viking hair. Same piercing blue eyes. But the sudden onslaught of lust that had caught her off-guard when she'd last been standing this close to him was, thankfully, absent. How was it possible she'd allowed that to happen?

It was she who'd made the first move, all those years ago. Afterwards, Mickey had joked that it was like a scene from a porn movie. Randy plumber and bored housewife in shower. 'Except I'm not a bored housewife,' she'd said. To which he'd replied, 'But I *am* a randy plumber,' and the two of them had laughed out loud. It was a once-only thing, they'd both agreed.

Except it wasn't. It had happened again, six months

later, when the toilet seat came loose and he'd had to come back.

'It's been a long time,' he said now. 'How've you been?' He shook his head. 'Stupid question. I'm such an idiot.' He gave her the usual 'Sorry for your loss' spiel. Then he stared at his feet. 'I should have made more of an effort to keep in touch.'

Scarlett cringed. 'It's okay, Mickey. I wasn't some lovestruck teenager. I wasn't sitting here waiting for you to call. And if I'd wanted to see you again, I'd have broken the showerhead.'

Mickey gave a nervous laugh. 'You didn't have to invent a plumbing emergency to get me to come round, you know.'

Shit! Why on earth had she said that?

She assumed he'd wait on the front step while she went to fetch the key to the summer house, but he followed her in. Ollie and Mickey had been best friends since childhood. Back in the days when Scarlett and Ollie were living here with Rebecca, Mickey had been a frequent visitor and, though she hadn't seen him in ages, that level of familiarity ran deep. That's what made what had happened between them so mortifying.

All she'd wanted back then was some physical contact. Some intimacy. Something to remind her that she was still alive, that she was still an attractive, desirable woman, despite her ill health. But one thing she'd learned from their two somewhat frenzied encounters was that casual sex left her feeling empty and used.

'I really am sorry,' he said.

'Please, don't be. I never expected, or wanted, you to call.'

'I meant about Rebecca,' he said.

'Oh, right. Yeah.'

There was an awkward silence. Scarlett put the cards on the floor to look at later. She didn't want them on her nice, clean counter, not when they'd been sitting outside on the pavement for weeks on end. She went to fetch the key and handed it to Mickey.

'You can go out through the back door if you like, but when you've finished, maybe you can use the side gate?' He needed to know that she didn't want him popping back in for a chat or a coffee. Or anything else.

But Mickey showed no signs of wanting to go outside and get on with the job he'd been sent round to do. He looked as if he needed to get something off his chest.

'She was an awesome woman, your aunt,' he said.

'Yes, she was.'

'Terrible way for her to go.'

His face reminded her of Ollie's when he'd been trying to hold back tears. She felt herself soften.

'Help yourself to a coffee before you start on the window,' she said. 'You can take it out there with you.'

'Nah, I'm good, thanks.' He opened the back door and made to leave. Then he paused and turned to face her. 'Ollie tells me you broke the window yourself, to get in. Is that right?'

'Yes.'

He shook his head. 'You could have broken your leg.'

Scarlett sighed. 'Don't you start. Ollie's already bent my ear about that.'

He smiled. 'You've got some gumption, I'll say that about you.' His left eye twitched. She hoped it wasn't supposed to be a wink. Flirting with her was the very last thing she wanted him to do. There it was again. No, it was definitely a twitch. Once again, she got the impression he wanted to say something.

'He is all right, isn't he? Ollie?'

She looked at him. 'Why do you ask?'

Mickey twisted his mouth to one side. 'I just wondered whether he needs a bit more time off. He might be putting on a good act, but this has hit him hard. He's not coping with things.'

'It's hit us all hard,' Scarlett said. 'It's been a total nightmare. But thanks for mentioning it. I'll keep an eye on him.'

Mickey shrugged. 'No need to thank me. It's what mates are for.'

'Yeah, but you're more than a mate. I don't think he could manage without you, I really don't.'

She watched him stride up to the end of the garden

in his stonewashed denims and big yellow boots, just as she'd watched Ollie stride up there yesterday morning, *and* the night before. Either Mickey was right and Ollie needed more time off for grieving, or her brother was worried about something else entirely. Unease flickered in her belly. What secret had Ollie and Rebecca been keeping from her? And what did it have to do with Gina Caplin?

Scarlett observed Mickey as he measured up the window. She had more than enough work to be getting on with, but while he was still here she knew she wouldn't be able to concentrate. Something occurred to her as he lifted out the black bin bag, the one in which she'd deposited all the broken glass and duct tape, and carried it back towards the house. Why hadn't Ollie done a better job with the summer house? Why hadn't he got one of those bigger, sturdier ones installed, with stronger glass in the windows? In fact, why hadn't he got a specialist to build it instead of doing it himself and rushing it?

Everything related to the house conversion had been done to the highest specification. Like many architects, her dad was a perfectionist, and Ollie, despite all his protestations to the contrary, was a chip off the old block. Having gone to such lengths to ensure that everything relating to the house was perfect, why would Ollie have accepted second-best for the garden? Especially seeing as a summer house was something Rebecca had always wanted. And, now she thought about it, why hadn't her dad ever said anything about it? It wasn't like him to keep his opinions to himself.

Scarlett returned to her desk in case Mickey caught sight of her watching him. Without really knowing why, she went into Google and typed 'Gina Caplin' into the search bar. She began to jot down notes and dates. If only she could have found Rebecca's old diaries. That was strange in itself, wasn't it? Hadn't Rebecca kept everything? And she hadn't just used her diaries for recording appointments and special occasions, she'd used them to record her thoughts and feelings too, hadn't she?

Scarlett rolled her shoulders back to ease the tension in her neck. She still hadn't looked in the bedroom. She felt a twinge in her stomach. The very thought of opening that door filled her with dread. But what if Rebecca had kept the diaries in there somewhere? The police would have found them during their forensics search, but entries relating to someone called Gina would have been of no interest to them. Not when they'd been looking for information relating to Rebecca and Clive.

Out of curiosity, she changed the filter on her search results to images and studied all the different versions of Gina Caplin's face that came up on her screen, various photos that her family must have provided. So many news articles over the years, so many different sites. There was, Scarlett thought sadly, always so much more news media when the women who went missing were young, white and middle class. She'd heard somewhere that this even had a name: missing white woman syndrome. What kind of world was it where a hierarchy of missing girls and women existed and only some got the coverage and national outrage they *all* deserved, every last one of them?

She wandered back out to the living room and over to the bay window. Mickey's van was no longer there, which meant he must have gone to get the glass cut. There was nothing to stop her going upstairs again right now and continuing her search, only ... only she didn't feel quite strong enough at the moment.

Are you making excuses? Her aunt's voice questioned her from beyond the grave. 'Very probably,' Scarlett replied, unsure whether she felt comforted or distressed by the conversation. Was hearing Rebecca's voice in her head a sure-fire sign that she was losing her grip on reality? Or did this sort of thing always happen when someone close to you had died unexpectedly?

Just then, she had an idea. She would check her *own* diaries. Her old work diaries. She never got rid of them. It was her accountant's brain, trained never to throw away anything that might one day be needed in the event of a tax audit. She would be able to cross-reference her own dates with what had been happening here at the house. She'd visited several times before actually moving in. She'd seen the work in progress, met the men doing all the labouring, talked to Ollie about paint colours and tiles, what style flooring she wanted. And on at least a couple of those visits, she'd seen the ground being prepared for the summer house: the digging up of the old shrubs at the end of the garden, the site being staked out.

She had a sudden vision of a body being lowered into a hole in the ground. A poisonous image that made her stomach churn. She pushed the dreadful thought away. What on earth was wrong with her? Was her life really so lacking in drama that she needed to imagine trouble where none existed? And yet, something odd was definitely going on with Ollie. And Rebecca had kept a pretty massive secret to herself.

She went into her office. As soon as she'd cross-referenced those dates, she could rid her mind of this madness. But as she caught sight of all those Gina Caplins staring back at her from the screen, she realized what it was about her that looked so familiar. Her breath caught in her throat. She couldn't believe she hadn't noticed it before.

28

DEE AND LINDSAY WERE sitting in the front office. Ever since Lindsay's confession yesterday, there'd been so many work-related interruptions they hadn't had a chance to talk properly about the Trevor Cooper situation. Now, there was only thing on the agenda.

'So what do we do about it?' Dee asked, not wasting any time.

Lindsay's eyes had lost their usual sparkle. 'I'll call him,' she said. 'I'll apologize and pay him whatever he spent on buying the crash helmet back. And I'll ask him to nominate a charity and I'll donate the same amount I got for the jacket. I'll explain what a terrible year it was, how I must have lost my mind. I'll make sure he knows that you knew absolutely nothing about it, that I betrayed you, too, and that you're distraught. I'll appeal to his better nature. If he has one.'

Dee slid Trevor Cooper's contact details across the desk. 'Let's hope that works.'

Lindsay folded the paper in half and pocketed it. 'I'll *make* it work, I promise. And I want you to know that I've never, ever, done anything like that since, and I'll never, ever, do anything like it again.' Tears spilled out of her eyes. 'This business means everything to me, Dee. And so do you. You *have* to believe me.'

Dee felt herself soften. She *did* believe her. 'Didn't you ever worry about something like this happening?'

Lindsay looked down and sniffed back the tears. She shook her head sadly.

'Didn't it occur to you that they might turn up again and that one of his friends might see them?'

'It should have done, but it didn't. I can't believe it didn't. I'm so fucking *stupid*.'

Yes, Dee thought. *You are*. But it was pointless agreeing with her on this. Lindsay was suffering enough. There was little to be gained by rubbing salt into her wounds.

'Did he seem like the angry, violent type?' Lindsay asked.

'He seemed pretty pissed off, and he had every right to be. I don't think he was the violent type, though, but how do we know *what* he's capable of? He sent those nasty reviews, didn't he? And he walked into reception and confronted me. Someone else might have just sent an email, or phoned. Do you want me to sit with you while you speak to him?'

'No, it'll be better if I do it on my own,' Lindsay

said. 'I feel embarrassed enough already. I'll let you know when I've done it.'

Dee didn't see much of Lindsay for the rest of the day. She didn't come up at lunchtime to suggest a walk, like she normally did. It was hardly surprising in the circumstances. Things were bound to be strained between the two of them, at least until this business with Trevor Cooper was sorted. *If* it could be sorted.

Even if he accepted Lindsay's apology and decided not to take things any further, Dee couldn't see her and Lindsay returning to the easy rapport they'd enjoyed before. Not for a while, at any rate. She felt let down. Disappointed. But most of all, she felt sad. It had changed the dynamics of their relationship. All the trust and camaraderie had vanished.

Dee got up to make herself a coffee. She toyed with the idea of calling down to see if Lindsay wanted one too. She even reached for Lindsay's mug, then decided against it. She couldn't help thinking that it would have been easier to accept if Lindsay had stolen something from *her* instead. Or if she'd upset Dee personally in some other way. But stealing the property of one of their clients somehow made things so much worse.

Then again, it had been a long time ago, and Lindsay was right, it had been a terrible, terrible year. Opening this business together should have been one of the best, most exciting times in their lives, and with Gina set to embark on her dance-teaching career, the three of them had been riding high. Then Gina had gone missing and all the happiness had evaporated, literally overnight. Perhaps she should cut Lindsay some slack. After all, nobody was perfect.

When the door to reception swung open and Lindsay appeared in her coat, Dee was surprised.

'I thought you were downstairs,' she said. 'I didn't hear you leave.'

Lindsay gave her a sheepish look. 'I went out the back way earlier. Didn't want to disturb you.'

Dee took a sip of her coffee. Was this what it was going to be like from now on, both of them trying to avoid each other? She really hoped not.

'It's all sorted,' Lindsay said.

Dee looked at her, confused. 'What do you mean?'

'The Trevor Cooper situation. He's agreed not to take things any further. He's accepted my apology and he's not going to say anything to Gabe's mum, or any of his mates.'

'What?' Dee stared at her suspiciously. 'When did he say all this? You haven't been round there, have you? I thought you were going to call him.'

Lindsay unbuttoned her coat. Dee noticed that her hair was different. This morning it had been swept back in a neat chignon. Now it was loose and messy.

'I tried to call, but his phone kept going to voicemail. I thought I'd pop round there on the off chance.

I just wanted to get it over with as soon as possible. And it *is* over. It was like you said, he was pissed off at first, but . . . but then he came round. He said he'll delete those reviews.'

Dee stared at her. Her hair. That look in her eyes.

'Oh my God, Lindsay, please tell me you didn't sleep with him.'

A red flush crept into Lindsay's cheeks and Dee knew. She knew straight away. 'I can't believe you'd do that. That's so . . . did he *ask* you to do that? Is that what he expected, because if it was—'

'Look, Dee, we had a problem and I've sorted it. End of.' Lindsay's tone was defiant.

'You didn't need to do *that*, for Christ's sake! That's sexual blackmail. What were you *thinking*, going round there on your own? Jesus Christ, Lins, we'd have found another way to deal with this.'

'Except now we don't need to, okay? And anyway, he didn't *ask* me.' She gave Dee a tight little smile. 'Actually, he was rather cute, so let's just call it "damage limitation".'

Dee glared at her in disbelief. 'No, Lindsay, let's just call it "whoring yourself out".'

Lindsay's jaw dropped, as well it might. Dee couldn't believe she'd used those words, but now that she'd started she couldn't stop.

'What did you do? Tell him you'd give him a blow job if he let the matter drop? My God, Lindsay! What kind of person are you? No, don't answer that. I already know what kind of person you are. You're the kind of person who steals things from dead people and fucks random strangers just for the hell of it. I can't believe you'd stoop so low. I can't believe you have so little respect for me or the business we've worked so hard to build. So little respect for *yourself*!'

Lindsay looked as if Dee had just slapped her round the face. 'How *dare* you talk to me like that. You're just jealous that I have a life and you don't. And for your information, I don't fuck random strangers just for the hell of it. I sleep with men I fancy, yes, and I enjoy it. What's wrong with that? At least I'm not stuck at home with my dad at the age of forty, too scared to go out in the dark. I'm an independent single woman. Why the hell shouldn't I have some fun? We're all of us a long time dead, Dee. In our line of work, we know that more than most. And as for not respecting you or the business, that's exactly why I wanted to sort this situation out before it went any further. And I didn't go round there *intending* to sleep with him. I really didn't. It just . . . it just happened.'

'How? How did it *just happen*? That sort of thing doesn't *just happen*.'

'Yes, Dee, it does. Not to you, maybe, because you never do anything, or go anywhere. And if you do, you don't engage. You might as well have a bloody great sign on your head that says: "Men, keep away!"'
She took a step closer to Dee, her face taut with anger.

'I made a colossal mistake back then. I admit it. I fucked up big time. There are no excuses for what I did. But, for whatever reason, I did it, and I have to live with that. It would be nice if I didn't have to live with your disapproval as well. It would be nice if, for once in your life, you could accept that not everyone is as fucking perfect as you!'

And with that, she stormed downstairs, her words still reverberating in the air.

29

Scarlett stared at all those faces of Gina Caplin on her screen. She looked like Ollie's most recent girlfriend, Nikki. It was a wonder she hadn't registered this before. And now that she *had* registered it, something else clicked into place. All the girls Ollie had gone out with in the past – all the *women* – had shared these same physical characteristics.

All the Katys and Lornas and Staceys and Jennas. All the Leonas and Tammys and Pippas and Nikkis. And those were just the ones Scarlett knew about. They all had longish blonde hair and pretty, smiling faces. They were all slim and sporty, with a tendency to giggle. Her brother had a 'type', and Gina Caplin had fitted the mould perfectly.

Scarlett tried to ignore the uneasy feeling in her stomach. If Gina Caplin had visited this house, then there was every possibility that Ollie had met her too. He'd carried on living here after Scarlett went to university and then moved to her flat in Clapham and, even when he'd moved out, he was still a frequent visitor to the house. Always popping round to do odd jobs for Rebecca.

She lowered herself into the chair at her desk. Was she seriously giving headspace to the possibility that Ollie might have had some kind of involvement with Gina? That he might know something about her disappearance?

She tried not to focus on the adrenaline surging round her body. No. She could put that ridiculous notion to bed, once and for all. Ollie might have hurt a few women emotionally by not being the loyal boyfriend they craved, but he'd never hurt them physically. Not Ollie. Not her little brother.

And if Ollie had been romantically involved with Gina Caplin, Rebecca would have known about it, wouldn't she? The uneasy feeling in Scarlett's stomach intensified. Her aunt's words came back to her then, the ones she'd used when Scarlett had tried to get to the bottom of the incident at Riverhill, the one that had resulted in her being asked to take sick leave: 'This girl, that girl. There's always *some* girl.' She'd been confused, yes. Unable to recall the facts with any clarity. But she'd been scared too. Had she been thinking of Ollie when she said this?

And what about those other things her aunt had said? Those strange remarks of hers. The paranoia. Then there was the time Scarlett had found her standing in the garden in her nightie. 'It's a secret,' she'd said. 'I'm not allowed to tell.' They had been symptoms of dementia, hadn't they? But what if she did have a secret and someone had told her never to tell? What if her deteriorating brain meant that the secret was no longer safe with her?

The faces on the screen swam before Scarlett's eyes. Another headache was on its way and her joints had started to ache. She closed down her PC. If only she could close down her mind so easily, drive out this unspeakable darkness. But now that she'd started, there was no going back. She found her 2009 diary, took some painkillers and decamped to the sofa with her laptop.

Gina Caplin had vanished on 16 March 2009, just three weeks before Scarlett had moved into the ground-floor apartment. All the work on the house had been completed then, bar the bathroom, which Mickey had still been working on, and one or two minor cosmetic jobs. The summer house had been erected too, hadn't it? And the lawn – what had been left of it – had been aerated and overseeded.

Three sharp knocks on the back door made her start. It must be Mickey, she thought, returning with the glazed panel. Surely he didn't need to speak to her again?

'Come in,' she called out. She'd just got herself into a comfortable position and didn't have the energy to haul herself up again.

Mickey came in and stood on the mat.

'All done?' she said.

'Yup. Good as new.' He cleared his throat. 'Listen,' he said. 'About what I said earlier.'

She waited for him to continue.

'You won't tell Ollie I said anything, will you? I don't want him to think I'm going behind his back or anything. You know what he's like.'

Scarlett frowned. She wasn't quite sure what he meant. What *was* he like? 'Of course not,' she said.

Mickey transferred his weight from one foot to the other. 'I know, when my mum died, I was in pieces. Absolute pieces.' He looked down at his boots. 'You know what us men are like, Scar. Never like to admit when we're struggling.' He looked uncomfortable. 'Your dad isn't helping much either.'

Scarlett looked at him in surprise. 'My dad? What makes you say that?'

Mickey shook his head. 'He's been giving him a hard time over something. Turning up at the yard unannounced. You don't know what that's about, do you?'

Scarlett frowned. 'I've absolutely no idea, sorry.'

'Oh well, like I said, I just wanted to give you the heads-up, so you can keep an eye on him.'

'I will,' she said. 'Thanks for letting me know.'

When Mickey had left, Scarlett pondered his words. Why was her dad turning up at Ollie's yard and giving him a hard time? The two of them had never exactly *got on*. Her dad had always expected Ollie to follow in his footsteps, to train as an architect and work with him, or follow some other high-status career. But Ollie had never liked studying and hadn't wanted to go to university. He didn't have the intellectual capacity for it and, instead of just accepting that and encouraging him in other areas, their dad had continually given him grief for not being the son he wanted.

They hadn't even been able to discuss Rebecca's funeral without getting into an argument. It was always the same. After a minute in each other's company, they'd been sniping at each other. But surely, after the trauma they'd all been through, her dad should be cutting him some slack.

Scarlett put her laptop and diary on to the floor and lay on her side on the sofa, drew her knees to her stomach. Her recent dream came back to her. The one where they'd all been in the summer house; her mother, too. All laughing and drinking wine. Except Scarlett hadn't been laughing. Scarlett had been the outsider, there but *not* there. The only one who'd sensed danger.

She wasn't dreaming now, though. She was wide awake. So how come her sense of danger was even stronger?

30

It had been two days since T. J. Cooper's visit to the office and his damning accusation, and a day since Lindsay had made things ten times worse by going round there and having sex with him.

Dee still found the whole thing hard to believe. Not the theft itself. She'd reconciled herself to the fact that Lindsay had made a stupid, stupid mistake, that she'd let her desperation not to lose her house cloud her common sense and decency. And at a time when she was consumed with stress about Gina. But taking it upon herself to visit a potential blackmailer in person, allowing herself to be persuaded into having sex with him, or seducing him as a means to an end – whichever it had been – was beyond stupid. They'd barely spoken to each other since.

Dee read the message that Lindsay had left on her desk.

'Gone on that course. Out all day. Jake will pick up the van and collect Mr Byatt from the hospital.'

And that was it. No niceties in the form of greeting or sign-off. Just that one stark message. Dee sighed. How were they ever going to get through this?

She crumpled the note in her hand and tossed it into the wastepaper basket. At least she'd have the place to herself today, wouldn't be on tenterhooks every time they bumped into each other. Lindsay had been in two minds about attending that course. It was to update her embalming skills and, since they rarely offered this service, it hadn't seemed particularly essential. It was true, they'd had a couple of repatriation enquiries lately, which involved tropical embalming, a much longer process with stronger chemicals to take account of the extra time the bodies spent in transit. But Dee had always been happy to recommend another firm for jobs like that. Lindsay had clearly wanted to be anywhere else but here right now.

She looked at her watch. If Jake was collecting Mr Byatt, he'd be arriving soon. She went and unlocked the back door. The sky was leaden, the temperature colder than it had been. Winter was on its way. Dee shivered as she drew back the bolts on the gate and opened them, ready for Jake's arrival.

A moment later, she saw the van turn into the access road and stepped away from the gate, wondering if Lindsay had come clean with him yet, if she'd told him the whole story. If Jake knew she'd slept with Trevor Cooper, he'd be appalled. But if she'd told him about their argument and the horrible words Dee had used, he'd be indignant on her behalf. However much Jake might condemn his sister's actions, he'd always support her. He'd always take her side over Dee's, wouldn't he? Dee hated the thought of falling out with Jake too.

He grinned at her from behind the steering wheel and gave her the thumbs-up sign before reversing into the yard. Dee felt herself relax. When he climbed out and said, 'Wotcha, mate!' just like he always did, she knew Lindsay couldn't have told him. She was probably too ashamed.

Dee helped him unload the gurney from the back of the van and wheel the late Mr Byatt along the corridor and into the lift.

'I'll see you down there,' she said.

Dee went downstairs and waited for the lift to descend. The prep room wasn't the same without Lindsay pottering around in it. It was never warm down here, and nor was it meant to be, but today it felt particularly cold. Dee turned the lights on just as the lift doors opened and Jake emerged with the gurney.

The two of them undid the securing belts and transferred the late Mr Byatt into one of the drawers in the refrigerated storage unit. Jake was so strong he could probably have managed entirely on his own, but it was nice for Dee to do something practical. It distracted her from her worries, at least for a little while.

'Young, wasn't he?' Jake said, taking one last look at Mr Byatt before closing the fridge drawer.

'Too young,' Dee said.

By the time Jake had folded up the gurney and given her the relevant paperwork from the hospital mortuary Dee was more than ready for a coffee. Jake joined her upstairs.

'I can't stay long,' he said. 'I've got to take Hayley for her antenatal check-up.'

'When's she actually due?' Dee asked.

'First of January.' He laughed. 'I'd better not drink too much on New Year's Eve. She'll kill me if I'm in no fit state to drive her to the hospital.'

Dee laughed along with him. 'Quite right. No partying for you this year, Jake Morgan. In fact, you'd better not drink at all.'

'Here, let me show you the latest Ruby pics. I was going to show you in the pub last week.' Ruby was Jake and Hayley's four-year-old daughter. Dee didn't think she'd ever met a prouder dad.

She scrolled through the latest photos he'd taken and made all the right noises. It made her sad to think she'd never have a child of her own. She might have done, if she'd stayed with Euan. There was still time – just about. It wasn't as if she hadn't thought about it. She'd thought about it when she'd seen him in the pub the other night. The way he'd looked at her when he thought she couldn't see him. Jake and Lindsay were right. He'd take her back in a heartbeat, and there were worse things in life than not fancying your husband, especially if, deep down, you really liked each other.

But it was crazy, thinking like that. Stupid. She handed him back his phone. 'I am grateful, you know, for all the work you do for me and Lins, for stepping up at short notice.'

Jake shrugged. 'No need to thank me.' He grinned then. 'It's not as if I do it for free.'

'True,' Dee said. Hayley had once told her and Lindsay that she wished Jake would give up on his acting ambitions and find a proper job so that she could reduce her own working hours and spend more time with Ruby. After all his experience at Fond Farewells, Jake would easily have been able to get a job in one of the bigger funeral firms. He was practical and capable and not in the least bit squeamish about the less savoury side of the business. But Dee knew how heart-breaking it must be to give up on your dreams. Gina had tried for years to make a go of it as a professional dancer, but it had been hard, living from short-term contract to short-term contract. That was why, in the end, she'd made the decision to train as a teacher.

Jake drained his cup of coffee and got up to leave. 'What's up with Lins, by the way?'

Dee gave him a wary look.

'She didn't seem her usual self when I spoke to her on the phone last night.'

Dee started shuffling some papers around on her desk. 'Maybe you need to ask *her* that question, not me.'

Jake nodded. 'She's asked me to pick her up from that course later. Said she wants to talk about something. I just thought you might know what's going on with her.'

Dee dry-swallowed. Jake might not be quite as friendly to her next time they met, not once he knew Dee had accused his sister of 'whoring herself out'.

'I don't really know what's going on with her,' she said, not meeting his eye.

Jake went to leave. 'Guess I'll see you at the match on Sunday then.'

'Let's just hope it stays dry,' Dee said.

With any luck, she and Lindsay would have called some kind of truce before then.

31

SCARLETT SLEPT BADLY THE night after Mickey
North's visit. She had to accept what she was feeling:
she didn't trust her own brother. And if her dad was
turning up at the yard unannounced, then maybe she
wasn't the only one.

As soon as she was dressed and had forced herself
to eat some toast and drink a small coffee she made
up her mind to phone Ollie and put her suspicions to
the test. And now that she'd reached this decision,
she wanted to do it straight away. She was both
dreading and, in a weird way, *looking forward* to the
conversation. What was wrong with her for feeling
like this? How was it possible to hold these two
conflicting emotions at the same time?

She waited for him to answer the call, not knowing exactly what she was going to say but preferring
to wing it. It wouldn't do to sound too rehearsed.

'Scar? What's up?'

She launched straight into it, surprised at how steady her voice sounded. How calm. 'Thanks for sending Mickey round to fix the window. Although I have a horrible feeling it was a complete waste of his time.' Her pulse quickened. She could almost sense him frowning.

'Why's that?'

'Because I've decided I'm going to relocate the summer house so that I don't have to walk all the way up the end of the garden to use it.' She thought she heard a sharp intake of breath on the other end of the line, but maybe it was her own breath she could hear. 'If I'm going to live here for the rest of my life – and, frankly, I can't see how I'll ever want to move – then I want to make sure it's accessible for when I'm not feeling so strong, or when I'm older.'

There was a noticeable beat before her brother responded. 'That's crazy. Why go to all that effort for something you'll probably only use a few times a year? And that's a big job, Scar. I won't have the time or the manpower for something like that. Not for a good long while.' There was exasperation in his voice, but something else too. Something she couldn't quite put her finger on.

'I know,' she said. 'I'm not asking you to do it. I'll get someone else in. I've got plenty of savings.' She carried the phone over to the sofa and sat down with it, warming to her theme, even though it made her nervous. 'I fancy one of those log-cabin-type ones. I can start that pottery hobby I've been talking about for years.' Her voice was too loud, too high.

'That's a terrible idea.'

She twiddled the silver ring on her middle finger, not trusting herself to respond.

'Sorry,' he said. 'It just seems a bit extreme. Building a log cabin for a hobby you don't even know you'll stick at.'

'But you know I've always fancied being a potter. I went to those evening classes.'

Ollie snorted. 'So throwing a couple of misshapen pots in an evening class makes you a potter, does it?' He was trying to sound sarcastic, but Scarlett recognized the tension in his voice.

'Why do you have to be so disparaging? And, for your information, I didn't just *throw a couple of misshapen pots*, I made a really nice vase and a collection of matching bowls.' She tried to control the rising tension in her own voice, to make it sound more like defensiveness. 'I made ceramic gifts for Christmas presents. You got an ashtray, remember? I did decorative application and glazing too. I'm actually quite good at it.'

Another pause. 'So go to a more advanced class. And if you want a pottery studio in the garden – which it sounds like you do – with a wheel and a kiln and everything – why don't you just look into getting one installed? You don't have to go to all the trouble of relocating the summer house. That's just making unnecessary work.'

'Possibly. But that's my decision to make, isn't it?' She paused. 'I fancy a low-maintenance gravel garden up that end.'

The line was silent. Then he spoke. 'Since when did you get interested in gardening?'

'I'm not. That's why I want a low-maintenance gravel garden. The clue's in the name, you twit.'

She could tell he was getting annoyed. Not just annoyed, but anxious. The apartment upstairs might be his now, but the garden belonged to her. She could do what she liked with it. He wouldn't be able to stop her, no matter how hard he tried. Scarlett was stubborn. Isn't that how he'd always described her?

'I suppose it's a better idea than Clive's fishpond,' he said.

Scarlett frowned. A fishpond. She'd forgotten all about that. Clive had also once suggested they get rid of the summer house. His plan had been to put a pond up there instead. Apparently, he'd always fancied keeping koi carp.

Ollie was still talking. 'If you really are set on this idea, then *I'll* dismantle it for you. If you're going to shell out for a log cabin, you won't want to waste money paying someone to get rid of the summer house as well. Not unless you want to blow your entire savings. I can do that. I'll put a patio over the concrete base. Then you can have somewhere to sit to enjoy your *low-maintenance gravel garden.*'

Something bad hovered just below Scarlett's conscious mind. It reminded her of how she'd felt when she'd stood outside Rebecca's bedroom door. The blood was so loud in her ears it was a wonder Ollie couldn't hear it too.

She struggled to keep her composure. 'Okay,' she said at last. 'I'll have a think and do a bit of research. There's no point doing anything before next year anyway. I'm just having one of those dreaming and planning type of days.'

Ollie made a harumphing noise. Was it her imagination or was this also laced with relief?

When the call was over Scarlett's hands were trembling. She raised her head slowly and stared at the pristine white ceiling above her, her breath trapped at the back of her throat. Her neck felt clammy under her T-shirt. Something vile was playing out behind her eyes. Something utterly preposterous, and yet . . .

She thought of those odd little things her aunt had started saying in the months leading up to her death. Things Scarlett had put down to Rebecca's failing mind. Things she sometimes giggled at behind her aunt's back with Ollie or, worse still, ignored altogether, dismissed as nonsense.

If Rebecca's confused mind had been remembering something that she'd forgotten was supposed to be a secret, and if that secret had something to do with Gina Caplin's disappearance, then wouldn't her aunt's life have been in danger?

A crack opened up inside her. Scarlett clamped her hand across her mouth and staggered to her feet. It couldn't be true. It just *couldn't*. How could she even be entertaining the possibility? There was no way. No way on earth. This was her brother. The same brother who'd clung to her when he was a little boy, frightened of the dark. The same brother she'd looked after when their mother died. The same brother who'd adored Rebecca as much as she had.

Besides, the police had investigated. Forensics had been all over the place. They were satisfied with their conclusions.

But what if they'd got it wrong?

32

It was Saturday and Dee was still mooching about the flat in her pyjamas. She hadn't been able to settle to anything after Jake had left the office yesterday. She'd kept hoping that Lindsay would come back from her course and tell her all about it. In the past, when either of them had been on any kind of training session, they would give the other one the lowdown on what they'd learned, describe the other attendees, and the lunch, maybe complain about the facilitator, and indulge themselves in all those other bits of gossip that came from spending a day away from the office.

But Lindsay had obviously decided to go straight home. She had deliberately avoided coming back.

'You all right, Dee?' her dad said.

'Yeah, just a bit headachey. Didn't sleep well last night.'

'Still worrying about Lindsay?'

'Yeah.' Dee had told him that Lindsay had

confessed to stealing the helmet and the jacket and sorted things out with Trevor Cooper, but she hadn't told him *how* she'd sorted them out. She usually told her dad everything, but she couldn't tell him that. How could she?

'We're hardly speaking to each other at the moment. We've both said some really mean things.'

'Don't worry, love,' he said, gently squeezing her shoulder. 'You two will get through this, I know you will. Just be patient. I know you're feeling let down by what she did, and I can't blame you for that, but imagine how ashamed she must be feeling. How embarrassed. Maybe the football match tomorrow will help smooth things over. You'll have to be civil to one another in front of Sue and Alan, won't you? Maybe it'll allow you both to start afresh.'

Dee nodded and gave her dad a hug.

'Tell you what,' he said. 'I'll make us both a cup of tea and a bacon sandwich, shall I?'

While her dad was pottering about in the kitchen Dee thought about what he'd said and knew he was right. Much as she was dreading standing around in a cold, muddy park watching a football match, she and Lindsay would be working together, handing out flyers and jangling a collection bucket. It would give them the chance to talk on neutral ground.

She curled up on the sofa and switched the telly on, tried to drown out her thoughts. It wasn't just this business with Lindsay, it was everything. It was as though she'd been catapulted back in time and all the emotions and worries she'd entertained in the weeks and months after Gina went missing had crowded back into her mind in one noisy procession. That awful feeling of fear and dread had started up again. She was a mess.

She knew the reason for it, of course. It was because of this event they were planning for March, not to mention the football match tomorrow. There'd been the phone calls and meetings with the Caplins. Constant reminders of Gina's name and face. For some time now, her missing friend had been more like a background noise. A dull ache that only occasionally intensified. Now, all of a sudden, she was up front and centre, demanding to be remembered.

Demanding to be found.

Dee got up and fetched the manuscript she'd left in her bedroom, brought it back to the sofa. It was because of this, too. Three hundred pages of double-spaced typing in Times New Roman font, waiting to be proofread for errors. A novel that demonstrated the romantic, gentle side of Gina's nature. The private side.

Dee thought of Gina sitting in her bedroom dreaming it all up, this fantasy world of hers. The singer who'd fallen in love with a married man. Dee leafed through the manuscript again. Had Gina also met and fallen in love with someone? Someone she wanted to keep a secret from her friends? From her parents?

She'd been so happy on that last holiday to Morocco. Her skin had been glowing, almost as if she'd been lit from within. She'd been excited about the teaching course she'd been about to start, the anticipation of a totally new direction. That was what she'd told them, and they'd believed her, because why wouldn't they? And she and Lindsay were equally excited about their change of direction. About the launch of Fond Farewells.

But now that Dee thought about it, and now that she'd read this novel, she couldn't help wondering whether it had been more than that. Had Gina also been in love with a married man? But if she had been, then surely Dee and Lindsay would have been the first ones to know about it. They'd told each other everything.

Although, of course, that wasn't strictly true. Dee hadn't told them she was gay. She'd kept her sexuality hidden from everyone. She'd broken Euan's heart because she hadn't had the courage to come clean and tell him the truth. And Gina hadn't told them she was writing a novel. Hadn't even told her parents.

Dee began to bite her nails. Was it significant that Gina had made her main character a singer rather than, say, a secretary or a lawyer or a nurse, or any of the countless other jobs she could have chosen? Singing and dancing. Both were creative professions. By making her character a singer, might Gina have been exploring that side of herself that wanted to be on the stage, in front of an audience?

The same side of herself she shared with Jake.

Dee put the novel aside. Her dad had just come in with her tea and sandwich. As she nibbled at the bacon, Dee thought of how, once, a long time ago, when they were in their early twenties, Jake had taught them all 'Chopsticks' – a friend had been teaching him to play keyboard, and he was really good at it, said it was useful for an actor to be familiar with at least one musical instrument, as it made you so much more versatile – but Gina had never been able to manage more than a few notes. In the end, he'd given up trying to teach her in despair. 'It's so easy,' he'd said, but however many times she practised, she hadn't been able to get the hang of it. Lindsay and Dee had teased her about it. Not long after that, Jake and Gina had started dating.

Dee put her plate on the coffee table and settled back on the sofa with her tea.

Was it possible that Gina had based the piano teacher in her novel on Jake? That a small part of her had sometimes wondered what it would have been like if they'd stayed together and he hadn't married Hayley? Hadn't Dee been thinking the same sort of thing herself recently, about her and Euan? It was natural to think like that sometimes, to wonder how your life might have turned out, had you taken a different path. Of course, it had been Gina who'd ended her relationship with Jake – that's if you could even call going out with someone for four months in your early twenties a *relationship*.

Dee thought of that tear sliding from the corner of Jake's eye in the pub and shook her head to drive the thought away. Of course he was sad. He was sad because he'd lost a friend. They were *all* sad. He'd only been married to Hayley a couple of years when Gina went missing. That was far too soon to start having an affair.

And yet people had affairs all the time, didn't they? Dee thought back to her last conversation with Lindsay. Her *argument* with her. When Dee had accused her of using sex to manipulate Trevor Cooper into keeping quiet and told her that that sort of thing didn't *just happen*, Lindsay had told her, in the most unequivocal of terms, that it *did*. She'd basically implied that it wouldn't happen to the likes of Dee because she never went anywhere or did anything.

Dee had to admit it, Lindsay did have a point. Maybe that sort of thing happened all the time if you were open to it, if you saw opportunities and took them. Some people seemed to recognize those moments when they happened and were able to act on them without qualms, or at least to shelve their qualms until after the event. Some people had higher sex drives than others and weren't so hung up on the potential embarrassment of rejection or misunderstanding. Not

211

everyone was as big a coward as Dee when it came to sex.

Dee stared at the TV, wishing she was half as interested in this cookery programme as her dad clearly was. Was it possible that Jake and Gina *did* have a fling? Maybe they'd run into each other somewhere while they were both on their own and whatever spark they'd felt when they were younger had reignited. Maybe they'd had a secret affair and Gina had wanted him to leave Hayley for her. Maybe she'd got clingy and . . . and . . .

Dee took another sip of tea, disliking the turn her thoughts had taken, because the more she thought about this scenario, the more uncomfortable she felt, until she had to force herself to stop thinking about it. *This is what you're like*, she told herself, *always imagining the worst. Always fearful and suspicious. Even of your own friends.* The very thought of gentle Jake doing anything to hurt someone, especially a woman, was outrageous. She felt guilty for even thinking it. It was absurd.

And yet men *did* hurt women. They did it all the time. Clive Hamlyn had killed Rebecca Quilter, hadn't he? Bludgeoned her to death in her own bed. And that wasn't an isolated case. Men killed their wives and their girlfriends and their ex-wives and their ex-girlfriends and women they thought *should* be their girlfriends all the time. Some of them killed their children too.

And people lied. People you thought were honest and good did stupid, stupid things – bad things. Dee got up and took her empty plate and mug out to the kitchen, started washing them up. She was getting things out of all proportion. She was upset, that's all, because of what Lindsay had done. Having that argument the other day had destabilized her. She wasn't thinking straight. The sooner she forgave Lindsay and apologized for the horrible way she'd spoken to her, the better. Maybe then she'd settle down and stop imagining the worst of everybody.

33

SCARLETT STOOD OUTSIDE HER aunt's bedroom, her hand hovering over the doorknob, discomfort prickling her neck. She didn't want to be up here again. Every fibre of her body was screaming at her to get out. But Ollie's reaction when she'd suggested relocating the summer house had scared her. She felt a burning need to make one last attempt at finding her aunt's diaries. What good it would do if she *did* find them she really didn't know, but she had to do something. She couldn't just sit about imagining the worst.

Her breath quickened. 'Go on, open it up and walk in!' Rebecca's voice in her ear made her jump. 'It's just a room, Scarlett. Four walls, a floor and a ceiling.'

She took a deep breath and opened the door wide in one firm sweep, stood at the threshold, peering in. The first thing she noticed was the astringent smell of cleaning fluids. The second was how different it looked without the carpet.

She swallowed down her fear and took a step inside. The room was dark on account of the drawn curtains, but the light from the landing was enough for her to see by. Something stopped her from flicking the overhead light switch on. It was partly the same feeling that had stopped her the last time she'd been up here, in her aunt's sitting room that time – a desire to keep her presence hidden from the outside world – and partly a fear of seeing the room fully illuminated.

She turned slowly to the left to see the large pine frame of her aunt's bed with its slatted base. Had the neighbours seen the stained mattress being removed from the house? She could just imagine them observing it all from their windows. Their horrified fascination.

She took another step, then another, until she was standing in the room, the curtained window to her left, the dressing table to her right. Scarlett glanced down at her aunt's hairbrush, lying at an angle on the glass top. The sight of it made her heart lurch. She picked it up and touched the strands of grey still entwined in its bristles, brought it to her face and breathed in the faint traces of her aunt's hair. Then she put the brush down and opened the drawers in the dressing table. They contained nothing more than emery boards and cotton pads, various pots and tubes of cream – her aunt's 'lotions and potions', as she used to call them – but still she rummaged

215

through them, not quite trusting herself not to miss something.

Satisfied that there was nothing of interest in the dressing table, she turned away from it and had full sight of the empty bed frame. A shudder of revulsion ran through her like an electric current. All she could think of was Rebecca lying there, oblivious of what was to come. From the corners of her eyes, Scarlett glimpsed the wall behind the bed. She didn't want to let her eyes dwell on it but found she was overcome by a ghoulish compulsion to take it all in. The blood splatter stains had been cleaned by the specialist firm, but their shadows were still visible where they had soaked into the paintwork.

Her mouth went dry as she walked towards the big old mahogany wardrobe that stood to the left at the bottom of the bed. She was dreading opening it up and seeing her aunt's clothes. If she remembered correctly, there was a shelf that ran across the top and several smaller ones down one side, where her aunt might, perhaps, have stashed personal notebooks or diaries. But after several minutes rummaging through jumpers and tops and old pairs of trousers, all neatly folded or rolled, Scarlett knew she wasn't going to find any paperwork.

She moved on to the chest of drawers next to the wardrobe, but all the time she was looking she was painfully and acutely aware of the empty bed behind her and the hideous shadows on the wall. She was in the process of pushing the final drawer back in place when the sound of the front doorbell made her jump. She stood stock still and waited for whoever it was to go away. She wasn't expecting any visitors and she didn't want any.

Was it Ollie, coming round to continue their conversation, to reassure himself that she wasn't going to do anything stupid? If it *was* him, and he'd yet again taken time out of his supposedly busy schedule to come and see her, she'd know she was definitely on to something. She'd know he was running scared.

She edged nearer to the window and stood at the outer edge of the curtain nearest the wardrobe. She moved it aside just a fraction and peered out but couldn't see who it was from this angle. She let the curtain fall back and waited. The doorbell remained silent. It was probably one of those door-to-door salespeople, or someone to read the electricity meter. If it was important, they'd have tried again, wouldn't they? Pushed the bell at least one more time for good measure. Scarlett had lost count of the number of times she'd answered the door and wished she hadn't, cursed herself for not ignoring the interruption. She thought she heard the sound of someone slipping something through the letterbox and breathed a sigh of relief. Whoever it was had gone away.

Gently, reluctantly, she took one last look at her aunt's clothes and shut the wardrobe door. There was only one place left to search in here, and that was the bedside cabinet. Scarlett went over to it now. The smell of disinfectant was even stronger over here. She pulled open the drawers, but all she could find were boxes and boxes of tablets, much like her own medicine drawer downstairs.

She sighed in frustration. If Rebecca had kept hold of her diaries from ten years ago, then she must have hidden them well. Perhaps she had got rid of them altogether. Scarlett had looked everywhere she could think of.

She turned to leave the room, then froze. A floorboard had just creaked on the landing.

There it was again.

Somebody was up here with her.

34

'SCARLETT! WHAT ON EARTH are you doing?'

Scarlett stared at her father as he appeared in the doorway.

'I could ask the same question of you! You nearly gave me a heart attack, creeping up on me like that. How did you get in?'

'With my key, of course.'

She blinked at him in confusion. She knew he had a spare key to the main front door, and to her own apartment, in case of emergencies. She hadn't realized he had a spare for this one too.

She bit down on her tongue to release some saliva. Her mouth had gone completely dry. Why had he let himself into the house in the first place? Wasn't Saturday his and Claire's 'special day'? The day they pootled about in Greenwich or had lunch with friends in town?

He took a tentative step into the room. 'I can't

believe you've come up here all alone,' he said. He narrowed his eyes at her. 'What are you looking for?'

'Nothing,' she said. 'I just wanted to see it for myself.'

He looked around the room, his gaze travelling haltingly over the slatted base of the bed then bouncing off the stained wall and back to Scarlett's face. He looked awful. She had a sudden memory of finding him in the hallway staring at Rebecca's front door, that evening he and Ollie had come round to discuss the funeral arrangements. The wary expression on his face.

He steepled his fingers over his nose and mouth and took a long, deep breath. 'Well, now you have. Now we both have. Come on, let's get out of here.'

Back in her kitchen, Scarlett made them both a coffee with shaky hands.

Her dad looked down at his shoes. 'It's going to take us all a long while to get over this.'

Scarlett stared at him in astonishment. 'Get over it? How will we ever get over it?'

He sighed and shook his head. 'I didn't mean that, I meant come to terms with it.'

Scarlett handed him his coffee. 'I've never really understood what that means. If it means accepting what happened, then I'm not sure I can. How can I accept that someone killed Rebecca?'

Her dad looked up. 'Someone? You mean that spineless excuse for a human being Hamlyn?'

'Yes, yes, of course that's what I meant. I guess I can't bring myself to say his name.'

'No. No, quite.'

Her dad sipped at his coffee. He looked as if he wanted to say something.

'You okay, Dad?'

'Me? Yes, I'm okay. Well, depends what you mean by "okay", I suppose. I'm hanging on in there. What else can I do? What else can any of us do?'

Scarlett walked over to the sofa and sat down. Her dad followed her and sat on the armchair.

'What made you go up there?' she asked.

'I was coming round to see you. To make sure you were okay. When there was no answer, I got worried because I could see your living-room light was on. So I let myself into the hall and was about to knock when I thought I heard something upstairs. I didn't know what to think, whether it was you up there or . . . or someone else. So I crept up to see what was going on.'

He sat back in the chair and crossed his legs. For a few moments, neither of them spoke.

Her dad broke the silence first. 'By the way, I spoke to Ollie on the phone earlier.' He cleared his throat. 'He said you've got some hare-brained plan to pull down the summer house and put a gravel garden in.'

Scarlett went very still. He'd been lying just now. This wasn't some random visit to check in with his daughter. He'd come round with the express purpose of talking her out of her plans. Why did everything seem to revolve around the summer house?

She moistened her lips. What was going on here?

'It's not a *hare-brained plan*. Bloody hell, Dad, don't you think I need something other than work to occupy my brain? I want to do something different with the garden, make it my own.'

He was about to say something, but she carried on. 'Every time I look out of the window I'm reminded of Rebecca pottering about out there with her trug and her gardening gloves and those little rubber clogs she used to wear. I want a clean sweep so I'm not ambushed by memories every time I set foot out there. And why the hell is Ollie reporting everything I say straight back to you?'

Her dad gave an exasperated sigh. 'Don't be daft! He's doing no such thing. I phoned *him*. It just came up in conversation, that's all. It's your garden now. You can do what you want with it. It's just that . . .'

Once again, he cleared his throat. 'It's not the grandest of constructions, I'll give you that. But it's sturdy enough to last. A lick of paint might cheer it up a bit. Maybe you could design a gravel garden *around* it and get a path laid from the house. I could ask one of my landscaper contacts to get in touch with you, if you'd like?'

For a few seconds Scarlett just sat there, unsure how to respond. Why was her dad taking so much interest in this?

She pressed on, determined to see how far he would go in trying to dissuade her. 'That's very kind of you, Dad, but I don't want to give you any more work to do. You've done enough for me already.' She watched him closely as she spoke. 'Don't you think it's about time I took control of my own life? I'm perfectly capable of project-managing my own garden. And I can't believe Ollie is that bothered about what is, let's face it, a fancy shed.'

Her legs had started to tremble slightly so she crossed them and tucked her ankle behind her calf – an uncomfortable position but one that seemed to hold them still and keep her grounded.

Her dad sat back in his chair. 'The truth is, I'm worried about you. We all are. Ollie tells me you broke the glass and climbed in. Is that right? Dear God, Scarlett, you could have injured yourself badly. If you didn't have the energy to go back to the house for the key, you certainly shouldn't have been climbing up on a chair and through a window. What were you thinking? And then I find you upstairs in Rebecca's bedroom. Putting yourself through even more unnecessary stress.'

He leaned forward and clasped his hands between his knees. 'Have you considered going to the GP and asking him to review your medication? How long is it since you've had a check-up?'

Scarlett clenched her jaw. 'Asking *her*, you mean. My GP is a woman.'

Her dad gave an exasperated sigh. 'What does it matter whether your GP is a man or a woman? Why do you always have to split hairs?'

Scarlett bit her lip.

'Have you thought about starting your yoga classes again? Maybe you need to think about some self-care. Start prioritizing your mental health.'

'There's nothing wrong with my mental health.'

'That's what Rebecca used to say.'

'Oh, great, so now you're suggesting I've got dementia?'

'No, of *course* not. For God's sake! Can't you just accept that I'm concerned about you?'

Scarlett forced herself to meet his eye, to soften her response. 'Okay, Dad. I'll make an appointment. But please don't treat me like a child. If I want to sort the garden out, I'll do it. And in my own way. You don't have to take over and do everything for me, you know.'

She watched as her dad finished his coffee. 'By the way, is everything all right with Ollie?'

He frowned at her as if she'd asked a stupid question. 'What makes you ask that?'

She shrugged. 'He's been acting really weird lately.'

'He's grieving, Scarlett. We all are.'

'When was the last time you saw him?'

'Ollie?' He frowned. 'When we were all here,

meeting that funeral girl.' Scarlett sighed. 'Woman,' he said. 'Funeral *woman*. Funeral *director*. Talking of which, has she sorted things out yet?'

Why was he lying? Mickey said he'd been turning up at the yard unannounced.

'She's waiting for me to confirm some possible dates. I was going to speak to you and Ollie about it next week.'

'Right. Okay then. Look, I'd better be off, but you'll think about what I said, won't you? About taking things easy and not pushing yourself?'

Scarlett nodded. 'Sure.' But she had no intention of taking things easy. Not before she'd found those diaries.

35

SCARLETT STOOD AT THE front door and watched her father walk away from her down the path. Something about his unexpected visit so soon after she'd told Ollie of her plans to rearrange the garden didn't sit right with her. What was so damned important about that wretched summer house to have rattled them both like this, to make two incredibly busy men with companies to oversee waste their time on something so seemingly insignificant? And all that guff about being concerned for her mental health. What had he been implying?

He'd almost reached the space where the front gate had once stood when she called out to him, adrenaline buzzing in her veins. She had to find out if this reservoir of suspicion and distrust that was growing larger and deeper in her by the minute had any kind of basis in reality. She had to ask him outright.

'Dad, you don't happen to know if Rebecca ever knew Gina Caplin, do you?'

He came to a halt and spun round, his face creased in confusion. 'Gina *Caplin*? You mean that girl who went missing? I hardly think so. She'd have told us, wouldn't she? What on earth makes you think that?'

Scarlett held on to the door frame to keep herself steady. He seemed genuinely surprised at the question, but was it all an act? 'It was a card I found in the summer house.'

'Show me,' he said. 'Show me this card.'

Scarlett went back inside and into the bedroom to retrieve it from her dressing table where she'd left it, but as soon as she stepped over the threshold, she could see that it wasn't there.

She opened the drawers, but, even as she was doing this, she knew it was a waste of time. She'd left it there – she was sure of it. She turned to see her dad standing in the doorway, observing her through narrowed eyes.

'It's gone,' she said. 'It's vanished.'

Overcome with dizziness and unable to stand a second longer, she dropped on to the bed behind her and put her head between her knees. Her dad was by her side in an instant, rubbing the space between her shoulder blades with his hand. It felt strange, him touching her like this. The only physical contact that usually passed between them was a brief hug or a peck on the cheek.

'Are you all right, darling?'

'Someone must have taken it. It must have been Ollie.'

'Scarlett – *darling* – what are you talking about? Are you sure you haven't been overdoing things lately?'

She turned to face him, furious. 'You think I'm imagining this?'

'No, of course not. But sometimes, when we're a little *overwrought*, our minds can play tricks on us.'

Scarlett tried not to react to his use of 'we', not to mention the word 'overwrought'. Any other time, she'd have accused him of acting like a Victorian patriarch. Men who called women *overwrought* or *emotional* or *hysterical* or any of those other gendered insults were patronizing bastards. As were men who described a forty-two-year-old woman's perfectly reasonable desire to relocate her own summer house in her own garden as 'hare-brained'.

'Hasn't there been something about her on the news recently?' he said. 'Some memorial event?' He sighed deeply. 'Ollie told me you've got enough painkillers in your drawer to stock an entire chemist's. Is it possible that you've taken too many? I must say, you don't look at all well, sweetheart.'

Scarlett clenched her fists. 'If you're trying to suggest I'm going mad, you're wrong.'

'I wasn't suggesting any such thing,' he said, getting to his feet. 'I was just saying you look a bit . . . peaky. Listen, darling, I've got to get back to Claire

228

or she'll be wondering where I've got to. I'm sure the card will turn up and, when it does – *if* it does – give me a ring and let me know.' He went to leave, then hesitated. 'And Scarlett . . .'

'Yes?'

'Get some rest. Please.'

Her dad put his hands on her shoulders and peered at her face, concern now softening his features. 'We're all in shock over what's happened,' he said. 'Promise me, darling, if you start obsessing over things, go and see your GP. Maybe you need a course of antidepressants or something.'

Scarlett pressed her lips together. Far better for him and Ollie to think she was suffering from mental distress than to realize that she suspected them of knowing something about Gina Caplin's disappearance.

'Yes,' she said. 'I think you're right.' The words nearly stuck in her throat, but she forced them out. 'I don't like the thought of going back on them, but . . . after everything that's happened . . .'

She made her voice crack. 'I keep imagining connections between random things.'

She sensed a loosening of his shoulders as he stepped forward and enclosed her in a hug. Her vulnerability seemed to calm him. She tried to slow her heartbeat by holding her breath. She didn't want him to pick up on her anxiety. He kissed the top of her head and released her from his arms.

'What you really need right now is peace and quiet. You need to give yourself the space to recover from what's been a hideous, *hideous* time. We *all* do.' He looked into her eyes. 'Why don't you get back into your yoga? That always seemed to relax you.'

'You're right, Dad,' she said. 'And I will, I promise.'

After her father had gone, Scarlett remained sitting on her bed. A solid, heavy sensation gathered at her throat and neck. Breathing was no longer an automatic function. She had to will her lungs to work, to focus on each and every breath.

This was crazy. Her fears were running away with her, mutating into ever more gruesome scenarios. This was dread she was feeling. Cold dread.

36

DEE'S DAD BLEW ON his hands and rubbed them together. 'It's a good turnout,' he said.

Dee agreed. Standing on the sidelines of a football pitch in a muddy park on a damp November morning wasn't how she would have chosen to spend her Sunday, or any other day, but then, they were doing this for Gina, and for her parents, to raise awareness and money, and by the size of the crowd, it was serving its purpose.

Lindsay was walking round handing out flyers to passers-by. Dee had the collection bucket. In a while, they'd swap over. At least they were talking to each other.

A sudden roar made her focus on the match. The other team had just scored and some spectators in a cluster a little further down the sidelines to Dee's right weren't happy.

'Fuck's sake, ref. That was offside, you could see it a mile off!'

Eva Kowalski tutted. 'I thought it was supposed to be a friendly match. Why are they getting so worked up?'

'Because it's football,' Dee's dad explained patiently. 'It doesn't matter if it's a friendly or the FA Cup. They still want to win.'

Dee noticed how close Eva was standing next to him, how every so often her dad would lean his head into hers and say something in her ear. Something that made her smile or giggle. They weren't holding hands or linking arms, but it was overwhelmingly clear from their body language that they were a couple now. Dee edged away, to give them some space.

She looked up to see Sue and Alan Caplin walking over. They'd been standing over by the trees a little way back up until now, talking to some of their friends. Sue was wearing one of those long, quilted coats and had a woollen hat pulled down over her head. They both waved at Dee, then Alan veered off to have a chat with her dad and Eva.

'At least the rain's held off,' Sue said as she approached.

Dee gave her a hug and the two of them stood there for several seconds, holding on to each other tightly. It was touch and go whether one or both of them would start crying, but then someone on the pitch hollered, 'Man's open, pass the fucking ball, you wanker!' and they released each other, laughing.

'Thank you,' Sue said. 'For organizing all this. It's really wonderful.'

Lindsay appeared at Sue's side and greeted her the same way Dee had.

'Actually, the match was Lindsay's idea,' Dee said. 'And Jake's done most of the organizing.'

'And Euan,' Lindsay said, giving Dee a little look. She wasn't exactly smiling at her, but her eyes looked softer today. Kinder. Maybe going on that course and getting out of the office for the day had been good for her. Good for both of them. It had given them time to reflect. With any luck, Lindsay had reached the same conclusion as Dee had, that their friendship was far too important to be derailed by what had happened.

For a while, they stood there together – Dee, Lindsay and Sue – watching the match. Someone was on the ground, rolling around and clutching his knee. At first, Dee couldn't see who it was, then she realized it was Euan. For a minute or so, it looked like he might have been injured. People on the sidelines were yelling, 'That was a foul! Send him off!' but then Euan got to his feet, and he and the man who'd brought him down slapped each other on the shoulders and started running around again. All the players were streaked with mud now, hair plastered to their heads with sweat, steam coming off their breath. It took Dee a while to pick out Jake. He was still glaring at the ref, his features distorted in rage.

She'd never seen him look so angry, and all because of a foul.

At half-time, Alan Caplin brought a tray of coffees over from the café. Dee sipped hers through the slit in the lid and watched as the two teams huddled at opposite ends of the pitch, swigging their energy drinks and listening intently to whatever instructions were being doled out to them. At one point, Euan looked over in her direction and raised his hand in a wave. She waved back and found herself blushing. How ridiculous, she thought. After all this time. Why couldn't she be more relaxed about things? So what if they'd once been an item? That had been eight years ago.

Just then, she spotted a familiar figure in a waxed waterproof jacket and beanie walking along the path, his eyes fixed on the pitch. She squinted at him and saw that it was Ollie Quilter. His glance shifted in her direction, and she was about to acknowledge him when it dawned on her that he was actually looking at someone else. Someone behind her. She glanced over her shoulder to see Lindsay, who'd also noticed him and was waving and grinning.

He made his way over, noticing Dee at last. 'Hello,' he said, peering at the bucket in her hand. 'What's all this in aid of then?'

Dee lifted the bucket in the air so that he could see the charity logo and the 'Gina Caplin 10 years missing' sticker directly underneath.

'Oh, I see,' he said, frowning. He shoved his hand in his pocket and pulled out a handful of loose change, which he dropped in the bucket. 'Sorry, that's all I've got on me, I'm afraid.'

'No worries. Thanks very much,' Dee said, aware of Lindsay materializing at her side.

'Here you go,' she said, handing Dee a fresh pile of flyers. 'My turn with the bucket now.' She pointed across to the other side of the pitch. 'I haven't handed any out over there yet.'

Dee put the bucket on the ground and relieved her of the flyers. 'How are things?' she asked Ollie. 'I need to catch up with your sister soon about dates for the funeral. She said she'd email over some suggestions.'

'All good,' he said. An awkward expression came over his face. 'Well, hardly *good*, in the circumstances, but we're hanging on in there. I'll, er, let Scar know I bumped into you,' he said.

Dee smiled, waiting for him to move away, to keep on walking, but he stayed where he was.

'What's the score then?' She couldn't help noticing that he hadn't directed the question at her.

'One–nil to the wrong team,' Lindsay said, and proceeded to start filling him in on the standard of play so far, how the goal had almost certainly been offside but the ref hadn't called it. As they were speaking, the two of them drifted off towards the pitch, leaving Dee standing on her own, clutching the flyers, the bucket still at her feet. She watched Lindsay's face as she chatted away to him, all animated and bright. Her usual flirtatious self.

She was still staring at her crossly when Lindsay caught her eye and gave her a look that seemed to say, *What's your problem now?* – although maybe Dee was just imagining that.

She snatched the bucket up and took it over to her, stood there holding it out until Lindsay took it. All Lindsay's attention was now focussed on Ollie's face. Dee marched round to the other side of the pitch, her trainers sinking into the mud. When she glanced back at them a few minutes later, Lindsay was laughing and playing with her hair. Ollie couldn't take his eyes off her.

37

Lindsay looked up in surprise as Dee walked into the prep room the next morning. She was in the middle of dressing Mr Byatt in the suit his son and daughter-in-law had brought in. It was always tricky, dressing a corpse, and Dee could see that she'd already slit the shirt at the back to make it easier.

Dee helped her feed Mr Byatt's arms, cold and clammy from the fridge, into the sleeves. If things hadn't been so strained between them, Lindsay would almost certainly have asked her to help. Lindsay was more than capable of doing this on her own, and clearly she'd been intending to, but it was hard work even with two of them. When Dee had first helped to dress a corpse, she'd been surprised at how heavy the limbs were.

They worked together silently, tucking the shirt under his back and neck, doing up the buttons. Then they eased his legs into the trousers.

'It went really well, didn't it?' Dee said. 'Yesterday's match.'

Lindsay glanced at her, before threading Mr Byatt's black leather belt through the loops on his waistband. Dee helped her by rolling his body first towards her and then away. They'd done this together so many times, it was second nature.

'It did,' Lindsay said.

Dee waited for her to say more. They clearly weren't going to start chatting away like old friends. Not after everything that had happened. But at least they were talking. She ploughed on.

'It was a great turnout, wasn't it?'

Lindsay nodded as she put Mr Byatt's purple tie around her own neck to fix the knot, her deft fingers producing the perfect half-Windsor in a matter of seconds.

'Very impressive.'

Dee gently peeled back the collar on Mr Byatt's shirt, then eased his head up from the table so that Lindsay could slip the tie over it and straighten it at his neck.

'I thought the Caplins managed really well,' Lindsay said. 'It can't have been easy for them.'

Dee breathed a sigh of relief. At least she wasn't having to do *all* the work in this conversation. 'No,' she said. 'It can't.'

Lindsay was now fussing with Mr Byatt's tie, smoothing out the knot and turning his collar down

over it, pressing any creases out with her fingers. Dee
had watched her prepare and dress bodies so many
times. She was always so capable, so attentive to the
smallest of details.

'Right, now for the jacket. Can you hold it up
while I cut the back?'

Dee did as she was asked and held the suit jacket
up by the shoulders while Lindsay took hold of a
large pair of dressmaking scissors and cut a vertical
line from the bottom of the middle seam at the back
all the way up to the base of the collar.

Once they'd fed Mr Byatt's arms into the sleeves
and tucked the ends of the jacket under his back, they
were ready to put his socks and shoes on. Dee hated
this part more than anything else. She'd always been a
bit squeamish when it came to other people's feet, and
dead feet were even worse. But she dutifully and
respectfully eased a black sock over Mr Byatt's cold,
rubbery left foot while Lindsay did the same with the
right.

Putting shoes on could be awkward too, particularly
if the feet had become misshapen in death, and even
more so if the shoes were a little tight, like these were.
Usually, they didn't bother with shoes unless the family
had specifically requested it. The Byatts *had* requested
it. Just like Gabriel Abiodun's family had requested he
be buried with his customized crash helmet, his favourite leather jacket and his biker boots, Dee thought,
spying on Lindsay from the corner of her eye.

'I need to do his make-up now,' Lindsay said.

Dee stepped away from the table. Lindsay liked to be alone when she did this. It was an intimate act, applying foundation to someone's face, giving them a healthy colour so that they were fit to be viewed by the family. Dee had no doubt that in half an hour's time, when Mr Byatt's son and daughter-in-law and various other members of the family came down to the viewing room, Mr Byatt would be looking a whole lot healthier than he looked right now.

It was obvious that Lindsay was waiting for her to leave, but now that the ice between them was starting to thaw, Dee was loath to go back upstairs. She wanted to prolong their conversation a little longer.

'Shall I bring Gina's novel in tomorrow? Would you like to read it?'

Lindsay, who was in the middle of unscrewing a pot of foundation, met her eyes, but only briefly. She nodded. 'Yeah, why not? I mean, romantic fiction's not really my cup of tea, but . . .'

Dee remembered the way Lindsay had been flirting with Ollie Quilter at the football match, in front of Sue and Alan Caplin and everybody else, and felt the urge to say, *No, erotic fiction's probably more up your street*, but she held her tongue. She knew it was just her own stupid jealousy, and catty comments like that would make everything between them ten times worse.

'I was thinking about it the other night,' Dee said.

'I was wondering whether she made the main character a singer because it's a similar sort of profession to dancing. I mean, in terms of the performance element.'

Lindsay shrugged. 'Maybe.' Then she smiled. Dee felt them inching back to how they were, before that wretched Trevor Cooper had turned up and ruined everything. Lindsay assumed a mock-curious tone. 'In which case, *who* was the mystery piano teacher?'

Dee smiled. 'It crossed my mind that she might have based him on Jake.'

Lindsay looked at her. 'Why on earth would you think that?'

Dee's cheeks flushed with heat as she remembered what else she'd briefly considered, but it was too late; Lindsay had clocked her discomfort. 'It was just something that went through my mind. He tried to teach us all to play "Chopsticks" once. Do you remember?'

'Why are you blushing?'

'I'm not.'

'Yes, you are.'

'I'm not. I'm just a bit hot, that's all.'

'In the cool room?' Lindsay said, still staring at her. 'No, seriously, Dee, I'm interested in why you think Gina might have written a novel with the love interest based on my brother.'

Dee sighed. 'I wish I'd never said anything now. It was only because they went out together. And because he plays keyboard. That's all.'

Lindsay rolled her eyes, but not in a friendly, jokey way, in a sarcastic, incredulous way. 'You'll be telling me next you think she was still in love with him.'

The way Lindsay was looking at her, it was as if she could read her mind, as if she knew the suspicions that had troubled her the other day.

'I hope you didn't say any of this to the Caplins,' Lindsay said.

Now it was Dee's turn to look incredulous. 'Why the hell would I have done that?'

'I don't know, Dee. Maybe because you never think before you speak. You just say exactly what's on your mind. Like accusing me of being a whore.'

'I never said that.'

'You might as well have done, and now you're implying Gina wrote a novel about my brother.'

'I didn't say that either. Why are you so touchy about me thinking that, anyway? So what if she *did* base it on him?'

Lindsay glared at her. 'Work it out! If people start thinking Gina was still in love with Jake, their minds might start working overtime. Like yours clearly has. Don't you think he went through enough before?'

'Oh, for God's sake! He wasn't the only one the police were interested in. Gina's dad, my dad, Euan – they all went through the same thing. The police were just doing their job.'

'Yes, but Jake went through more of it because he used to go out with her.'

'I think it was probably a whole lot worse for Alan, actually. Imagine how *he* must have felt. It was only a year after that horrendous Josef Fritzl case, and people always suspect any men in the family first, don't they?'

'They suspect boyfriends too. Which is why you need to think about how your words might be interpreted.'

Dee felt her jaw harden in anger. 'Well, you need to think about how your *actions* might be interpreted.'

Lindsay glared at her. 'And what's that supposed to mean?'

'Coming on to Ollie Quilter on Sunday. In front of the Caplins, too. Flirting with a client after what's just happened with Trevor Cooper.'

Lindsay's face was taut with anger. 'What the hell has Ollie Quilter got to do with Trevor Cooper?'

'It's about boundaries, Lindsay. Professional boundaries.'

Lindsay put her hand out. 'Can you leave now, please?'

Dee went upstairs. Far from healing their friendship, the conversation had made things even worse. If only she'd kept her stupid mouth shut.

38

EVER SINCE HER DAD'S unexpected visit on Saturday, Scarlett had been in turmoil. Where was the card from Gina? Had Ollie taken it the last time he'd visited? Was that why he'd popped over with those chocolates, so that he could have a snoop around when she wasn't looking? She'd left him napping on the sofa. He'd had ample opportunity to nip into her bedroom while she was distracted in her office. He was the only person who'd visited her since she'd found the card. Apart from Mickey, of course, and he hadn't been anywhere near her bedroom. She'd kept him firmly in her sight the whole time, hadn't she?

And why was her dad so intent on dissuading her from reorganizing the garden? She tried to make sense of it, but couldn't. Her mind was a mess. A total jumble. What the hell was going on? Was she losing it, as her dad had seemed to imply? She'd even found herself considering whether *he* might have taken the card. After all, she hadn't heard him coming up the stairs when she was in Rebecca's bedroom. What if he'd let himself into her apartment first and taken it before coming up?

All weekend, she'd tried to focus on displacement activities: unnecessary little tidying jobs, folding and sorting laundry, ordering her groceries online. The rest of the time, she'd wandered around the apartment in a daze.

Was Ollie responsible for Gina Caplin's disappearance? And had Rebecca known something about it? Was that why she'd never mentioned her? And what about her dad? Was he in on it too? No, it wasn't possible. Not her own family. Not the people she was closest to in the whole world.

But still, the images came swarming in. Rebecca standing in the garden in her nightie in obvious distress. Ollie prowling around the garden at night, letting himself into the summer house with the key he'd stolen from the hook. She didn't want this in her head, any of it. Couldn't cope with it squatting there. An ugly, toad-like creature. But there it was, and it showed no signs of budging.

She went into her office and sat at her desk. If she didn't get on with her work soon, she'd fall even further behind. Then she saw it. The envelope with the card inside. It was sticking out from under a pile of her papers. She stared at it, unable at first to quite take in what she was seeing. So Ollie *hadn't* taken it.

Nobody had. She must have brought it in here and forgotten all about it.

She put her elbows on her desk and rested her head in her hands. Maybe her dad was right. Maybe she had been taking too many painkillers. Maybe she really *was* cracking up. Or was it simply a case of brain fog, another bloody symptom of ME?

For the rest of the day, she tried to focus on her to-do list. Her office had always been a refuge. A place to switch off the worries in her mind and focus on numbers and calculations. But it was no longer working. She couldn't concentrate for more than a couple of minutes at a time, had to keep stopping and staring into space. She'd never experienced such restlessness before, but then she'd never experienced this level of disquiet before either.

Somehow or other, she got through the day and managed to complete a couple of long-outstanding tasks. At any other time, she'd have been disappointed at how little she'd managed to achieve but, right now, achieving anything at all seemed pretty amazing.

Later that evening, after an early supper she had to force herself to finish, she decided she *would* go to yoga after all. There was a class tonight, wasn't there? She checked the timetable online to confirm. Yoga was the only activity, apart from her work, that had the effect of clearing her mind and giving her a sense of purpose. Maybe she needed to get out of the house for a couple of hours, have a complete change of scenery. It couldn't be good for her, being cooped up here all day.

She changed into a loose pair of yoga trousers and a baggy T-shirt. Then she twisted her hair into a ponytail, made sure she had her purse and her keys in her bag and left the house with her walking cane. She felt better as soon as she was standing at the bus stop in the fresh night air. Why hadn't she done this before? Why did she never remember that it was routine her body and mind needed? Routine that she craved.

And it would be nice catching up with her yoga acquaintances. The last time she'd been to a class was a few days before that party in Bedford. A few days before Rebecca was killed and Scarlett's life had been turned upside down. Thankfully, nobody there knew her that well. They were on what Scarlett called 'yoga friend' terms, which encompassed smiling and passing each other mats from the pile, maybe sharing the odd comment about the teacher, or the temperature of the hall, or the tendency of the earlier aerobics class to take too long to leave the room. That kind of thing.

Nobody knew that Rebecca Quilter, the woman who'd been brutally murdered in her own bedroom and whose tragic story had been all over the news, was Scarlett's aunt and, what's more, that Scarlett lived in the house where the murder had taken place. Nobody knew any of that, thank God.

It was the first time Scarlett had been on a bus since returning home and, as soon as it started moving and she looked out at the familiar landmarks, she felt her muscles start to relax, which was odd, because leaving home and using public transport usually had the opposite effect. Usually, it made her tense and tired, having to smarten up and act like other people, hold herself upright and give the impression of being someone who was in control of her body.

But while she wasn't always in control of her body, she'd always been in control of her mind. Or so she'd thought. She stared at her reflection in the dirty window. Her dad might be annoying and patronizing, but he was right. It was about time she started looking after herself and got back into an exercise regime. An hour of gentle stretching and breathing. An hour of being somewhere else. Anywhere but in that house.

The bus was passing the barracks now, about to turn into John Wilson Street, when something occurred to her. Something that brought her up sharp and made her grab the top of the seat in front. She hadn't wanted to go to that party in Bedford back in September. She'd almost decided to decline the invitation, but Ollie had persuaded her to accept. Not in so many words. He'd made a jokey comment about how if she turned this one down too – there had been various others in the past year or so, events she'd always managed to wriggle out of – then her friends would probably get the message that she wasn't bothered about them any more and not invite her to anything else. Then she'd never have to go through this dilemma again. He'd made it sound like a good idea *not* to go.

And that had rankled with her, because she *did* want to be their friend. She just didn't fancy the journey and staying in a bedroom that was never going to be as comfortable as her own. She didn't want to make the effort, because effort tired her out. Social occasions tired her out. Her friends knew that; she'd told them enough times. But it was hard for people to understand that ME fatigue was on a different scale from *normal* fatigue.

And yet friendship *relied* on people making the effort, didn't it? And if she didn't occasionally do things that took her out of her comfort zone, then that was giving up on life, wasn't it?

Twenty minutes later, as she was lying on her back on a yoga mat with her knees drawn into her chest and focusing on her breath, everything seemed to crystallize in her mind. Ollie had made that comment on purpose. He knew the way her mind worked. He didn't need to say, 'Come on, Scar, don't you think you should go? You haven't seen them in ages.' Because if he'd said that, she would almost certainly have declined the invitation. Ollie had known that, being the stubborn and contrary creature she was, she'd have refused to be guilt-tripped into going.

Oh yes, he'd known exactly how to play her. Which begged the question, what difference had it made to him whether she went or not?

Unless he'd wanted her out of the way.

39

SCARLETT PUSHED HER KEY into the lock of the main front door and stepped into the darkness of the hallway. She felt as tightly coiled as a spring. So much for the relaxing benefits of yoga.

She went into her apartment and locked the door. Then she changed into her pyjamas and made herself a mug of hot chocolate, carried it over to the sofa. Perhaps she might be able to lose herself in front of the TV long enough to quieten her mind. She needed to gather her thoughts, corral them into some kind of order so that she could make a rational decision about what to do.

She had just picked up the remote control when she heard a noise upstairs. Trembling, she put her mug on the coffee table and strained her ears. Maybe she'd imagined it. Or perhaps it was one of the hot-water pipes. They made odd noises sometimes, didn't they?

There it was again. Someone was moving around

in Rebecca's bedroom. She remembered the terror she'd first felt when she'd been up there a week ago, the sensation of evil that had so unnerved her. But she'd been inside the room since then. She'd conquered her irrational fears and, apart from the shock of her dad creeping up on her, she'd been fine.

She stood up. She wouldn't allow herself to believe that the room was haunted by a malign presence, so either it was an intruder, or it was one of the only two people who had a key apart from herself. Her brother or her father.

She went to get her own key and stepped out into the hallway again, anxiety lying in the pit of her stomach like sediment. She unlocked Rebecca's door and called up the stairs before she could talk herself out of it.

'Ollie? Dad? Is that you?'

Silence. Whichever one of them it was, Scarlett sensed their surprise. They must have thought they were alone in the house. But how had they known she'd be out? Had they been watching her?

'Yeah. I'll be down in a sec.' It was Ollie. He sounded casual, matter-of-fact, as if there was nothing in the least bit strange about what he was doing. Scarlett took a few deep breaths. Ollie couldn't possibly have anything to do with Gina Caplin's disappearance. And yet . . .

'What are you doing?'

'Just taking a look around, seeing what needs to

be done. It's going to take ages to get this lot cleared out.'

Scarlett went up a couple of steps. 'You should have said you were coming round. I thought you were a burglar.' She waited a beat. 'You know that, legally, you shouldn't be up there at all.'

Ollie peered down at her from the top of the stairs. 'What're you talking about? This place is mine now. I need to get it cleared and decorated and rented out.'

'Yes, but you're meant to wait until after probate is sorted. Seriously, Ollie, you need to come down.'

'Don't be daft. What difference does it make? And how are they going to find out? Who's going to tell them?'

He gave her a look that Scarlett couldn't help interpreting as a challenge. He was searching for something, she felt sure of it. Was it the same thing he'd been looking for in the summer house?

Her heart beat faster, but she knew that if she backed off now, she'd be acting out of character. And besides, she didn't *want* to back off. She didn't want him up there. If there was something to be found, something else that linked her aunt to Gina Caplin, Scarlett wanted to be the one to find it.

'It's not right, Ollie. You could get into all sorts of trouble. We don't want to fall foul of the law.'

'For fuck's sake, Scar! What is *wrong* with you? I'm just having a look and doing some measurements and calculations. I'll be down in a sec.'

'No, Ollie. You need to come down now. We're joint executors, so this is my decision too. You need my consent to go through Rebecca's things and I'm not giving it.'

Ollie came to the top of the stairs, an incredulous look on his face. 'What the fuck are you talking about? This is *my* property now.'

She felt a flutter of fear. Did she even like Ollie? She loved him, of course she did. And they were bonded by more than just blood. That old childhood alliance ran deep. But did she truly *like* the man he'd become? Not right now she didn't.

'Not until probate is granted it isn't. It's a legal process and you have to do things properly. I'm a professional accountant, Ollie. If I'm found to have acted unlawfully by turning a blind eye to something like this, it's my reputation on the line. My career. You have to get out of there now.'

Ollie came thundering down the stairs so fast Scarlett barely had time to get out of his way.

He stared at her in disbelief, anger distorting his features. 'You're fucking *shitting* me, aren't you?'

Scarlett stood her ground. Was this really her little brother talking to her like this?

She swallowed hard. 'No, I'm not. There's a reason things are done like this, and we have to comply.'

His silence was mutinous. He pushed past her and yanked the front door open. Then he stopped and turned around. 'Just because you're a pen-pushing bureaucrat, it doesn't mean you can tell me what to do. I'm talking to Dad about this.'

Scarlett raised her eyebrows. He was no longer her handsome, roguish brother. Now, his expression was grim. He looked sullen, like an angry little boy. Scarlett scarcely recognized him.

'How old are you, Ollie? Do you really think Dad is going to come round and tell me off for making sure we stay within the law?'

'Dad's right. You're not yourself lately, Scarlett.'

Scarlett bristled. 'And what's that supposed to mean?'

Ollie sighed. When he started speaking again, his voice was softer, kinder. 'We're worried about you, Scar. Smashing a window and climbing into the summer house when all you needed to do was go back to the house and get the key. Planning gravel gardens before we've even buried Rebecca. It's a bit weird, you've got to admit.'

Scarlett opened her mouth then closed it again. She'd been about to say, *How could I get the key when you'd already stolen it?*, but something told her to keep quiet. Something told her that whatever was going on here, antagonizing Ollie wasn't the way forward.

'I'm tired, Ollie. I need to get to bed. Let's talk in the morning.'

She shut the door before he could say anything more and pulled the bolts across. She stood for a few moments until the roaring sound in her head subsided and her pulse rate slowed. A sob welled up in her throat, but she swallowed it down. There was only one person she wanted to talk to right now. Only one person who would understand how she was feeling and who would know what to do. But that person was Rebecca.

40

DEE HEARD LINDSAY LEAVE the office. Her shoulders sagged. This was intolerable. It was the second day in a row that Lindsay had gone home without saying goodbye. Ever since their argument yesterday morning, the two of them had barely spoken to each other.

Dee logged off her PC and put her coat on. She made a decision. She would go round to Lindsay's house this evening and see if they couldn't get over this somehow. Or, at the very least, get through it. Together. Just like they'd got through everything else together. They couldn't go on like this. It wasn't good for their friendship, and it certainly wasn't good for their business. She would apologize for offending her, for lecturing her about professional boundaries, even though Lindsay was the one in the wrong here.

Dee locked up the office and walked to her car. She would drive home first, get changed, then take the bus back to Woolwich. She'd stop off at Tesco and pick up a bottle of Lindsay's favourite wine, maybe some chocolates too. The only thing that mattered was getting their friendship back on track. She'd already lost one best friend. She couldn't bear it if she lost another.

An hour and a half later, Dee got off the bus and turned the corner into Lindsay's street, hoping she'd be in the mood for her peace offering and that in a little while the two of them would be over this bump in their friendship and ready to move beyond it. Perhaps they'd end up ordering a pizza and watching something on Netflix. Perhaps Dee would sleep over on the sofa and they'd go out for breakfast together in the morning before work. Cement their reconciliation with a big fry-up.

But as she approached the house Dee saw a man get out of a car a little further along on the other side of the street and cross over. It looked suspiciously like Ollie Quilter, and he was carrying what appeared to be a handful of plastic rulers in his hand.

Dee quickly crossed to the other side and stood just out of sight behind a tree. It *was* Ollie Quilter. She watched as he sauntered up to Lindsay's front door and rang the bell. What was he doing at her house? How did he even know where she lived?

A few seconds later the door opened and Lindsay emerged, smiling and laughing. She was wearing her tight-fitting jeans and knee-length boots, a big baggy jumper and a scarf Dee had never seen before. Her blonde hair was piled on top of her head, stray locks escaping in front of her ears. One of those haphazard, just-put-it-up-any-old-how arrangements that Dee knew for a fact took her ages to perfect. She watched in appalled fascination as Lindsay stood on her tiptoes and greeted Ollie with a kiss on each cheek. Then he showed her what he had in his hand and Dee realized at once what they were. Packets of sparklers. Of course. It was 5 November. Bonfire Night. Ollie Quilter must be taking her to a firework party. They must have arranged it on Sunday at the football match. She must have given him her address then.

Dee stood, rooted to the spot, her left hand grazing the trunk of the tree she was hiding behind, her right holding tightly on to the bag of wine and chocolates, and watched as the two of them crossed the street and got into Ollie's car. She waited until they'd driven off, then turned round and walked back to the bus stop. Tears burned the back of her eyes. She sniffed crossly and blinked them away. Why the hell was she reacting like this? As if she'd been snubbed. Rejected. As if it were a date, for Christ's sake! Lindsay hadn't even known she'd be coming round.

But it was more than that. It was knowing that Lindsay was already going out with someone else, so soon after sleeping with Trevor Cooper, so soon after Callum and all the rest. It was knowing that Lindsay obviously didn't give a toss about getting involved with one of their clients, or how that might be perceived. Okay, so she wasn't actually breaking any rules, but it was common sense, wasn't it, not to mix business with pleasure?

Dee increased her pace. What a great evening this had turned out to be. She'd have been better off staying at home and never venturing out in the first place. It would be embarrassing, returning so soon. What if her dad was making the most of her absence and had invited Eva Kowalski round for a drink? Dee would turn up, clutching her sad plastic bag of white wine and chocolates, like the forty-year-old loser she was, and they'd both feel sorry for her. Was there anything worse than being pitied by your own father and his late-middle-aged girlfriend?

Dee reached the bus stop and perched on one of the red plastic seats under the shelter. Who was she more cross about here? Lindsay, for her lax attitude to men and sex, for her total disregard for the reputation of their business? Or herself, for being sad and lonely, for having no one else she could call up and hang out with, for having no fucking life?

When the bus pulled up about five minutes later Dee briefly considered not getting on. She could always go back to Tesco and mooch about for another hour. It was massive, that store. She could look at the clothes and the books and the stationery, kill a bit of time. Maybe she could go and eat a burger somewhere and go home after that. But what was the point? She wasn't in the mood for shopping or eating burgers. She'd been in the mood for having a drink with Lindsay, for making things all right between them, and now that wasn't going to happen she might as well go home.

She got on the bus, tapped her Oyster card on the reader and found a seat towards the back. At least if she had her own place, nobody would ever know how pathetic she really was. Nobody would know she spent her evenings in her pyjamas, cross-legged on her bed, watching crap on TV.

As the bus pulled away, Dee had an image of Ollie Quilter and Lindsay standing in someone's back garden, heads tilted back, watching the fireworks. He would probably have his arm around her shoulders and she would be nestling against him for warmth. She pictured them waving their stupid sparklers around like kids and swigging beer from bottles. Later, when the party was over and everyone had drifted away, he'd drive her home and she'd invite him in for a coffee. Except it wouldn't be coffee she was really offering him, and it wouldn't be coffee he'd be saying yes to.

41

THE ANSWERPHONE WAS BLINKING when Dee went into the office the next morning. If today turned out to be anything like yesterday or the day before that, she was in for another tense and awkward eight hours, with her and Lindsay doing their best to avoid each other.

She pressed play then went to hang her coat up. Scarlett Quilter's voice filled the room. There was something different about it today. She sounded anxious. A little breathless.

'Dee, I need to talk to you. It's urgent.'

Dee rang her straight back. 'Hi, I've just heard your message. Is everything okay?'

'No. No, it isn't. I'm afraid we need to put the funeral arrangements on hold.' She paused. 'Something's come up.'

Dee frowned. When people said, 'Something's come up,' it usually meant they didn't want to give any details. It was on a par with 'family emergency' or 'personal issues'. Scarlett had been so open with her thus far, it seemed odd for her to be holding back now.

Dee sat down at her desk, immediately fearing the worst. Had she seen those two bad reviews? Was she having second thoughts about using their services? Dee would have been mortified whichever of their clients, past or present, had seen those hateful words, but for some reason Scarlett Quilter's opinion was even more important to her.

Maybe it was the father putting pressure on her to play safe and go with the Co-op. Dee could still remember the disparaging way he'd said the word 'alternative'. If that were the case, then the conversation was going to be difficult, seeing as Scarlett had already signed the agreement forms and paid her deposit.

Dee swivelled round in her chair and pulled open the middle drawer of the filing cabinet behind her, walked her fingers to the hanging file marked P–Q and extracted the relevant paperwork, placed it on the desk in front of her.

'Would you like me to pop round for a chat?' As soon as she'd said this, Dee regretted it. She'd made it sound like she was available at the drop of a hat, that she had nothing more pressing to do. But it was too late now – the offer had been made. In any case, she *wanted* to see Scarlett. And at least it would get her out of facing Lindsay for a bit longer.

'Would you?' Scarlett said. 'I'd really like that.'

Dee breathed out in relief. It couldn't be the reviews. It sounded like Scarlett was on the verge of tears. Maybe the police had unearthed new evidence about Rebecca's murder. That could really delay things.

'I'll be with you shortly,' she said, wondering what could be troubling Scarlett Quilter so much that she was practically crying over the phone.

The shop door swung open just as she was finishing the call, and Lindsay came bowling in. Dee hated how tense she felt just seeing her.

'I'm going to see Scarlett Quilter,' she said. 'She sounded really upset on the phone. Wants to put the funeral arrangements on hold.'

Lindsay sniffed. 'Well, if anyone can cheer her up, it'll be you, won't it?'

Dee caught her glance and held it. Lindsay turned away first. She shrugged her coat off and slung it over the spare hook by its hood. Then she went into the kitchen and started clattering around, humming tunelessly, as if she didn't have a care in the world.

Dee clenched her jaw in irritation. Then before she knew quite what she was doing, she'd followed her into the tiny cupboard of a kitchen and started saying things she knew she'd regret but which were coming out anyway. She couldn't seem to stop herself.

'Maybe she's found out you're seeing her brother.'

264

Lindsay slammed her mug down and spun round to face her, but Dee carried on, undeterred. 'I know you went out with Ollie Quilter last night. How many more men are you intending to sleep with?'

Lindsay stared at her. 'Have you been spying on me?'

Dee's cheeks flushed with heat. 'No! But I saw you. I saw him come to your house.'

Lindsay shook her head in disbelief. 'So you *were* spying on me. Jesus Christ, Dee, haven't you got anything better to do with your time than hanging around in Woolwich trying to catch me out?'

'I *wasn't* spying on you. I was coming round to apologize. I was bringing you wine and chocolates.'

There was a long silence. Dee blinked back the tears. 'I'm sorry for saying those mean things to you. I don't like what you did, but I don't want to fall out with you over it. I hate how we're arguing all the time. I just want us to go back to how we were before.'

Lindsay rested her hands on the counter and closed her eyes. 'How *can* we go back, now that I know what you really think of me? How can we ever go back to how we were before?'

42

As soon as Scarlett opened the door to her Dee could tell that she hadn't been mistaken. Scarlett had definitely been crying, and for some while, by the looks of her red, blotchy eyes. Her hair was untidy, as if she hadn't brushed it since getting up.

'Thank you for coming round. I'd have come to you, but . . .' She waited until Dee was in the hallway before closing and bolting the door behind them. Dee gave her an enquiring look.

'The fact is, I'm not sure I want to leave the house at all right now.'

'Oh, I'm sorry to hear that. Are you unwell?'

'Not exactly. Well, no more than usual.'

Dee followed her inside. Scarlett gestured towards the armchair. 'Please, take a seat. I'll make us some coffee. You like it strong, don't you?'

Dee nodded, and Scarlett went off to the kitchen. Dee's gaze wandered around the room while she waited. This was now the third time she'd been here, but she was still taken aback by the beauty of it. Each time she visited, she noticed little things she hadn't fully registered before. The contemporary glass sculpture on a small round table tucked in the corner. The way the mirror above the fireplace reflected the huge piece of abstract art on the wall opposite, so that it looked almost like a second picture. How the cushions on the sofa were all different colours and patterns and sizes but somehow complemented each other perfectly.

Even with bits and pieces left out on the coffee table and a big pile of messy papers on the floor, the room didn't look untidy. At home in her dad's flat, mess just looked like mess. Here, the clutter seemed almost artful. Dee couldn't help feeling envious. But when her eyes glided towards Scarlett she checked herself. Just because someone lived in a gorgeous home like this and had nice stuff it didn't mean their lives were perfect. Of course it didn't. Something about Scarlett Quilter wasn't right. It wasn't just her red eyes and messy hair, it was the anxiety etched into her face, the awkward, stiff way she was moving. Perhaps her ME symptoms had flared up again. Or was it something else?

Scarlett was now wheeling the coffees through on the little trolley. 'Do you mind moving all that on to the sofa for me?' she said, gesturing at the papers on the floor with her chin.

Dee sprang out of her chair to lift them up and, as

she did so, she recognized something about the font and layout of the printed words that made the hairs on her arms stand up. No. It couldn't be. There must be some mistake.

She scanned the first few sentences on the top page and her ears began to buzz. How was this possible? Why did Scarlett Quilter have a copy of Gina's novel?

She glanced up at Scarlett, who was clearly waiting for her to move out of the way. 'Where did you get this?'

Scarlett looked at her in surprise. 'It's my aunt's novel.'

Dee stared at her.

'Do you remember me telling you that she wanted to be a writer?'

Dee nodded, unable to speak.

'It's a rather sweet romance.' Scarlett smiled, weakly. 'Reading it makes me feel like she's still here.'

'May I . . . May I have a quick look?'

'Sure,' Scarlett said. 'Do you read much romantic fiction?'

Dee scarcely heard what she was saying. She took the manuscript back to her chair and leafed through it while Scarlett pushed the trolley into position and sat down on the sofa. She wasn't mistaken. This was Gina's novel. It was identical.

'I've seen this before,' she said, forcing herself to

meet Scarlett's curious eyes. 'In fact, I've got the very same one at home in my bedroom.'

Scarlett pulled a face. 'Why would you have a copy of something my aunt wrote well over ten years ago?'

'Because ... because it isn't her novel.' Dee stood up, suddenly remembering how Scarlett had bolted the door when she'd come in. 'It's Gina's novel. Her parents gave me a copy a couple of weeks ago.'

'No, no, that's not possible. This is definitely Rebecca's. I'd recognize her voice anywhere. The language. The cadence. Everything about it.' Something strange happened to Scarlett's face then, as if a troubling thought had just that moment occurred to her.

And as she watched her, something occurred to Dee, too. Gina had been so sharp, so funny. Dee had expected at least some of that to come out in her friend's writing. She'd been surprised and, if she were honest, disappointed at how dated and flowery Gina's novel had seemed. How old-fashioned.

Almost as if it had been written by a much older woman.

Scarlett had her face in her hands now, and Dee's stomach dropped. She had no idea what Scarlett was about to say, but she knew it couldn't be good.

'I discovered something a little while ago,' Scarlett said at last, looking up at Dee. Dee felt the muscles in

269

her chest tighten. 'Your friend Gina and my aunt were in touch with one another. I don't know how their friendship started – whether they kept in touch after Rebecca stopped teaching you, or whether they met again some time afterwards. All I know is, Rebecca gave Gina a copy of her novel to read, and Gina sent her a card, telling her how much she'd enjoyed it.'

Dee sat back down again. So it was true. The novel she'd read and thought was Gina's had been Rebecca Quilter's all along. All her silly theories about who the characters might be based on were utterly meaningless. As was the argument she'd had with Lindsay about the love interest being based on Jake.

'Can I see it? This card?'

Scarlett reached for a book on the end of the sofa and removed an envelope from inside. She handed it to Dee, who drew the card out with trembling fingers. She recognized the picture on the front straight away. Somewhere in her box of treasured items back home in her bedroom was an identical card that Gina had once given her. She must have bought a whole set of them. Dee looked at the familiar handwriting. The neat, evenly spaced letters with the distinctive full stops. Gina had never filled them in, always wrote them like tiny circles.

'How long have you had this?' Her voice was barely audible.

'I only found it recently. It was in the summer house. With the novel.'

'How come I didn't know about their friendship?' Dee said. 'How come *you* didn't know? Or Gina's family and friends?'

Scarlett wrung her hands. 'I don't know. I don't know anything. It's as much a mystery to me as it is to you.'

Dee straightened her spine. 'When was the last time your aunt saw her? Was it near the time she disappeared?'

Scarlett was biting her bottom lip and shaking her head.

'Why didn't she ever come forward to say she'd known her?' asked Dee.

'I promise you, Dee, I don't know the answers to *any* of those questions. I wish I *did*.'

'So why didn't you say anything when you found it? Why didn't you tell me? Oh my God. You don't think Rebecca had something to do with Gina's disappearance?'

The image of the bolted front door once again flashed into Dee's mind. She sprang to her feet. 'Why did you bolt the door as soon as I came in? What the hell is going on here?'

'I can't, I . . .' Scarlett's hands covered her face.

Dee's stomach dropped like a stone. Ollie Quilter. He'd carried on living here after Scarlett had left. If Rebecca had kept in touch with Gina, there was every chance she'd come to this house. He'd have met her, wouldn't he?

271

'Is it your brother you're scared of? Or your father? Was that why Rebecca never said anything? Scarlett, you *have* to tell me what you know!'

Scarlett clasped her hands together on her lap. 'Ever since I mentioned the card, Ollie's been looking for something. In the summer house. In Rebecca's apartment. I have a strong suspicion that it's the very same thing *I* was looking for when I went up there. Rebecca's old diaries. It was the day you rang me about Rebecca's ashes. I wanted to find out the last time Rebecca had seen Gina.'

Dee moistened her lips with her tongue. 'That's why you were asking me questions about what Lindsay and I remembered about your aunt teaching us.'

Scarlett nodded. 'I wanted to know if you knew anything about their friendship, but you didn't. Please, Dee, you have to believe me. I don't *know* anything. I'm struggling to understand this too. All I know is, Ollie hasn't been himself since I mentioned the name Gina. He stole the key to the summer house. I saw him prowling around out there in the middle of the night, and he's been acting strangely ever since.' She plucked at the hem of her T-shirt, not meeting Dee's eyes. 'And my dad's been . . .'

Dee leapt to her feet. 'For Christ's sake, Scarlett. Do you think this has got anything to do with Gina going missing? And what about what happened to Rebecca and Clive? Maybe it's all connected somehow.'

'No, it can't be. It *can't* be.'

Dee grabbed her bag from the floor and took out her phone. Her hands were shaking so much she almost dropped it.

'Phone the police, Scarlett. Phone them now, or I will.'

43

THE ROOM BEGAN TO sway. There was a whistling in her ears. Now that Scarlett had confessed her fears, there was no taking them back. She felt a cold hand on the nape of her neck. Dee was beside her on the sofa, perched on the edge.

'Put your head between your knees,' she said. Dee's voice sounded distant and muffled, as if it were coming from another room. Scarlett did as she was told and waited for the feeling to pass. When it did, a few moments later, she sat up. Dee was staring straight into her face.

'Are you all right? Can I get you some water?'

Scarlett nodded weakly. She pressed her forehead with her fingers and closed her eyes. When Dee returned from the kitchen with a glass she took it from her hands and drank greedily. Her arms were shaking and water sploshed on to her chin and down the front of her top.

'I'm so sorry,' she said. Her voice sounded high and feeble. 'I'll be okay in a minute.'

Dee took the glass from her hands and put it on the trolley. 'Take your time. I'll stay with you while you phone the police.'

Scarlett shook her head. 'No, please, I'd rather be alone when I make the call. I need a few minutes to myself before ... before ...' She clamped her hand to her mouth and lurched over her lap, aware of Dee leaping to one side.

'Are you going to be sick?'

Scarlett focussed on breathing deeply and slowly through her nostrils. She would *not* be sick. She would not. When she looked up, Dee was staring at her bleakly.

'I'll be okay. I just need to compose myself. I'll ring them. You have my word. I just need some time alone with my thoughts before I make the call. It will change everything for me. Everything. You do see that, don't you? If I've got this wrong and there's another explanation, Ollie will never forgive me. But if I've got it right ...'

Dee moved towards the door. 'You'll call me as soon as you've spoken to them?'

Scarlett nodded. 'I will.' She sensed Dee's hesitation, her reluctance to leave. She met her eyes and held her gaze. 'I promise.'

Gingerly, she got to her feet and followed Dee into

the hallway. As soon as she had seen her out Scarlett locked the front door and dragged the bolts across. Her hands were still shaking. She glanced at the door to Rebecca's apartment and pictured the scene all over again, just as she'd done every single day since it happened. Only this time, it was as though it were a painting. A gigantic canvas depicting horror and destruction on an unimaginable scale. Her brain registered it detail by grotesque detail, until it was spread out before her in all its hideous enormity. But what Scarlett saw in her mind's eye wasn't a work of art. It was so real she could almost smell the blood, the fear.

She staggered back into her apartment, her grief and loss now compounded by what she was about to do. What she *had* to do. She had no choice. A sob welled up in her throat and she sank to her knees, giving herself up to the emotion, experiencing the full force of it there on the kitchen floor. An avalanche of misery and pain and revulsion reducing her to her simplest form: a rocking, swaying, howling creature.

She wasn't sure how long she'd been crying when her sobs finally began to subside. By now, she'd reached the heaving, juddering stage and her knees were beginning to hurt where they were pressed into the ceramic tiles. It took all of her effort to stand up and hobble back to the sofa.

She raised her eyes to the ceiling, remembering that afternoon when she'd left her dad's house and returned home for the first time since Rebecca's murder. She had sat on this very sofa and contemplated the tragedy that had unfolded upstairs, tried to work out what it was that had motivated Clive to do what he'd done, scarcely able to believe him capable of such an act.

But what if he *wasn't* capable? What if Clive *hadn't* killed Rebecca in a frenzy of humiliated rage? What if Dee was right and what happened to Rebecca was somehow connected to Gina Caplin's disappearance?

That small creep of mistrust, the one she'd felt when first setting eyes on the card and reading the message inside, seeing the name Gina, had steadily grown in size, until now it was full-blown dread. A deep, dark chasm splitting open inside her.

This was what had been brewing in her subconscious all this time. That appalling sensation of evil. What if Rebecca had been killed in a premeditated and systematic way? Clive, too. Slaughtered like animals, both of them, and by her own brother. No, it was unthinkable. But why else would he be so concerned about her dismantling the summer house? Her father, too. Did he know something as well? Was it all to do with the secret Rebecca couldn't tell?

Scarlett dry-retched into her hand. She hoped to God she was wrong, but somehow she doubted it. What else could account for her aunt's ten-year silence on the topic of Gina Caplin? And those comments

she'd made about 'this girl, that girl' – were they the
result of her deteriorating brain struggling to make
sense of it all?

She wrenched her gaze away from the ceiling and
counted, very slowly, to ten. Her heart still raced, so
she did it again, even slower this time. Then, when
she could delay the moment no longer, she reached
for her phone.

44

DEE DROVE BACK TO work too fast. When she turned into the side road where she normally parked there was only one space left and it took her ages to reverse into it. She had to keep telling herself to calm down and focus. Eventually, she managed to manoeuvre the car in. She was still way too far from the kerb, but it would have to do. After the bombshell Scarlett Quilter had just dropped, there were more important things to think about than parallel parking.

She rushed to the office, desperate to talk to Lindsay about what it all meant. They'd have to put their differences aside in the face of such shocking news; surely they would. But when she got there, sweating and panting, the 'Back in Half an Hour' notice was hanging on the door. Dee let herself in, hoping Lindsay had put it there because she didn't want to be disturbed and not because she'd actually gone out. But Lindsay's coat was missing from the hook.

Dee ran downstairs to check, just in case. After convincing herself of what she already knew, that Lindsay was most definitely not in the building, she stood in the empty prep room and waited for her breath to return to a more normal pace. Then she pulled her phone out of her pocket and called Lindsay's numbers, mobile first, then her landline. The mobile went straight to voicemail and the landline rang out.

Dee thought of how Ollie had sized Lindsay up when he came to the shop that time they were dressing the window. And to think she'd been out on a date with him, that he knew where she lived. He might even have spent the night with her. Dee felt sick to the stomach. What if Lindsay was with him now?

If Scarlett was right and Ollie had something to do with Gina's disappearance, God only knows what might have happened – what might *still* happen. Scarlett had been so scared of her brother letting himself into the house she'd bolted the front door as soon as Dee had arrived. And the second Dee had gone, she'd done it again.

Dee rang the mobile again and left a message. 'Lindsay, you've got to ring me. It's about Gina. Gina and the Quilters. She knew them. Gina and Rebecca kept in touch. Scarlett thinks her brother might know something. She's ringing the police.'

She paced the floor of the prep room, expecting Lindsay to call back as soon as she heard the message. Except she didn't. Dee rang again, but once more it went straight to voicemail. She left another message. 'Lindsay, this is urgent. You have to ring me back. Please!'

She sent a WhatsApp too. If Lindsay was ignoring her calls and not listening to her voicemails, then at least she'd see the message notification flash up on her screen. The name Gina alone should make her get in touch.

But when fifteen minutes had passed with no response Dee really started to panic. Lindsay was never without her phone. It was like an extension of her body. She called Jake. Maybe he'd know where his sister was.

Jake answered straight away. It sounded like he was in a pub.

'Where are you?' she said.

'What?'

'Where are you?'

'What do you want?'

His voice was cold and hard. She'd never heard him speak to her like this before. Not Jake. They'd known each other for as long as she'd been friends with Lindsay, and that was for ever. He was like a brother to her. But, of course, he wasn't her brother. He was Lindsay's brother. And when Lindsay was upset or offended, he was upset and offended on her behalf. He looked out for his little sister, always had.

Only this time it was Dee who'd upset and offended her. Lindsay must have told him about their argument

281

and what Dee had said. Had she also told him what Dee had suspected? That she'd entertained the possibility that Jake and Gina had been having an affair before she went missing? No wonder he was being off with her.

'Something's happened, Jake. I need to speak to Lindsay. Is she with you?'

'What's that?' Why did Dee get the feeling he was *pretending* not to hear her just to be awkward? 'Sorry, you're cracking up.'

'Jake, listen to me. This is important. Is Lindsay with you?'

'No. She's at work. Where else would she be?' His voice sounded slurred. How many had he had?

'She isn't at work, she's—'

'Listen, Dee, it was me who flogged that stuff. Not Lindsay. I made her give them to me. I had a gambling debt and I didn't want Hayley to find out. It would have really stressed her out. Lindsay told me to spray-paint over the initials and the angel wings, but I was so desperate for the money I flogged it all right away to some bloke in the pub. How was I to know that ten years later he'd put the helmet on eBay?'

Dee sighed. That explained the look on Lindsay's face when Dee told her where they'd turned up. But there wasn't time for all this now. She had to speak to Lindsay.

'I don't care what happened. Not any more. I just need to speak to Lindsay.'

Jake sighed. 'I don't know where she is. Sorry. Got to go.'

'Jake, no, don't hang up.' But the line had already gone dead.

Dee swore and called him back, but now *his* phone went straight to voicemail. She was about to leave a message when she thought about checking Lindsay's Outlook diary. She pressed the keyboard to wake up her laptop and found herself looking at the Fond Farewells Facebook page and another damning review, this time from someone called Philip Smith.

It said: '*If you want your late relatives to be treated with respect and dignity, DO NOT USE THIS FUNERAL FIRM. They are a joke. The two women who run it are liars and thieves and only out for what they can get. What I've been offered as compensation so far is an insult. They need to pay what they owe, or I'll be taking this further.*'

Dee balled her fists in anger. There was only one person this review could be from, and that was Trevor Cooper. Her earlier fears had been justified. This was nothing short of blackmail. He'd obviously been lying to Lindsay when he said the matter was now closed. Lindsay would be furious, which meant there was every possibility she'd gone round there straight away to give him a piece of her mind, to tell him where to shove his stupid reviews and his demands for 'compensation'. It was exactly the sort of thing she would do.

Dee took the stairs two at a time. The situation was far from ideal, but at least she wasn't with Ollie Quilter.

45

Trevor Cooper's address was still etched in Dee's memory, like everything else from his visit. It was a house in Church Manorway, up near the West Thamesmead Business Park. She grabbed her keys, locked up the office and went back to her car. If Lindsay was stupid enough to sleep with him again, who knew where this might end? He'd have a hold over her, and over the business, for as long as he wanted. No way was that going to happen.

She turned the key in the ignition and tapped the street address into the satnav, waited until it loaded. She wasn't entirely sure what she was going to do about this, but one thing was certain: she needed to make sure Lindsay was safe. She might not be with Scarlett's brother, but she could still be in danger.

As she pulled away from the kerb it occurred to her that she really ought to try Jake again. He could easily summon up a few of his mates – Euan and the rest of the football team – to put the frighteners on

Trevor Cooper. They weren't the type to deliberately seek out trouble, but if one of their own needed help, they'd be up for it, she was sure they would. If they turned up on Trevor's doorstep en masse, they'd be pretty intimidating. And it was *Jake's* fault this was happening in the first place. If he hadn't persuaded Lindsay to let him take that biking gear . . .

But even if they managed to keep the sordid details from his mates, Jake himself would have to be told the full story. Dee already knew his thoughts on Lindsay's attitude to sex and men. It was the only source of tension between him and his sister. Lindsay wouldn't want him knowing what she'd done. And it would make things even worse between her and Lindsay if Dee involved Jake without talking to her first. Anyway, this was *their* business. Hers and Lindsay's. *Their* problem. And he'd sounded half pissed when she'd spoken to him on the phone.

Dee was driving too fast. She had to keep reminding herself to slow down and take care. Having an accident right now would be a nightmare. This whole bloody thing was a nightmare. All she wanted to do was find Lindsay, get her back to the office and tell her what Scarlett Quilter had told her. She didn't need all this aggravation with Trevor sodding Cooper.

Dee parked up as near to the house as possible. It was a shabby-looking end-of-terrace. Dingy grey nets at the window. A badly paved front garden stained with lichen and oil. She noticed Lindsay's car parked a little further along the street.

Dee ran towards it, hoping to God that Lindsay was still inside, but when she drew level with it she could see that it was empty. She started walking back towards the house, calling Lindsay's phone as she did so. She could hear it ringing behind her. Lindsay must have left it in the car. Why on earth had she done that?

Starting to panic now, Dee went up to the front door. She couldn't believe she was actually doing this, turning up at a stranger's house all on her own. A lone female. But she needed to know if Lindsay was inside.

There was no doorbell to press, and no proper knocker either. She tried to make a sound with the letterbox, but it was useless, so she rapped on the cheap glazed door with her knuckles. Nobody came.

She bent down and pushed the letterbox open to peer inside the hall. From somewhere upstairs came the sound of voices. A man's and a woman's. Dee held her breath and strained her ears. It was definitely Lindsay, and she sounded really stressed.

Dee's hackles rose. What the hell gave him the right to blackmail Lindsay like this? To make her do things she didn't want to do? What was Lindsay thinking, coming round here again? Did she really feel so guilty about what she'd done that she was prepared to compromise her own safety, to allow herself to be degraded like this, rather than discuss it with Dee and decide what to do together, like they'd always done?

Dee rapped on the door again, harder this time. But still no one came. How could they not hear her if she could hear them?

She went round the side. The gate was shut, but it wasn't locked. She slipped down the side passage, a narrow strip of dirty old concrete with weeds sprouting up through the cracks and crates of empty beer bottles stacked up against the wall. She peered in through the kitchen window. It was empty and dark. Dated kitchen fittings. A sink full of washing-up and loads of stuff out on the counter. Cereal boxes and saucepans. Empty takeaway cartons. The sort of kitchen students in a house-share might have. Or a slob, living on his own.

She tried the handle of the back door, expecting it to be locked, but it wasn't. She hesitated, but only for a second. Now that she was actually doing this, she was surprised to find that fear wasn't her primary emotion. It was anger. Rage.

She stepped inside. This was nothing whatsoever to do with Trevor Cooper's indignation on his late friend's behalf. Nor was it concern for Gabe's family and the fact that their last wishes had not been respected. Trevor Cooper's actions were now worse than the original crime. He was exploiting Lindsay, using her desperation to keep the good name of Fond

Farewells as a means to his disgusting, depraved ends. Well, he wasn't going to get away with it. Not if Dee had anything to do with it. She'd tell him, here and now, that if he wanted to tell Gabe's mum and girl-friend what had happened, then that was entirely his decision. But Lindsay and Dee would *not* be held to ransom like this. Didn't he know that blackmail was a crime too?

Lindsay had started to cry. Her sobs tore at Dee's heart. Dee should never have let something like this cause a rift between them. It was her fault for react-ing so badly in the first place, for not being more forgiving.

Fuelled by outrage at Trevor Cooper's motiva-tions, not to mention her pressing need to get Lindsay out of here and tell her that she might be romantic-ally involved with Gina's abductor and a possible triple murderer to boot, Dee took the stairs two at a time. She followed the sound of Lindsay's sobs. They were coming from behind a closed door at the end of the corridor. Dee swung it open, her whole body bristling with rage.

46

DEE FROZE IN PANIC. She'd just walked into her worst nightmare.

There were two men in the room. Trevor Cooper and a darker, leaner guy with acne scars on his cheeks and around his mouth. Lindsay was cowering on the floor, hair dishevelled, cheeks stained with tears. Trevor towered over her, handfuls of her hair in each of his big, meaty hands, the belt of his jeans hanging down, unbuckled.

He looked up in surprise, but the expression of shock on his face soon turned to something else. A wry, mocking sneer. He looked different from the last time she'd seen him. Meaner. Unhinged. Dee clocked the dilated pupils and knew straight away he was on something.

She shrank back, too petrified to run away. She couldn't anyway. How could she leave Lindsay to this? The other guy took a step towards her and held out his arms as if she were a long-lost friend. 'Come to join in the fun, have you?'

He was like an animal, moving in on his prey, smelling her fear.

Lindsay looked horrified. Desperate. 'Get out of here, Dee. Run!'

But no sooner had the words left her mouth than Trevor slapped her viciously round the face, the force knocking her sideways. Dee recoiled. It felt almost as if he'd hit her, too. She watched, appalled, as he hauled Lindsay back into a kneeling position.

'Shut up, bitch,' he said.

The other guy moved slowly towards Dee. He wasn't as well built as Trevor and he seemed more out of it, more unsteady on his feet. There were beads of sweat on his top lip and his eyes kept darting around as if he couldn't focus properly.

'Come on, darlin', give us a cuddle.'

He shoved her against the wall and put his arms out either side of her. He pushed his face nearer hers. His breath smelled rank.

Dee turned her face away in disgust. Over his shoulder, she saw Trevor Cooper's jeans slither to the floor. His hands were still in Lindsay's hair. Bile rose in Dee's throat. A lifetime of being careful and avoiding dangerous situations, and now here she was, in a house with two men high as kites on God knows what and with only one thing on their minds.

What's more, nobody knew where she and Lindsay were. Nobody.

She pushed her assailant away with a force that took them both by surprise. He staggered backwards, almost losing his balance. He was so out of it the push had completely disoriented him.

Dee's eyes strayed to what was happening to poor Lindsay. The sheer horror of it. 'Leave her alone!' she shouted. 'We don't care if you tell Gabe's mum what happened. We don't care what you say. You can't do this to us!'

Trevor Cooper just laughed. He started impersonating her. 'We don't care what you say. You can't do this to us.'

Then his voice changed back. He glowered at her. 'Forget Gabe's mum,' he said. 'We just want some fun now.' He winked at her. 'That's what you want too, innit, darlin'? That's why you're here. I don't normally go for dykey types, but I might make an exception in your case. When I've finished with your mate.'

Acne Guy had regained his balance. He lunged forward, taking hold of the neck of Dee's jumper and pulling her towards him. Dee could smell his sweat. She struggled to get out of his grasp, but he wouldn't let go.

'Try something like that again and you'll regret it,' he said, spittle flying out of his mouth.

Without thinking, Dee brought her right knee up

and jammed it with all her force into his crotch. He howled in pain and staggered back, his hands on his balls, folding in on himself.

Just then, the room was filled with an agonized roar like nothing Dee had ever heard. She turned to see Lindsay rocking back on her heels, blood trickling from the corners of her mouth, Trevor now doubled up on the floor, screaming in agony.

Acne Guy staggered towards Dee, fury distorting his face. Dee clenched her hand into a fist and, with all the strength she could muster, punched him, hard and fast, feeling her knuckles connect with his cheekbone and sending him reeling back.

'Dee, let's go. Now!' Lindsay yanked the door open and shoved Dee ahead of her. The two of them tore out of the room and down the stairs.

'Back door!' Dee yelled. At least she knew for certain that was unlocked and, as far as she could remember, she'd left the gate open.

The last thing they heard as they ran out of the kitchen was Trevor Cooper bellowing, 'Don't just stand there, call me a fucking ambulance, you twat!'

47

SCARLETT WAS ABOUT TO phone the police, when the ringing of the doorbell made her flinch. She dropped her phone on to the sofa and went to the window, peered out through the slats in the blind. It was Mickey. He was pacing up and down the path and biting his nails. When he caught sight of her looking out at him he rushed over to the window, saying something she couldn't hear through the double glazing. She'd never seen him look so frantic. So desperate. The only word she could make out was 'Ollie'. Had something happened to her brother?

She went out to the hall and opened the door, eyes wide with concern. 'What's the matter?'

'I think he's having some kind of breakdown,' Mickey said. He sounded hoarse. Breathless. 'I've never seen him like that. Not in all the years I've known him.'

'Where is he now?'

'I've just driven him home. Told him to get his

head down for a few hours. That's if he'll take any notice.' He put his hand in his pocket and drew out Ollie's car keys, handed them to her. 'I took these off him. He's in no fit state to drive. I don't think he's slept in days.'

Scarlett took the keys from him. All this just reinforced her decision to call the police.

'I feel so disloyal,' Mickey said, shaking his head. 'He's going to kill me when he finds out I've taken them.'

'I'll talk to him. Don't worry. You've done the right thing.'

'You think so?'

'I *know* so.'

He bent forward over his knees and exhaled noisily. 'I hope you're right.'

'You okay?'

'No. Feeling a bit Tom and Dick after all that rushing around. I'll be all right in a sec. I've got a drink in the van.'

'Wait here. I'll go and get you some water.' She hesitated. 'Sorry I can't ask you in, but . . . I'm expecting a call from a client any minute.'

'No worries. I've got to get back to the office anyway. Poor Shaz'll be wondering what the hell's going on.'

By the time she came back with a glass of water Mickey was sitting on the front step, his head between his knees.

'Here,' she said. 'Drink this.'

She watched as he gulped back the water. 'Gimme a minute and I'll be right as rain.'

'Take your time, it's okay. I'm going to call Dad, let him know what's going on.'

Mickey stood up and handed her the empty glass. He was sweating. 'I'm not so sure that's a good idea. I told you they've been at loggerheads lately. Fuck knows what's going on with those two.'

From upstairs came the sound of a loud bump, as if something had fallen on to the floor. Mickey's head jerked up.

Scarlett gasped. 'What the hell was that? It sounds like someone's . . .' It was only then that she noticed that the door to Rebecca's apartment was ajar.

'What the . . .'

Mickey's face changed then. He looked . . . ashamed all of a sudden. Apologetic.

She stared at him in disbelief. It felt like all the air had left her body in one go.

'Sorry, Scar,' he said. 'I couldn't say no, could I? He's my boss, and it's his gaff now, after all.'

Scarlett's legs began to shake. This whole thing had been a set-up. Mickey had deliberately distracted her so that Ollie could get in while she wasn't looking. He must have known she wouldn't let him go back up there on his own. Must have realized she suspected him of something, so he'd resorted to a cheap trick, and she'd been stupid enough to fall for it.

She went to shut the door on Mickey, to stop him coming in, but he was too strong for her. He pushed it back open and stepped into the hall. He looked wretched.

'Like I said, Scar. Ollie's my boss and my best mate. He just wants time to find something up there. I didn't want to trick you, I promise. *Please* don't be difficult.'

Her mind spun. She turned to go back into her flat and lock herself in. She would phone the police right now, before this went any further. Even if she'd made a stupid mistake and got completely the wrong end of the stick, she couldn't put up with being manipulated like this in her own home, and by her own brother. But before she knew what was happening Mickey had got past her and was blocking her way.

'Sorry, Scar. I really am. But I can't leave you down here on your own. Not until he's finished. I promised.'

She stared at him in disbelief.

He couldn't meet her eyes. 'Just until he's found what he's looking for.'

'What *is* he looking for?'

He shook his head.

'What's he done, Mickey? You have to tell me.'

Mickey closed his eyes. 'It's just business, Scar.'

Scarlett glared at him. 'What kind of business involves rifling through your dead aunt's possessions?'

'You'll have to ask him that, not me.'

It was no use. Mickey was too loyal a friend. He and Ollie went back a long way. He knew her brother better than anyone. Better than she did.

'I *will* ask him,' she said. 'I'll ask him right now.' She turned to go upstairs.

'I don't think you should do that.' Mickey put his arm out and touched her wrist.

She shrugged him off. 'I don't *care* what you think. You've caused enough problems as it is.'

He inhaled deeply. 'Okay,' he said. 'But I'm coming up there with you. He's in a right state. I wasn't lying about that. We don't want to aggravate him.'

Scarlett pursed her lips. 'I think I know how to handle my own brother, thank you very much.'

She turned and climbed the stairs to Rebecca's apartment, Mickey so close behind her she could feel his breath on her neck.

They'd reached the small landing at the top now. Scarlett's heart was beating so fast she thought it might explode. Why hadn't she phoned the police when Dee was still here? Why had she opened the door to Mickey in the first place? She should have kept it bolted fast until the police arrived.

Ollie was in Rebecca's sitting room just off to the left, turfing things out of the drawers in the bureau like a man possessed. He was looking for her diaries. He must be. What else could it be?

'Ollie?' she said.

He froze at the sound of her voice. He'd been so

intent on his search he hadn't even heard them come up. When he turned around, she saw that his eyes seemed to have sunk into his head. He looked shattered. Mentally and physically exhausted.

'For God's sake, Ollie! You've got to tell me what's going on. Why are you doing this? You can talk to me. You *know* you can.'

Ollie stared at her in fury. 'You've been up here too. All that shit you gave me about the sodding probate, and you've been up here on your own. I know you have. Rebecca would never have left those box files open.'

Scarlett stared at him. Had she really not closed them? She felt sure that she had.

'I haven't,' she said. 'I was going to come up, but I changed my mind.'

'Liar!'

She winced at the venom in his voice. 'Ollie, what's going on? Why are you acting like this? You're freaking me out.'

Mickey took a step towards him. 'Yeah, mate, you're freaking both of us out. Let's just calm down, yeah?'

Ollie shoved him in the chest. 'What did you bring her up for? I told you to keep her downstairs.'

Scarlett was incensed. 'You're talking about me as if I'm a *thing*!' she shouted. 'You don't get to decide where I go and what I do!'

But Ollie looked past her, as if she weren't there.

His focus was solely on Mickey. 'Why can't you ever do what we agree?'

'Careful,' Mickey growled.

Scarlett slid her eyes to the right. Blood pounded in her ears. It wasn't just Mickey's voice that was different. His whole demeanour was, too. Gone was the concern she'd seen in his eyes earlier. Gone was the awkward, apologetic expression. The 'he's my boss, what can I do?' act. Too late, she saw that he'd sensed her watching him. He swivelled his head to the left and looked straight at her.

'*You* need to be careful, too.'

48

DEE POINTED HER KEYS at the car as they ran towards
it. Two minutes later, they were inside. Dee put the
central locking on and tried to put her key in the
ignition, but her hands were shaking so much she
couldn't feed it into the slot.

Lindsay kept looking over her shoulder. 'Get away
from here, Dee!' she said. 'Drive!'

'I'm trying, I can't—' At last, the key went in and
the car started. But Dee seemed to have forgotten
how to drive. She stalled as she pulled away from the
kerb. 'Fuck!'

'Take a deep breath and start it again,' Lindsay
said. 'You've got this.'

This time, her muscle memory kicked in and she
managed to drive off. She headed back in the direction of Woolwich and Lindsay's house on autopilot,
not daring to think about what had just happened.
Not yet.

Lindsay began to shiver in the passenger seat. She was in shock. They both were. Somehow or other, Dee kept driving. It must have been the adrenaline. Fight or flight. They'd done both today.

'There's a blanket in the back seat,' she said. 'Can you reach it?'

Lindsay twisted round and threaded her arm through the space between the two front seats.

'No, it's too far away.'

'Do you want me to pull over and get it for you?'

'No! Just drive. Get me home quick.'

Lindsay shrunk down in the seat. She was trying to fasten her seatbelt and failing. The car began to beep its security warning. 'My car's still there,' she said. 'I left my bag on the front seat. My phone and everything.'

'Don't worry about any of that,' Dee said. 'It's not important. What the hell happened? Is that how it was before? The first time?'

'No, of *course* not. He was nice the first time.' Lindsay started to cry. 'I was so fucking stupid, flirting with him in the first place. But once I'd explained what a tough year it had been back then, and how sorry I was for stealing Gabe's things, I broke down and started crying. He comforted me, told me he hadn't been going to say anything anyway, that he'd just wanted us to know he knew, and, well, one thing led to another. Yes, I know what you're thinking,

Dee. It was crazy, but you know what, I actually *did* fancy him. He was . . . he was really gentle.'

Lindsay's teeth started to chatter. 'I don't know what happened to change things. Maybe he bragged about it to his mate. They obviously decided they were on to a good thing, that I was so desperate for them to keep quiet about what I'd done that they could have some fun with me whenever they fancied it.'

She hung her head in her hands. 'When I saw that review I tried to phone him, but he wouldn't pick up. I left messages and he never replied. I was just going to talk to him at the door, tell him enough was enough and that I'd call the police if he kept hassling us. No way was I going to go inside. That's what I was doing, telling him I'd speak to the family myself. Offer to give them the money back and make a donation to a charity or something. But then the other guy appeared from nowhere and they pulled me inside. They were off their heads. I was so frightened. Trevor had a knife.'

Dee gasped. Thank God she hadn't seen that, or she might not have had the courage to fight back.

Lindsay cried like a child then. Great rasping, juddering sobs. 'Oh God, Dee, when I saw *you* there too, I thought . . .'

'They won't get away with this,' Dee said. 'We have to report them.'

They'd reached Lindsay's road now. Dee found a space and, when they were parked up, she slumped over the steering wheel in relief. 'We've got to get you inside and warmed up,' she said. She swivelled round and got the travel blanket from the back seat, pulled the Velcro straps off and wrapped it around Lindsay.

'Shit!' she said. 'You haven't got your keys, have you? They'll be in your bag.'

'It's okay. There's a spare buried in the pot of lavender. Just under the top layer of compost.'

As soon as Dee had fished the key out of the pot and shepherded Lindsay inside, Lindsay shot upstairs like a flash, and into the bathroom. Dee followed her up and found her washing her face, rubbing it so hard with a soapy flannel it was a wonder she wasn't taking the skin off.

'I don't think you should be doing that, Lins. We need to report this, don't we? They'll need to examine you.'

Lindsay was now brushing her teeth like a demon, scraping her tongue clean with the bristles, swilling her mouth out with water and spitting pink foam into the sink. Dee wondered how much of the blood was from the savage brushing she was doing, and how much was from what she'd just bitten into. She shuddered at the thought.

Lindsay was throwing up in the toilet now. Heaving into the bowl. Dee held her hair back and stroked her sweaty back until she stopped. Lindsay clambered to her feet and started the washing and scrubbing all over again. Dee ran her a bath and went downstairs to make them both some tea.

There'd be no traces of that bastard on her now.

They were sitting, the two of them, on Lindsay's sofa, both nursing huge mugs of hot, sweet tea. Lindsay was in her pyjamas and bed socks. The skin around her mouth looked red and sore. Her eyes were pink and watery.

'I don't want to report it to the police,' she said.

Dee stared at her. 'But they can't get away with it. They *can't*.'

Lindsay sighed. 'Think about it, Dee. I'll be questioned. They'll do a bit of research into my sexual history, and that'll be that.'

'But that's got nothing to do with—'

'I know that, and you know that, but that's what happens. I don't want to go through all that. It could drag on for months on end, years maybe. I want to forget it. I want to wipe it clean away and pretend it never happened.'

Dee frowned. 'I'm not sure you'll be able to do that.'

'I will. And anyway, if we report it, all the stuff about that fucking crash helmet will come out, won't it? I don't want to put us through all that. And anyway, I doubt T. J. Cooper's going to be asking anyone to give him a blow job any time soon.'

Dee caught her eye and, in spite of everything they'd just been through, the sheer horror of it, they found themselves laughing. Hysterical laughter that consumed them utterly for minutes on end, then made them both start weeping.

When they'd recovered, Lindsay touched Dee's arm. 'You were brilliant back there, Dee. I couldn't believe it when I saw you turn on that other guy. It was like a switch going on in my head and I knew what I had to do. We *did* it, Dee. But if you hadn't done what you did first, I'm not sure I'd have had the courage. It's so hard to fight back when you're paralysed with fear.'

Her breath caught in her throat. Tears were running down her face.

'You were so brave, Dee. So bloody brave. And you're right. The way I've been carrying on, all the risks I've taken, it's a bloody miracle something like that's never happened to me before. You were right to say those things to me, because they're true. You can't possibly think any worse of me than I think of myself.'

'Jake told me, by the way,' Dee said. 'He told me he pressured you into letting him sell that stuff. Why didn't you tell me, Lins? I know he's your brother and you love him, but why did you take all the blame?'

Lindsay sniffed back her tears. 'Because it doesn't make it any better. I shouldn't have *let* him pressure me, should I?' I don't know what's wrong with me, Dee. Why am I so fucked up?'

Dee squeezed Lindsay's hand and sighed. 'We're both fucked up, but in different ways. It's like Gina went missing and part of us did too. We had to carry on with our lives with this huge Gina-shaped hole in it.'

Dee sat bolt upright. She felt as if someone had pulled out a plug and all her blood was draining away.

'Dee? What's the matter? You look—'

'I can't believe I forgot!' Dee clamped her hand over her mouth. It seemed so long ago that she'd been with Scarlett Quilter this morning and seen Gina's novel or, rather, Rebecca's novel, and listened to Scarlett unburden her suspicions about her brother. Had that really only been a couple of hours ago? And to think how desperate she'd been to warn Lindsay about the danger she could be in.

She told her now, the words spilling out in her haste to bring Lindsay up to speed.

Lindsay's face fell. 'You mean, he might be the one who took Gina?' She wrapped her arms around her body and swayed backwards and forwards. 'I can't believe I went out with him. I actually went out with him. Jesus Christ, Dee! How sure is she about this?'

'She isn't sure about anything, but you should have seen her, Lins. She was in a real state. It's possible he might have something to do with what happened to Rebecca and Clive too.' Lindsay gasped. 'She was

307

going to call the police as soon as I'd left. That's why I was looking for you. To let you know.' Dee clasped her hands together under her chin. 'It might still be nothing, of course. It could turn out to be another false lead.'

'It won't be nothing,' Lindsay said. Her voice was quiet and solemn. 'I don't mean to get all Mystic Meg on you, but I can feel it in my bones. We're getting closer to finding out what happened to Gina.'

49

SCARLETT'S SKIN PRICKLED WITH fear. Was she hearing right? Was Mickey North threatening her?

'Leave her out of it,' Ollie said. 'You lay one finger on my sister and I'll kill you.'

Mickey laughed. 'Bit late for that, mate.'

Ollie looked at her, aghast, but all she could do was shake her head. 'What are you looking for, Ollie?' she said, her voice little more than a whisper.

'Her diaries. The ones she promised to get rid of.'

Scarlett's mouth went dry. 'Why did she promise you that? What's in them that you're so scared of?'

Ollie yanked the drawer clean out of the chest and threw it on the floor in frustration. Scarlett tried again. 'What makes you think she *didn't* get rid of them?'

'Because she kept that fucking card, didn't she? The one you found in the summer house. And she kept her stupid novel. What's the betting she kept her diaries too? I should never have trusted her.'

His eyes had a haunted expression. Scarlett no longer knew what to think or feel. How was it possible to have landed here, in this terrible moment? A woman like her, who'd never done a bad thing in her life. How was it possible to feel afraid of her own brother? Her own flesh and blood.

Her heart kept banging away. An image of Rebecca flashed into her mind. She was carrying one of her endless cups of tea into this very sitting room, her reading glasses perched low on her nose, her long grey hair fastened at the nape of her neck. Her beloved aunt. What in God's name had Ollie trusted her *with*?

The fear took hold of her then. Her eyes drifted towards Rebecca's bedroom door. She felt disoriented and weak, as though her bones weren't strong enough to keep her standing, but somehow she mustered the energy to stay on her feet. She couldn't collapse now. All she could think of was what had happened behind that door, barely seven weeks ago. Surely her aunt wouldn't have protected Ollie if he'd done something truly awful, if it was anything at all to do with Gina Caplin? But what else could be making him act like this?

Mickey, who'd been standing right behind Scarlett on the landing at the top of the stairs, squeezed past her and took a step towards the sitting room. His fists were clenched at his side. 'Too right you shouldn't have trusted her! If you hadn't blabbed to her in the first place, none of this would have happened.'

Scarlett wanted to go into the sitting room with Ollie, to try to calm him down, but Mickey was now standing between them, blocking the doorway.

'None of what?' she cried, dreading the answer but needing it all the same. 'What *did* happen?'

Mickey glanced at her over his shoulder. 'Trust me, some things, you're better off *not* knowing.'

Scarlett swallowed nervously. Whatever Ollie had done, Mickey knew all about it. He was in on it too.

'What's so important about those diaries? What are you frightened of? Please, Ollie, tell me. Did you two have something to do with what happened up here?' She clamped her hands either side of her nose and backed away. 'Tell me you didn't kill Rebecca! Oh, Ollie, tell me you didn't!'

Mickey rounded on her so fast she stumbled back near the top of the stairs and almost lost her balance and fell. It was Mickey who caught her. He held her in his arms, his face just inches from her own. She could feel his breath on her neck, see the blood vessels in the whites of his eyes.

'What the hell are you talking about, you stupid cow! Of *course* we didn't! *He* murdered her, that loser Hamlyn. You *know* he did.'

Ollie was at her side in an instant, pulling her out of Mickey's grasp. In his haste to get her away from him he pulled her too hard and she slipped sideways on to the floor, crashing down on her hip bone, but all his attention was now on Mickey. 'What the fuck are you doing? Let her go!'

'What the fuck are *you* doing?' Mickey yelled. 'You're losing it, mate. You'd better get a grip before it's too late.'

Scarlett struggled to her feet. 'Too late for what? Is this something to do with what happened to Gina Caplin?' She was sobbing now. 'Oh God, Ollie, Mickey, tell me you didn't . . .' She saw the look that passed between them – a look of despair – and she knew she was right.

Ollie sank to his knees. He hooked his forearms over his head and clamped the back of his scalp as if he were bracing himself against a blow. All he kept saying was 'no, no, no.'

Scarlett tried to fight the wave of nausea rising up inside her. She looked at him in horror. 'You knew her, didn't you? You liked her.'

Mickey advanced on her again, his face distorted in anger. He took hold of the neck of her T-shirt and pushed her until she was standing at the very top of the stairs, her back towards them. 'You're not helping, Scar. You don't know what you're talking about. We'll tell you what you need to know and no more. You got me?'

Scarlett heard the fear in his voice. The desperation. Still holding her by her T-shirt, he pushed her again so she was dangling over the stairs. Her toes were barely touching the floor. He only had to let go of her and she'd tumble backwards. 'You want to be careful what you say.'

Ollie uncurled himself then, slowly and deliberately, until he was on his haunches. Scarlett flashed a warning to him with her eyes. She was in too precarious a position. If he made any sudden moves, Mickey might let her go. Surely he could see that?

She forced herself to speak. 'Whatever you've done, we can work it out. The three of us.' She was looking directly at Mickey now, imploring him with her eyes. He was the one in charge here. She had no doubt about that. Maybe he'd *always* been in charge and she'd been too blind to notice.

A bead of cold sweat trickled from her left armpit down the side of her body. Fear and revulsion were all she felt now, but somewhere in the back of her brain a small, quiet voice was telling her what to do, giving her directions.

'We're family, aren't we?' She glanced at Ollie, willing him to understand. 'You too, Mickey.' The words almost stuck in her throat. 'Family comes first, right?'

Mickey narrowed his eyes, then hoisted her back on to her feet. He flipped her round so that now she was facing the stairs. She edged backwards down the corridor leading to the kitchen and the back of the house, her breath loud and ragged.

He nodded grimly. 'Good girl. You've got more

balls than your brother. We'll sort this out.' He looked at Ollie. 'Like we've sorted everything else out. No need to panic.'

In an instant, Scarlett saw what was going to happen. Ollie's fist flew through the air towards Mickey's face. Mickey, quick as a flash, intercepted it with his hand and the two of them teetered on the top of the stairs.

'Stop it, for Christ's sake! Stop it!' she cried, but it was too late. Mickey lost his footing and tumbled backwards down the stairs.

She rushed forward, hardly daring to look. Ollie held her back. Mickey lay in a crumpled heap. He'd crashed through the half-open door to Rebecca's apartment and landed on the floor. For a few seconds there was no sound at all. Then he started writhing and groaning in agony.

Ollie looked at her in horror. His skin had turned a horrible shade of grey and he was shaking uncontrollably.

Scarlett wrenched herself free. 'We have to call an ambulance.' She waited a beat. 'And we have to call the police. You know that, don't you?'

Ollie wouldn't stop shaking. She put her hands on his face, looked directly into his eyes. 'What happened, Ollie? You can't keep this to yourself any more. You need to tell me what happened.'

She moved her hands down to his shoulders, gave him a little shake, but still he wouldn't speak to her.

Mickey's groans were getting quieter and quieter, then they stopped altogether. Scarlett peered down at him. He was no longer moving. She was about to go and check he was still breathing when Ollie put his arm out to stop her.

'He killed her,' he said.

They both started at the sound of the doorbell and turned, wordlessly, to face the front door. Two dark shapes filled the stained-glass panel.

Scarlett watched her brother's face go slack.

50

IT HAD BEEN DEE Boswell who'd called the police, Scarlett later discovered. She obviously hadn't trusted Scarlett to keep her word. Mickey was now in hospital and Ollie had been taken in for questioning. As soon as Scarlett had finished giving her statement to the police, she'd collapsed from the stress. Now, coming round on her sofa after a sleep, she was unnerved to find the police gone and her dad sitting in the chair opposite, observing her.

She struggled to sit up. 'What are you doing here?'

'The police contacted me. They were worried about leaving you alone. What's going on, Scarlett? What have you told them?'

'I want you to leave,' she said. 'Now.'

His eyebrows knitted together in a concerned frown. 'Leave? Why? They said they were investigating an unsolved crime. They're coming back with ground-penetrating radar equipment. What the hell is going on, Scarlett?'

'You told me the last time you saw Ollie was when we were all here, talking about the funeral, but it wasn't. You were *lying*. Mickey said you turned up at the yard, that you and Ollie have been at logger-heads.'

Her dad gave a long sigh. 'One of my business contacts wanted Ollie's firm to do some renovation work for him. Ollie asked him if he'd consider paying for it in cash and he was quite rightly put out. As was I when he told me. I was so embarrassed. My own son, whom I'd recommended. So I went round there and had it out with him. Told him what I thought of his shady deal-ings, how he'd better smarten up his act before he got himself into very deep water. But, but what's that got to do with all this? I don't understand.'

'There's something else going on too. What do you know about Gina Caplin that you aren't telling me? Is she buried under the summer house?'

Her dad's face blanched. 'Dear God! Is that what you think? Is that why they're ... But who ... how ...?'

She watched his face crease in confusion and knew he wasn't faking it. He didn't have a clue what she was talking about.

'I thought you might know something ... that you might be ...' Her voice faltered. She couldn't finish the sentence. She didn't need to. Her dad knew exactly what she'd meant and he was stunned. Dismayed.

'Dear God! How could you think for one second

that I . . .' He brought his hands to his mouth and pressed his fingers against his lips. He shook his head from side to side.

'Because you were so worked up about the possibility of me moving the summer house. Both of you.'

'Only because I was worried you were taking on too much, too soon. I might not be the most tactful man in the world, and I know I come across as overbearing sometimes – Claire's always telling me that – but it's only because I care about you so much. I thought you understood that.'

Scarlett began to cry. 'Oh Dad, Mickey killed her and Ollie knew about it. He admitted it.'

The blood drained from her dad's face. He closed his eyes.

Scarlett stood in front of the window, watching as her father left the house to buy some provisions, braving the scrutiny of the neighbours and those who'd come to gawp. Since their conversation two days ago about Ollie's attempts at tax evasion, a suspicious-looking shadow had been detected under the summer house, and within hours the whole thing had been dismantled and a forensics tent erected.

Then came the breaking up of the concrete, with all the noise and dust that came with it. Every time Scarlett summoned the energy, and courage, to peep out between the slats of the wooden shutters, the level of concrete and soil inside the skip on the road had risen. A small crowd of onlookers had gathered on the opposite side of the street. Some of them were holding their phones in the air.

The whole circus had started up again. The tape across the front path. A police officer stationed outside. The gawpers on the bus. It was on the news and in the papers. She was a prisoner in her own home. Except, this time, it was ten times worse. People in the neighbouring flats and houses were watching the back of the house too. She felt like an animal in a zoo. If it hadn't been for her dad looking after her, she wouldn't have been able to cope.

The bedroom bloodbath story now had a terrifying new development. Ollie's last words kept playing on a loop in her mind: 'He killed her.' It didn't matter that Scarlett had known nothing about it; as far as the media and everyone else were concerned, she'd be tarred with the same brush. Her name would forever be associated with this horror. This death house. Whatever happened now, she would just have to live with the consequences. They all would.

She moved away from the window and resumed her position on the sofa. The TV had been on continually in an attempt to block out first the relentless whine of the angle grinder, then the trundling of wheelbarrows up and down the side passage. Not that she'd been watching it. Occasionally, something would hold her attention for a couple of minutes, but the reality of what was happening outside soon seeped back into her mind and obliterated all other thoughts.

And yet, in spite of the noise, she had slept, in short, fitful bursts, her dreams vivid and intense. After the nerve-wracking events of the past few days and the sleepless nights she'd endured as a result, she ached all over. But how she felt physically was nothing compared to the darkness in her mind. That terrible sensation of dread.

She heaved herself into a sitting position and made the short trip to the kitchen for another cup of tea and something to eat. She had no appetite but was forcing herself to graze at regular intervals to keep her strength up. Compelled to check on progress, she stood at the back door while she waited for the kettle to boil and her dad to return.

Scarlett's eyes were now fixed on the end of the garden, which was crawling with police officers and specialist forensic scientists. It all seemed so surreal, like a scene from a movie or a crime drama. Except this was no fiction.

Someone came out of the massive blue-and-white tent and Scarlett caught sight of a square trench where the summer house had once stood. She saw the top halves of white-suited figures bobbing up and down. It looked like an archaeological dig, which was, of course, exactly what it now was.

The ringing of her phone made her jump. When

she saw the name Ollie on the screen, she answered it straight away.

'Where are you? Are you still in custody?'

'No, they've let me go. Pending further investigation.' His voice was hoarse. 'They're watching me.'

'What are they going to find, Ollie?' she said, her voice little more than a whisper.

'You have no idea what you've done,' he said.

'Oh God, Ollie. Why did you . . .'

Her voice trailed off at the sound of a shout from outside. She moved back to the door, the phone slipping from her hand and dropping to the floor. An eerie stillness had descended on the scene. The figures that had been bent over in the trench now straightened up and made eye contact with those standing on the perimeter peering down. Scarlett went cold all over. They had found something.

Ollie's voice shouted at her from the floor. The handful of officers milling around outside the tent now went in, their bodies blocking the entrance and Scarlett's view. Now one of them was coming out again, phone clamped to his ear. Scarlett recognized him as DI Guyver, the one who'd taken her statement. He looked up at the house and seemed to be composing himself. Then he started walking purposefully towards it.

Scarlett's knees buckled. She hauled herself upright by grabbing the edges of the countertop, her heart pounding so fast that for a moment she thought she might be having a heart attack.

'Scar? Answer me. What's happening?'

She picked up her phone from the floor and ended the call just as Guyver's face appeared at the kitchen door. She opened it and stared at him expectantly, waiting for him to say the words.

He nodded at her grimly. 'We've found a body.'

51

SCARLETT HELD HER BREATH. The detective inspector was still talking to her, but she no longer heard what he was saying. All she could see was his mouth opening and closing. Then she was aware of him stepping forward, catching her by the elbows.

DI Guyver led her gently to the sofa. Her hearing returned in a loud rush.

'There'll be a Home Office post-mortem, of course. Identification could take some time.'

Scarlett looked at him blankly. Surely the identification was just a formality.

'He'll be taken away soon, but our guys'll be here for a while yet. I'm afraid the garden's going to be out of bounds for a day or so.'

'Sorry, what did you say?'

'I said your garden's going to be out of—'

'No, no, before that. Something about being taken away. I didn't catch what you said.'

'He'll be taken away soon, I said. To the mortuary.'

Scarlett stared at him in shock. 'He?'

DI Guyver narrowed his eyes.

Just then, her dad returned with supplies from the corner shop. The two men acknowledged each other, then Guyver continued speaking. 'The body we've discovered is that of a male. Possibly in his forties or fifties, although of course that hasn't been confirmed yet.' The plastic bag her dad had been holding slipped out of his hands and on to the floor.

DI Guyver paused briefly. 'I'm not sure what arrangements you've made for your aunt's funeral, but I'm afraid this will delay the release of her body.'

He peered at them from under his eyebrows. 'The investigation into Rebecca's and Clive's deaths will need to be reopened in the light of this latest ... discovery, and in light of what you've already told us.'

Scarlett blinked at him in confusion. 'So, it's not Gina Caplin?'

'No, Ms Quilter. It isn't Gina.'

A female police officer appeared at the back door. DI Guyver beckoned her in. 'Ms Quilter – Scarlett – this is DI Mel Gartside, one of our investigating officers. She'll be your family liaison officer, so if you have any queries about anything, she'll be your main contact, okay?'

'But ... but what about the connection to Gina? What about ...'

'We'll obviously need to talk to you all again. Mel will go through the next stages with you.'

When Guyver had left and Mel Gartside was making them some tea and talking to her dad, Scarlett locked herself in the bathroom. With shaky fingers, she pulled out her phone and called Ollie back, keeping her voice low.

'Who is it?' she said. 'Who is the man buried in the garden?'

She heard the rush of air expelled from Ollie's lungs. 'Andrew Pulteney,' he said at last.

Her brain struggled to make sense of what he'd said. 'Oh my God, the guy Rebecca was going to marry? The one who was cheating on her? But how . . . why?'

'It wasn't meant to happen, I swear it. I just wanted to give him a piece of my mind, for humiliating Rebecca. But he was such an arrogant bastard. Came out with a load of abuse about her. Lies, all of it. And he started mouthing off about me too. Telling me I was a loser. That was the trigger. I swung for him. Hard.'

Scarlett heard his ragged breath on the other end of the line. 'I think I knew then that he wasn't going to get up, but Mickey was there too and he kept on kicking him in the head. I had to pull him off. In the end, we didn't know . . .'

There was a long silence, then: 'We didn't know which of us had killed him. All we knew was that he was dead. You should have seen the state of him, Scar. We'd have gone down for it.'

Scarlett heard him taking one deep breath after another, trying to calm himself down. 'The business was just taking off. Thanks to Mickey, I was making some real money. That's what Dad's never understood. I don't have a head for business. Never have done.' He gave a loud sniff. 'The answer was staring us in the face. The garden was a building site. The foundations for the summer house had already been dug out.'

'So you buried him.'

'Yeah. Then we got rid of all his stuff. All except his phone. We started posting stuff on his Facebook page, made it look like he was travelling.'

Scarlett shook her head in disbelief. And she and Rebecca had believed it. It's what he'd always talked about doing. Taking early retirement. Buying himself a yacht.

'But what about his family? Didn't you think they had a right to know what happened? Didn't anyone miss him?'

'He didn't have any family to speak of, only his mum, and she was in a nursing home. He was a loner. A chancer. You must remember what he was like. You met him, didn't you?'

There was a knock on the door. 'You okay in there, Scarlett?' It was Mel Gartside.

'Yeah, I'm okay. I'll be out in a sec.' She flushed the chain. 'So where does Gina fit into this?' She was

326

whispering now. 'How come Rebecca kept quiet about knowing her? I don't understand.'

Ollie gave the longest, deepest sigh. 'This was never about Gina.'

'But ... but Rebecca *did* know Gina. You knew her too. You must have done.'

'Yeah, I met her a couple of times. Asked her out once, but she had someone else on the go.'

'So why didn't Rebecca ever *tell* me she knew her? Why didn't *you*?'

There was a long pause.

'I was with Rebecca the day the news broke about Gina going missing. She wanted to call the police. She'd only seen her recently. But I knew the police would question me. I'd have been a suspect. I'd even given her a lift to some bloke's place in Welling a couple of times. Her DNA would have been in my car.'

The fog in Scarlett's head began to clear. 'Oh, Ollie, that *bloke* could have been the one who abducted her!'

'Yeah, he could have been. But don't you see, the garden was a building site. When you've just buried a body, you don't want the police sniffing round after some missing girl, do you?'

'So how did you stop Rebecca going to the police?'

Ollie was sobbing now. His words came out in fits and starts. 'I told her what we'd done. I told her everything.'

Scarlett gasped. Once again, she thought of how she and Rebecca had stalked Pulteney on Facebook. But Rebecca had known he was dead the whole time!

'She was horrified,' Ollie said. 'Disgusted. But I think she also felt partly responsible because it was *her* we'd been defending. She wasn't stupid. She knew how things might pan out for me if she went to the police. So she agreed to keep quiet.'

'You mean you *made* her keep quiet. Like Mickey tried to make me.'

'No, that's not what happened. I promise you. We discussed it, the three of us, and that's what we decided.'

Once again, Scarlett heard her aunt's voice saying 'Family comes first' and shuddered at the memory, now tainted for ever by Ollie's revelation.

Mel Gartside was knocking on the door again. 'Scarlett, are you sure you're all right in there?'

Scarlett ran the taps. 'Just coming.'

Ollie was still talking in her ear. 'She promised to get rid of anything related to Gina. Any messages. Meetings she'd recorded in her diaries. But when you told me you'd found her old novel and that card in the summer house I realized she couldn't have got rid of *everything*.'

Scarlett closed her eyes. Rebecca probably hadn't even realized the card had been caught up in the manuscript.

Ollie was still talking. 'Then she started losing it. Kept talking about the "secret" she wasn't allowed to tell, kept staring at the summer house with that strange look in her eyes and going on about "contaminated soil" and "this girl, that girl". All that stuff about Clive cheating on her ... he *wasn't*. She was getting confused. She was remembering what happened with Pulteney. Don't you see? It was only a matter of time before she blurted something out.'

Scarlett's blood ran cold. Surely he didn't mean what she thought he meant. And yet, it all made sense now. When Mickey had fallen down the stairs and Ollie had stopped her from going down to see if he was all right by saying the words 'he killed her', she'd assumed he'd been talking about Gina Caplin. But what he'd really meant was, he killed *Rebecca*! And if Mickey had killed Rebecca, then he must have killed Clive too. And Ollie was part of it. Ollie had let it happen!

She drew back the bolt on the bathroom door and walked out into the hallway like a zombie. Mel Gartside was standing right outside. Her dad was behind her, an anxious look on his face. Scarlett turned the loudspeaker on and Ollie's voice filled the hallway.

'She was becoming a liability. She had to be stopped, don't you see?'

Her dad's eyes flared in shock and he gesticulated frantically behind Mel's back for Scarlett to cut the call. She ignored him and ducked away as he stepped forward to grab the phone out of her hand, noticing as she did so that Mel had taken out her phone and pressed record.

As Ollie continued to speak, her dad went very still. He looked as if he'd aged ten years. 'She had to be stopped or the whole fucking thing would come out.'

'So you made sure I was out of the way at that party, and then you let Mickey kill her. You let him beat Rebecca to death and make it look like it was Clive!'

'No! It was going to be a gentle death. A *kind* death. We were going to give her an overdose of pills, make it look like she'd forgotten how many she'd taken. I managed to convince myself it was a sort of mercy killing.'

'Don't you *dare* try to justify it! Don't you fucking dare! Just because she had dementia didn't give you the right to—'

'I *know* it didn't. But we were desperate, don't you see? She'd forgotten it was a secret. They would have found Pulteney's body.'

'They *have* found Pulteney's body!'

'Yeah, they have *now*.'

He didn't need to say *thanks to you*, but Scarlett heard it anyway. 'So what went wrong with your *mercy killing*?' She spat the words out.

'I was in the kitchen getting the pills ready. Mickey

330

was in the bedroom talking to her. All of a sudden, I heard her shouting. Like I said, she was getting her stories all mixed up, accusing him of leading me astray, of murdering some girl and burying her under the summer house. Mickey says she started attacking him with the baseball bat, so he grabbed it and hit her across the head. When I got in there . . .' His voice broke. 'I saw the bloody footprints first. He was wearing Clive's slippers. Then I saw—'

Her dad, who'd started pacing up and down the hallway, stopped and looked directly at Mel Gartside as he spoke. 'But it was Mickey who actually killed her, not you. Is that what you're saying?'

Scarlett knew he was clutching at straws, trying to stop his son from incriminating himself still further. But it was useless. Nothing could help him now. And by Ollie's silence on the other end of the line, it was obvious he knew that too.

'So who killed Clive?' Scarlett said.

When Ollie spoke again it was hard to make out exactly what he was saying, he was crying so hard, but they got the gist all right. She watched the hope in her father's eyes fade as the full story emerged. Clive had been out drinking that night. When he came home pissed, Ollie had manoeuvred him into the bathroom and slit his wrists. Mickey had told him what to do, how to make sure he positioned himself behind Clive and sliced from the right angle.

'Mickey said it worked out better this way. Like a

crime of passion, he said. He knows things, Scar. Things about the business. I'm up to my ears in shit.'

'You are now, son,' their dad said, looking at Mel Gartside, who was still holding up her phone to record it all. 'You are now.'

52

DEE SAT AT THE table in her dad's kitchen and stared at the headline in the paper: 'GINA CAPLIN: POLICE EXCAVATE GARDEN IN HOUSE IN CHARLTON LINKED TO POTENTIAL SUSPECT.' It had been two days since Dee had made the decision to contact the police. Scarlett Quilter had given her her word that she would do it, but how well did Dee really know her? She'd only met the woman a couple of times, and it couldn't be easy when it was your own brother you suspected, maybe even your own father. It couldn't be easy at all.

Her phone rang. Sue Caplin's name flashed up on the screen, but it was Alan who spoke to her. Dee held her breath. The last time he'd called had been two days ago, to warn her of the breaking news. Not that she'd needed any warning. This time, she had no idea what he was going to tell her. But whatever it was, she knew it wasn't going to be good.

'It wasn't her,' he said, his voice hoarse from crying. 'It wasn't her.'

Dee kept it together the whole time Alan was on the phone, but as soon as the call ended the disappointment that had opened inside her like a valve welled up until she thought she would burst.

It wasn't Gina.

Dee folded her arms on the table in front of her and rested her forehead on her wrists. She wanted to sit with the knowledge a little while longer before she told her dad. It was a man's body, Alan had told her. 'At least someone, somewhere, will soon know what's become of their loved one,' he'd said. That was typical of Alan. Always trying to find the positive.

But for him and Sue, and the rest of Gina's family, and for Dee and Lindsay and all her other friends, the not knowing would continue. Maybe for ever. It was too much to bear and yet bear it they must, for there was nothing else they could do. It wasn't a question of 'being strong' or 'keeping faith', or any of the other meaningless platitudes people came out with. They had to get up each morning and drag the dull weight of frustration and sorrow around with them like a ball and chain. Whoever was responsible for Gina's disappearance had made prisoners of them all.

She was about to go and give her dad the heartbreaking news when her phone rang again. She saw the name Scarlett Quilter and almost didn't answer it, but something made her accept the call, some instinct that it was the right thing to do.

'I wanted you to know that I didn't go back on what we agreed,' Scarlett said. Her voice was quiet and shaky. 'I had every intention of calling the police after you left, but ... I was interrupted and then it was too late.'

Scarlett didn't give Dee the chance to respond.

'I want to let you know something before you hear it on the news. A body *was* found, but it wasn't your friend.'

'I already know,' Dee said. 'Gina's dad just phoned me.'

Scarlett paused. 'I'm so sorry for giving you all false hope.' Dee sensed her trying to compose herself. 'There's been a rather dreadful development,' she said. 'My brother did something terrible.'

Dee held her breath, dreading what she was about to hear.

'I probably shouldn't be telling you this – in fact, I *know* I shouldn't – but I must. Anyway, you'll find out soon enough. Ollie *did* know your friend.' Dee's hand tightened around her phone. 'But he had nothing to do with her disappearance. Absolutely nothing. I can assure you of that. What he did was unrelated to Gina. I can't tell you any more than that right now. I'm sorry but I can't.'

'How *well* did he know her?' Dee demanded.

'He gave her a lift to a man's house. That's all he told me.'

'What man?'

'I don't *know*. Some "bloke's place in Welling" was all he said.'

If Dee hadn't already been sitting down, she might well have fallen. The only person she knew who lived near Welling was Jake. His and Hayley's house in Camdale Road was on the Plumstead–Welling borders. Her mouth filled with saliva. She felt sick to the stomach.

'Whereabouts in Welling?'

'I have no idea. Look, I've said too much already. The police will work it out. Ollie's been arrested. I'm so sorry, Dee. I shouldn't have phoned. I have to go. I'm truly, truly sorry.'

Her dad came into the kitchen just as Scarlett terminated the call. 'Who was that, love?'

'Scarlett Quilter,' she said. 'And before that it was Alan.'

Her dad sat at the table opposite her and reached for her hands.

'There is a body, but it's not Gina,' she said. She didn't recognize her own voice.

Her dad hung his head and sighed. 'Oh, God.'

'Scarlett Quilter has just told me that her brother *did* know her, but that he had nothing to do with her disappearance.'

'Well, she *would* say that, wouldn't she?'

'He's been arrested.'

'There you go then.'

'It was for something else though. But she said

336

he'd admitted to giving her a lift to a man's house in Welling.'

There was a knock on the front door. Her dad got up to see who it was. Dee heard a woman's voice and looked up as her dad returned to the kitchen with two police officers. They introduced themselves as Sergeant Pam Dehal and Detective Inspector Martin Guyver and asked if she wouldn't mind answering a few questions.

'We won't take up too much of your time,' DI Guyver said. The two of them sat down at the kitchen table. DI Guyver cleared his throat. 'First of all, I want to thank you for phoning us the other day. You'll be hearing on the news shortly that a body has been found in the garden of the property.'

'Yes,' Dee said. 'But not the one we thought.'

DI Guyver gave her a quizzical look.

'Alan Caplin just phoned me,' she said.

'Ah, right. That new case is, of course, being investigated, but thanks to your call, we now have new information relating to the disappearance of Gina.'

53

'YOU THINK THE TWO cases are connected then?' Dee said. Had Scarlett been lying to her just now?

'I can't answer that, I'm afraid. But we'll be talking to all of Gina's friends and family again. Hence this visit.' He leaned forward. 'Can you confirm what you told us on the phone, that you, Lindsay Morgan and Gina Caplin were once taught by the late Rebecca Quilter?'

'Yes, that's right. She was a supply teacher.'

DI Guyver nodded. 'Did you know that Gina had kept in contact with Rebecca?'

Dee shook her head. 'Not until Scarlett told me.'

'Was Gina in the habit of keeping secrets from her friends?'

'I don't *think* so. I mean, she could be a little mysterious at times. I suppose I can understand why she might have kept their friendship to herself in the beginning. We'd given Miss Quilter a bit of a hard time. She was new to teaching and we were a bit – you know ...'

Dee blushed. 'We were seventeen-year-old girls. I don't expect we were the easiest class to teach.'

DI Guyver and DS Dehal both gave small, knowing smiles.

'But later on, as we got older, I'm surprised she didn't mention it then. Maybe she didn't think it was relevant to our friendship. We were close but we weren't joined at the hip. We had our own, independent interests.'

'Now I know you were asked all these questions before, but can you cast your mind back to the time before Gina went missing and tell us whether you ever got the feeling that she might have been involved with anyone romantically?'

'No, I didn't get that feeling.'

'But you did say she could be mysterious at times. What did you mean by that, Dee? And again, I know you've answered these questions before, but if you could just bear with us.'

'I suppose I meant that where Lindsay would give us all the details of her relationships and what was going on in her life, Gina kept things a little closer to her chest. She was more like me in that respect.'

'Did you ever hear her mention someone called Ollie, or Oliver?'

Dee thought of how Ollie Quilter's powerful arms had caught her as she stumbled on the ramp leading up to Scarlett's house. Just because the body under the summer house wasn't Gina's didn't mean he wasn't responsible for her disappearance. If he'd killed that man, whoever he was, he was a cold-blooded murderer. He could have killed Gina, too.

'No, never.'

'But she did, once, have a relationship with Jake Morgan, didn't she?'

Dee and her dad exchanged a worried glance. This was old ground. The police were already well aware of Jake and Gina's brief dalliance. Jake had been interviewed at length about it when she first disappeared. If the police were questioning her about him all over again, they must know something.

She thought of what Scarlett had just told her and swallowed nervously. 'Yes, they went out for a few months, in their early twenties, but you know all this already, don't you?'

'And can you remind us where Jake was living at the time Gina went missing?'

Dee went cold all over. They really did think it was him.

'Dee?'

'In Plumstead,' she said. 'The same address he lives at now.'

'The Camdale Road address?'

'Yes. Why are you asking me this?'

'We're following up a new line of inquiry linked to a property in the south-east London area.'

Unease settled in the pit of Dee's stomach. She couldn't begin to imagine what it would do to

Lindsay if Jake turned out to be involved in Gina's disappearance.

'And your ex-fiancé Euan Harding was living in a house-share in Lewisham at the time. Is that correct?'

Dee looked up in surprise. Why were they asking her about Euan. 'Ye–es.'

'And now he lives in . . .?'

'Charlton. He lives in Charlton, not far from the park.'

DI Guyver nodded.

'Would you mind telling us again how long you were in a relationship with Mr Harding? As I said, I'm sorry to have to go over all this again.'

Dee caught her dad's eye. Where were they going with this?

'Three years, or just under. We started seeing each other about a year before Gina went missing and we split up a couple of years after,' she said.

'You were engaged, I believe. May I ask why the two of you split up?'

Dee sighed. 'Everyone thought it was the stress of Gina going missing, the effect it had on all of us. It changed everything. But that wasn't the real reason. That was just an excuse I made. I suppose, deep down, I . . . I knew I didn't really love him enough to get married to him.'

'Were there any other reasons?'

Dee blinked at him in confusion. What was he getting at?

'Take your time, Dee. We're not trying to catch you out here. We're really not. We're just trying to understand the nature of your relationship with Mr Harding.'

'I was starting to realize that I might be . . .' Dee took a deep breath and exhaled slowly. In all the countless times she had wondered how this moment would play out she had never for one second imagined that it would be in front of two police officers with her dad sitting next to her. 'I was starting to realize that I might be gay,' she said at last, the words coming out in a rush. 'I *am* gay.'

She was aware of her dad's little sigh, but she couldn't look him in the face. Not yet. So she focussed instead on DI Guyver's face, which was, she thought, possibly one of the kindest faces she had ever seen.

'I see,' he said. 'May I ask whether Jake Morgan or Euan Harding ever frightened you, Dee? Was either of them ever violent towards you?'

'No! They never hurt me. Not once. But I suppose I *was* sometimes a little nervous around Euan.'

Her dad gasped. 'What? You never told me that! Why didn't you ever say anything?'

'Because I thought it was just me being me. It was . . . it was only ever when we were in bed. I never really enjoyed it. He was the first man I'd ever slept with.' She blushed. 'The *only* man I've ever slept with.'

She looked up then, straight into DI Guyver's face.

'You don't think Euan or Jake had something to do with Gina going missing, do you? Please tell me that's not why you're here.'

'I'm afraid I can't discuss any of the details, I'm sure you understand.'

DI Guyver adjusted his position on the chair. 'Just one more question, Dee. We know that Jake Morgan and Euan Harding were good friends, so can you tell us whether Euan regularly visited Jake Morgan at his house in Camdale Road?'

'Well, yes, of course, they're best friends. They play football together. And Euan often used to call in on Jake on his way back from visiting his grandmother.'

DI Guyver looked up. 'Did he often visit his grandmother?'

'Yes, all the time. She was bedridden and had carers going in. He was her only grandson. She died a couple of years ago.'

'I see. And did you also visit his grandmother's house?'

'Once or twice, yes.'

'And where did she live?'

Dee gripped the edge of the table. The room had begun to spin. No, it couldn't be. There had to be some mistake.

'She lived in Welling. Near the train station.'

Dee sensed a change in DI Guyver's and DS Dehal's expressions and her stomach flipped. She locked eyes with her dad. 'She left the house to Euan. He rents it out.'

Sergeant Dehal was already standing up and heading towards the front door. She was making a call.

DI Guyver also stood up. 'Thanks very much, Dee. You've been really helpful. We may need to ask you some more questions in the next few days. Is that okay?'

Dee also made to stand, but her legs were shaking uncontrollably. Her dad saw the police officers out and returned to the table. His face was grey.

One hour later, Dee got a message from Lindsay. 'Call me,' it said. 'Euan's been arrested.' She handed the phone to her dad so that he too could see it. Her dad put the phone down and wrapped his arms around Dee's shoulders. He held her close against him and the two of them stayed like that, without speaking, for the longest time.

MURDER-SUICIDE NOW DEEMED DOUBLE MURDER

By Frances Lilley
South London Press

The tragic deaths of Rebecca Quilter (56) and Clive Hamlyn (59) in Charlton, south-east London, previously believed to be murder-suicide, are now being treated as double murder.

A third body, identified as that of Andrew Pulteney (47), former fiancé of Rebecca Quilter, has been found in the garden of the property.

Two men, Oliver Quilter (nephew of the murdered woman) and his longstanding employee Michael North, have been charged with all three murders, one of which is historic.

It is understood that the accused deliberately framed Clive Hamlyn for the murder of Rebecca Quilter. A spokesperson for Clive Hamlyn's family said: 'We are shocked by this news and deeply saddened that mistakes in the original investigation have tarnished Clive's good name.'

In a bizarre twist, evidence arising from this investigation has led to a fresh lead in the case of Gina Caplin, who has been missing since 16 March 2009, although a police spokesperson has confirmed that the accused are not suspected of involvement with Gina's disappearance.

This shocking news has left the local community stunned.

GINA CAPLIN: BODY FOUND IN CELLAR OF HOUSE IN
WELLING CONFIRMED AS THAT OF MISSING WOMAN

By Frances Lilley
South London Press

A body found by police in a sealed coal chute in the cellar of a house in Welling on Thursday has been confirmed as that of missing woman Gina Caplin.

The 30-year-old dancer disappeared on 16 March 2009. She was last seen leaving the fitness studio where she worked part-time, for her lunch break. Her parents were expecting her for supper that evening and raised the alarm when she never arrived.

A local man, who was questioned at the time of her disappearance, remains in custody having been held on suspicion of Ms Caplin's murder.

MAN CHARGED WITH GINA CAPLIN'S MURDER CLAIMS IT WAS SEX GAME GONE WRONG

By Sam Walker
The Sun

Euan Harding, 42, will stand trial next week charged with the murder of Gina Caplin, 30, in 2009, and the concealment of her body.

Harding had known Gina since childhood and was having an affair with her while in a relationship with one of her friends.

Gina's body was found in the cellar of a house owned by Harding in Welling, following a lead arising from an unconnected case.

A post-mortem examination confirmed she died from asphyxiation.

Harding denies deliberately killing Gina. He claims it was an accident arising from a consensual game of 'erotic asphyxiation', but has confessed to panicking and hiding her body in the cellar of the house previously owned by his grandmother.

54

Four months later: 16 March 2020

DEE LOOKED AT THE people milling around outside the crematorium, clearly hesitant about standing too close to one another. Some were embracing, but most were hanging back, avoiding the social contact that usually came so instinctively on occasions like this. The hugs and the kisses. The clasping of hands.

Dee caught Lindsay's eye and they shared a sad little smile. It was awful, not what Gina or her parents deserved. Then again, there was talk of banning funerals altogether if this wretched virus wasn't brought under control, or, at the very least, restricting the number of mourners. At least Gina's had still been able to go ahead, with all her family and friends allowed to pay their last respects. All her friends, minus one.

It was odd to think that if Gina hadn't been found, this would still have been her day. Not here, of course,

348

but the same group of people would have been gathered together at their old school, thinking of her, wondering where she was. Now, of course, they knew exactly where she was. Gina had come back to them.

Dee watched her dad as he talked to Sue and Alan Caplin, relieved and saddened to see him standing the requisite two metres away from them. It seemed so strange and unnatural. She couldn't begin to imagine what the next weeks and months were going to be like. Although, after what they'd all been through, a global pandemic seemed almost tame in comparison.

Dee wandered over to look at the flowers and the messages. More and more people were eschewing flowers altogether at funerals now, on account of their carbon footprint. But Sue had wanted them, and neither Dee nor Lindsay had had the heart to persuade her otherwise. They'd recommended their own supplier of ethically sourced flowers and, seeing them now, laid out in all their glory, Dee knew that Sue had made the right decision. It was a fitting tribute for Gina and added a vibrant splash of colour to an otherwise grey and sorrowful day.

Dee didn't think that it would ever truly sink in, the reality of what had happened. She'd been shocked to the core. Repulsed. They all had. To think that it had been Euan all along. The friend she'd known since childhood, the man she'd been out with, slept with. The very thought nauseated her. Knowing that she'd remained his girlfriend for almost two years afterwards and that he'd cried alongside her, when all the time, he'd known exactly where Gina was.

What he'd done was beyond comprehension. Beyond evil. What he'd put Gina's parents through for ten long years. It was unforgiveable, the sort of horror story that happened to other people, not people she knew and cared for. Not to Gina. It didn't matter that Gina had betrayed her, that she and Euan had been seeing each other behind her back, meeting for secret rendezvous at his grandmother's house. It didn't change how she felt about her one little bit. How could it? Dee had never loved Euan in the first place. She'd known all along that there was something off about their relationship, but it had been nothing to do with her own sexuality. She knew that now.

It was him. It had always been him and the anxiety he'd induced in her. That subtle undercurrent of fear she'd felt whenever they were in bed. The fear she'd never truly understood or even acknowledged – the one she'd put down to her own discomfort with the sexual act – but which Gina, dear, sweet Gina, must have felt too, at the end.

He'd confessed everything, said it was a game that went wrong. A game! He'd once asked Dee if she wanted to try something like that, said it might help her come, but she'd been so horrified he'd laughed it off, assured her he'd been joking, and she'd believed him. Maybe if she'd said something about it, confided in someone . . .

Dee blinked away the tears. Tears of both sorrow and rage. Tears of guilt, too, because how could she not have suspected anything? How could she have missed the signs? She'd never get over the horror of it. None of them would.

She looked up. Lindsay was talking to some of their old schoolfriends. Dee knew she ought to join them, but something held her back. Jake and Hayley appeared at her side.

'Well done for arranging all of this,' Hayley said. 'It can't have been easy.'

'It wasn't just me,' Dee said. 'It was both of us.'

Hayley smiled. 'Lindsay's just told us that you did most of the work.'

Jake cleared his throat.

'Will you excuse me a moment?' Hayley said. 'I want to ring Mum and find out how the baby is. This is the first time we've left her.'

She walked away, leaving the two of them alone.

Jake looked up. 'I still can't get my head around it. Can't believe how blind we all were.'

Dee nodded, unable to speak.

'I feel so guilty. He was my best mate.' Jake's voice was tight with emotion. 'I should have known something was up. I should have sensed it, but I didn't. How could I have missed something like that?'

Dee put her hand on his shoulder. 'That's exactly

how I feel too. But it's not our fault. We have to keep telling ourselves that. If we'd had the slightest suspicion, we'd have spoken out.'

Jake nodded, barely holding back the tears. Dee threw her arms around him and he hugged her back. 'All that silly stuff I said to Lins, about thinking you and Gina were—'

'Forget it,' he said, still holding her close.

At last, they separated. Jake looked over to where Lindsay was standing. 'I hear you're moving in with Lins in a few weeks.'

Dee smiled. 'She's been on at me to be her lodger for ages. I've finally caved in to the pressure. I don't want her living on her own if there's a lockdown. At least my dad's got Mrs Kowalski to keep him company.'

Jake laughed through his tears. 'Yeah, your dad looked pretty pleased with himself when I saw him at the match.'

'And I can keep a closer eye on her Tinder dates.'

Jake pulled a face. 'Someone's got to,' he said.

'Someone's got to what?' Lindsay said. Neither of them had seen her approach.

'Look out for you,' Jake said.

Lindsay glared at him. 'I'm perfectly capable of looking out for myself, thank you very much.'

Dee raised her eyebrows, and Lindsay blushed. They turned to look at the flowers and Lindsay slipped her hand into Dee's. Dee squeezed it tight and stared at the flowers until the colours merged.

'You'd better let me go,' Lindsay said. 'She'll be here in a minute.'

'It's not *like* that,' Dee said. 'I don't even know if she thinks of me in that way.'

'Maybe not. But there's only one way to find out, isn't there? It's time to start living, Dee. Time to let go of the past.'

Dee released Lindsay's hand and nodded. She was right. It was time to let Gina go. And it was time to let Lindsay go, too. Being her friend was all that mattered now.

55

SCARLETT BUTTONED UP HER coat and selected a suitable scarf and pair of gloves. Then she put her woollen hat on and stared at her reflection in the mirror. She looked pale and tired, but that was hardly surprising, all things considered.

With Ollie in prison awaiting trial for, between him and Mickey, three murders, and one case of preventing lawful burial, Rebecca's funeral arrangements had been radically changed. Scarlett and her dad had no appetite for a formal service now. The new plan was for the two of them to scatter Rebecca's ashes in Venice, from the pontoon at San Michele.

Rebecca had loved Venice and Scarlett could think of no better resting place for her beloved aunt. Scarlett had, naïvely, thought it was simply a question of flying out there, finding a suitable location, then shaking out the ashes, but Dee Boswell had soon put her right about that. Scarlett should have realized that nothing in life – or death, for that matter – was ever straightforward.

But after the bureaucracy of seeking permission from the Italian consulate, the seemingly endless form-filling and email correspondence that Dee had heroically navigated alongside her, after settling the requisite fees to the City of Venice mortuary police, not to mention all the travel and hotel bookings, all flights to Italy were now banned because of the pandemic. The whole bloody palaver had been one big exercise in futility.

Right now, Scarlett and her father should have been on an express train from Santa Maria Novella station in Florence to Venezia Santa Lucia, watching the Tuscan landscape roll by, Rebecca's ashes carefully stowed in a discreet scatter tube in Scarlett's rucksack. Rebecca would have travelled with them in a taxi from south-east London to Gatwick and, from there, accompanied them on the EasyJet flight to Peretola airport. It would have been physically and emotionally exhausting, she knew it would, but her dad would have been there, looking after her.

The three of them would then have checked into her aunt's favourite hotel on the hills above Florence and Scarlett and her father would have spent a few days sightseeing in the pleasant spring weather, soaking up the treasures of the Uffizi before the hordes of tourists began to arrive. A chance for them to spend some much-needed time together. To reconnect. Then they would have embarked on the two-hour train journey to Venice, the penultimate leg of their final journey with Rebecca, the last being the funeral boat to the pontoon.

Scarlett locked the front door and walked to the bus stop. When the bus arrived five minutes later, she stuck her cane out and waited for it to draw up. Hopefully, they would still carry out their plan, when this ghastly Covid business was over and life went back to normal, but for now Rebecca remained on a bookshelf in Scarlett's living room, in a hand-painted ceramic urn purchased from Fond Farewells. An expensive buy, and one that Rebecca herself would surely have scoffed at. 'Put me in a shoebox and have done with it,' Scarlett could almost hear her saying.

She pulled her scarf up and wound it around the lower part of her face, cross with herself for feeling self-conscious about it. The threat of this damn virus was more important than worrying about what people might think of her. If the news was to be believed, they'd probably all be wearing masks soon.

She tapped her Oyster card on the reader and found a spare seat, as far from any of the other passengers as she could get. The bus pulled away. Soon it would be level with the crime scene. The house where the 'bedroom bloodbath', and now the 'gruesome garden discovery', had occurred.

Scarlett stared out of the window as the bus passed

by it, observed the house in a detached, curious way, much like the strangers she was travelling with. There was no way she'd be able to sell at market value. Not with that kind of history attached to it. And with a national lockdown imminent, the chances of moving any time soon were virtually non-existent. But as Ollie was so fond of saying, she was a stubborn woman.

What he really meant, of course, was that she was a *strong* woman. He might not have been right about many things, but he had been right about that. And if anyone could carry on living in such a place, it was her.

She exhaled into the fabric of her scarf. There would still be a ritual today, but not for her aunt. This morning belonged to a young woman called Gina Caplin. A woman her aunt had once taught, and with whom she had kept in touch, the two of them united by their love of writing. A woman whose life had been cut short in the most heinous way and whose parents would never recover from the loss. A daughter, a dancer, a writer, a friend – and who knew what else she would have become if circumstances had been different?

Scarlett blinked away her tears. Rebecca would have wanted her to pay her last respects, and after everything Scarlett had been through these past few months, she felt close to Gina, too. To the woman she'd never actually met and who might, perhaps, have been found ten years ago, if her aunt and her brother had done the right thing and contacted the police, if they had given them a statement.

Scarlett wasn't just going along for Gina, though. She wanted to see Dee again, to support her on this saddest of days. Like her, Dee knew what it was like to lose someone she loved in the worst possible way. She also knew what it was like to have slept with a murderer. Maybe today's funeral would be the beginning of a new friendship. A friendship that would encompass more than death and grief.

The kind of friendship that Scarlett had been waiting for all her life, even if she'd never quite realized it till now.

Acknowledgements

HUGE THANKS TO THE following people:

Sarah Adams, for her thoughtful, generous and exceedingly wise comments and suggestions.

Imogen Nelson, for her additional editorial input, and the rest of the glorious team at Transworld, with an extra shout-out to Alison Barrow and Louis Patel.

Amanda Preston, for keeping me sane and knowing exactly when to call me and what to say.

Louise Ford, for telling me what her working day looks like so I could pinch a few details for Scarlett.

Nathalie Andrews, for answering my random questions about funerals and celebrants, and for showing me round the business end of a crematorium.

Graham Bartlett, for our discussion about murder scenes and missing persons.

Rashid Kara, for all the other stuff.

Lesley Kara is the *Sunday Times* bestselling author of *The Rumour, Who Did You Tell?* and *The Dare*. *The Rumour* was the highest-selling crime-fiction debut of 2019 in the UK, and a Kindle No.1 bestseller. Lesley is an alumna of the Faber Academy 'Writing a Novel' course. She lives in Suffolk.

IF YOU LOVED

The Apartment Upstairs

DON'T MISS LESLEY KARA'S GRIPPING NEW THRILLER

The Vacancy

Available to pre-order now!

Read on for an early look at the first chapters . . .

DO YOU HAVE WHAT IT TAKES TO BE A PROPERTY GUARDIAN?

We have vacancies all over London starting from £50 a week and are looking for tenants with a difference – responsible people willing to sign up as property guardians.

You would occupy a shared living space (solo occupancies are sometimes available) under a non-exclusive licence agreement, and would be required to look after the property as per the rules of being a property guardian.

Please note, your live-in presence would act as a deterrent for anti-social behaviour in empty buildings, e.g. squatting or asset-stripping, but at no time would you be required to intervene in preventing criminal activity.

You must be 18+, employed and with no live-in dependents or pets.

Please telephone Harry Kiernan at Guardian Angels Inc on 0207 528 4298 for an informal discussion.

HAYLEY

This place gives me the creeps. Pools aren't supposed to be empty. They're meant to be full of water. Blue and inviting. Silky smooth against the skin.

It isn't just the air of neglect that hovers in the air, or the dated, institutional vibe; there's something about the shape of it I find unsettling. The hard, unforgiving angles of the exposed rectangular basin. The dramatically sharp slope to the deep end. Then there are those clinical white tiles with black mould in the grouting, like food stuck between teeth. And the metal ladders, flat to the sides.

I walk as far from the edge of the pool as I can possibly get, convinced I can still smell chlorine, still hear the echo of shrill voices, the splashing as young bodies propel themselves through the water. Every time my trainers squeak against the tiled floor, I flinch.

The tiered seating area to my left is shadowy in the fading light. I force myself to swivel my head, braced for the sight of a lone spectator watching my every move, even though I know I'm quite alone in here. I've been observing it from outside for ages and no one has either come in or gone out. If only my rational brain would communicate that fact to my heart, which is beating fit to burst through my chest.

When I've satisfied myself that there's nothing of interest to be found in the immediate vicinity of the pool, I climb the stairs to the spectator area, letting my gaze travel along each row of seats. Then I look under the seats, but apart from old sweet wrappers there's nothing there. I go back down to the pool and into the girls' changing rooms, where a thorough search reveals nothing more exciting than a couple of slimy old swim caps and a pair of dirty knickers left scrunched up in a locker. It would help if I knew what I was looking for.

Feeling much calmer now that I can no longer see the exposed shell of the swimming pool, I explore the rest of the building. The door to the plant room stands open and I can see all the equipment inside. The bank of switches on the wall. The maze of pipework, pumps and valves that looks like the back of a giant washing machine. The massive filtration cylinder and circulation pump.

Even with everything turned off and disconnected, it feels dangerous to be standing so close to all this equipment. For a moment I think I hear a ticking noise, like a radiator warming up. I stand perfectly still and listen intently. No, the only sounds I can hear are my own breath and the beating of my heart.

I reach out and touch one of the cylinders with the

tips of my fingers. Stone cold. Of course it is. This pool has lain empty and unused ever since the school closed down two years ago.

I'm about to leave and do a quick check of the toilets when I hear footsteps coming from further down the corridor. The brisk, echoey slap of shoes on linoleum. I freeze. I'm definitely not hearing things this time.

Panicking, I look around for somewhere to hide.

I push the plant-room door till it's almost closed, then tuck myself behind the filtration cylinder. I crouch down on the floor and hold my breath as the steps draw nearer. I hear a door opening and closing and the footsteps stop. I can't be sure, but I think they've just gone into the changing rooms.

Shit! I left my tote bag on one of the benches while I was searching the lockers. My phone is in that bag. What if it starts ringing?

My knees are getting stiff from crouching down, and I shift position. Further along the corridor, a door swings shut. I hold my breath, too petrified to move a muscle. *Please God, don't let them have found it. Please God, don't let anyone call me until they've gone.* The footsteps start up again, only now they sound like they're heading away from the plant room and back towards the entrance.

I rock back on my haunches, relief flooding through me. I must be crazy doing this. I should have got the hell out of here days ago. Slowly, gingerly, I stand up.

And that's when I see it, tucked behind one of the pipes that runs horizontally along the wall about four inches from the floor, and suddenly I know exactly what's going on here. I know what this is all about.

The tap on my shoulder makes me gasp. I freeze. If this is who I think it is . . .

I turn my head slowly, reluctantly, desperately trying to think of a good reason why I'm here, a reason that will reassure them I'm not—

'Oh! It's you!' I almost laugh out loud when I see who it is. 'Thank God—'

Then I see the look on their face and register what they're holding. But . . . but surely that's for something else. It can't be . . .

My mouth goes dry. I've got it wrong. So very, very wrong.

'I won't tell,' I say, my voice little more than a squeak.

The loud rasp of the gaffer tape as it peels away from the reel makes my stomach contract.

'I promise I won't—'

-1-

MARLOW

The agency is supposed to give me a month's notice and, to be fair, they usually do. But not this time. I've got less than a week to pack up my stuff and find somewhere else to live before the developers move in and turn this place – my home for the last ten months – into two swanky apartments, the likes of which I'll never in a million years be able to afford.

I look into the eyes of the angelic figure staring down at me, and even though I don't believe in the supernatural, a small part of me secretly hopes for divine intervention.

'Come on, Angie.' My voice echoes in the rafters. 'Prove you're not a figment of the collective imagination and bloody well *do* something. Save me!'

For one split second, I think I see a flicker in Angie's glassy eyes, but of course, it's just a trick of the light. I squint up at the benevolent figure in the blue robe. Perhaps he isn't keen on being called Angie, although it's a bit late to give him a new name now.

From somewhere outside comes the sound of a police siren. I don't usually register the noise. Sirens are a regular part of life in the city, a recurring motif in the urban soundscape. Today, it cuts straight through me like a jolt of electricity.

I turn away from the window and face the empty pews. My invisible congregation.

'Right then, you lot, we've got work to do.'

When I first spotted the old chapel on the agency's website, I knew straight away that I'd be happy here. It was just a feeling I had. An inexplicable sense that out of all the possible places I could choose to live, this one would suit me the best. I guessed it would be draughty and it is. But the cold keeps me sharp, makes me feel alive. In any case, the beauty of the building, its *history*, more than make up for its chilly interior.

There was another, more compelling reason why I was so keen to move in. It was a solo occupancy and that alone made it an attractive option, never mind the gothic architecture or the way the light shines through the stained-glass window. Never mind the solidity of the thick stone walls and the sturdy, double-planked door with its iron studs and bands to repel intruders.

When I draw the heavy bolt across each night, I feel an overwhelming sense of peace and security. Now though, everything's up in the air again. If the agency can't find me another suitable vacancy, I'll be homeless. There's always Dev's place, of course. I won't exactly be on the streets, but even so . . .

In the tiny vestry, I retrieve my large, framed rucksack. It's the most expensive thing I've ever bought. The most useful, too. As I lift it clear of the hook on the wall, the backs of my eyeballs start to tingle. I screw up my face and shake my head till the sensation passes. Tears are no use to me – they won't change anything. I've always known this day was coming. Everything in life is temporary. Provisional. At least, it is in mine.

I plonk the rucksack on the vestry table and unzip its various compartments, running my hands inside each one to check they're empty. Once, I found a tenner folded up small and caught in one of the seams. No such luck today.

Half an hour later, I've made a good start and have packed my underwear, my second pair of jeans and what few T-shirts and jumpers I still possess. I've also packed my sturdy walking shoes – I had to scrape the dried mud off the soles first and give them a good clean – plus the waxed jacket with the fur-lined collar I found on a bus. Yes, I know I should have handed it to the driver so he could take it back to the depot as lost property, but I really needed a coat and it's my size and somehow I found myself putting it on and getting off at my usual stop, casual as anything but with my heart thumping wildly. It's not quite the same as stealing, is it?

My phone vibrates in my pocket and I pull it out. It's Harry from the agency.

'You're in luck,' he says. 'I've found you another place, but you're going to have to make your mind up quick. It won't hang about.'

My heart soars. When he called me with the bad news earlier this morning, he offered me a room in an empty office block in North Acton and I turned it down. He wasn't best pleased. I'd heard what he was thinking in his voice: *beggars can't be choosers*. But that's where he's wrong. I'd rather doss with Dev for a few weeks than shack up on a floor with a load of other people snoring and farting on the other side of a flimsy partition wall. I've lived in an office block before and it was a dismal experience. Almost as bad as working in one.

Sometimes, being a property guardian feels like a brave, exciting thing to do. I'm an adventurer, living on the edge, spurning the tedium of a humdrum existence. A non-conformer. A *bohemian*. Other times, it feels sordid and sad. Camping out like a refugee in my own country. A glorified squatter, as my dad would say. As he *has* said, on more than one occasion.

'Sounds promising,' I tell Harry. 'What is it?'

'A school in North London. You'd have a whole classroom to yourself in a nice old Victorian build-ing. We've already got a small team installed there, but one of them's had to leave at short notice.' I hear him sigh. 'I'm really annoyed with her actually,' he drawls in that bored-sounding, public-school voice of his. 'She was adamant she wanted this licence. I turned down several good, reliable applicants on the strength of that.'

I don't say what I'm thinking, that it's a bit rich of the agency to expect one hundred per cent commitment from their guardians when long-term security is the very last thing they offer us. Harry's given me hardly any notice to vacate the chapel and I wouldn't mind betting that I'm as good and reliable a guardian as any on his books.

'I can whizz the details over to you in a sec,' he says. 'But it won't be available for much longer.' He pauses. 'I've got at least six other people interested in this one.'

'I'll take it.'

'Sure you don't want to look at the details first?'

I hesitate, but only for a second. A whole classroom to myself, and the architecture in some of those Victorian schools is stunning. If I wait till he sends the details over, someone else might beat me to it. Harry always makes out he's on my side and that he's doing me a big favour, but all he really cares about are bums on floors. Whether it's mine or someone else's won't matter a jot to him.

'I'll take it.'

When the email comes through a few minutes later and I click on the link, my legs start to wobble and I have to sit down. I assumed it would be an old primary school. They're always being sold off and turned into luxury flats. But this is a secondary school. And not just any old secondary school. It's *my* old secondary school.

I stare at my phone in shock, the old panicky feeling rising up through my body, swelling like a wave. I'll have to call him back and tell him I've changed my mind, tell him the accommodation isn't suitable after all. Of all the places to be offered . . .

I shake my head and try to blank out the images that blaze through my mind, because if I don't, the physical sensations will surely follow: the tight chest, the racing heart, the sweating.

I get up so fast I knock the chair backwards. It lands with a crash on the stone floor, but I don't stop to pick it up. I leave the vestry and go back into the nave. *Think of something else, quick. Look at this place. Just look at it. Focus on what you can see. Right here. Right now.*

In the late-afternoon sun, the chapel is more beautiful than ever. I press the camera icon on my phone and line up another shot of the window. I'll miss it so much, the way the light refracts through the stained glass, the way it lends everything it touches a heavenly glow. I've taken hundreds of pictures since I've been here, and no two are identical. It's like watching the sea every day from the same position on the shore. The light changes everything.

I post the picture on Instagram, then stuff my phone back in my pocket and lie down on my favourite pew, the one I've draped with scarves and covered with scatter cushions. I gaze up at the vaulted ceiling and reflect on my situation. If I turn this offer down I'll almost certainly end up in that ghastly office block. I'll have to get rid of half my stuff or ask Dev to store some for me. All my lovely finds. A whole classroom though . . . now that would be something. It might even be good for me, seeing the place empty and unused. Consigned to history. It might even, in some weird, masochistic way, be healing.

I look up at the window. 'What should I do?'

Angie stares down at me like he always does. Silent. Benign. Do I honestly expect him to give me an answer?

'Please, Angie, give me a sign if you think I should go. A wink or something.' My voice rings out in the silence. Pleading. Almost child-like. A *wink*? Am I mad?

I'm about to fish my phone out of my pocket and read Harry's email again when an arrow of light falls across the pew and makes me start. I squint up at the window. It looks like a laser beam is coming straight out of Angie's left eye. In all the time I've been here, I've never seen it do that. Not once.

It's a fluke, that's all. A freaky coincidence. To interpret it as a sign would be absurd.

And yet . . .

Have you read all of Lesley Kara's addictive thrillers?

The Rumour

When single mum Joanna hears a rumour at the school gates, she never intends to pass it on. But one casual comment leads to another and now there's no going back . . .

'Everyone is going to be talking about *The Rumour*. An intriguing premise, a creeping sense of dread, and a twist you won't see coming!' **Shari Lapena,** bestselling author of *The Couple Next Door*

AVAILABLE NOW

Who Did You Tell?

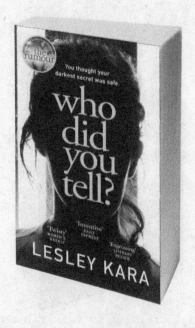

Someone knows Astrid's darkest secret. And they're going to have fun with it . . .

'An inventive and compelling psychological thriller. Kara skilfully builds tension through a series of twists before delivering a finale certain to leave you reeling'
Daily Express

AVAILABLE NOW

dead good

Looking for more gripping must-reads?

Head over to Dead Good –
the home of killer crime books,
TV and film.

Whether you're on the hunt for an intriguing
mystery, an action-packed thriller
or a creepy psychological drama,
we're here to keep you in the loop.

Get recommendations and reviews from
crime fans, grab discounted books at bargain
prices and enter exclusive giveaways
for the chance to read brand-new releases
before they hit the shelves.

Sign up for the free newsletter:
www.deadgoodbooks.co.uk/newsletter